I0762625

BIG MONEY, SMALL TOWN

BIG MONEY, SMALL TOWN

A TALE OF POWER AND CORRUPTION IN MAINE

THOMAS E. RICKS

PEGASUS CRIME
NEW YORK LONDON

BIG MONEY, SMALL TOWN

Pegasus Crime is an imprint of
Pegasus Books, Ltd.
148 West 37th Street, 12th Floor
New York, NY 10018

First Pegasus Books cloth edition June 2026

Interior design by Maria Fernandez

Map on page ix © Gene Thorp, Cartographic Concepts, Inc.

Library of Congress Cataloging-in-Publication Data is available.

ISBN: 979-8-89710-127-6

10 9 8 7 6 5 4 3 2 1

Printed in the United States of America
Distributed by Simon & Schuster
www.pegasusbooks.com

Dedicated to the proposition that the American government should be of the people, by the people, and for the people.

PRINCIPAL CHARACTERS

Ryan Tapia: ex-FBI agent living outside Bangor, Maine

Ed Healey: aging general practice doctor in Bangor

Ted French: a local lawyer in Finney Junction, Maine, north of Bangor

Betty Groleau: a reporter for the *North Country Times*

Lincoln Addison: owner and editor of the same newspaper

Bap Salim: graduate researcher in geology at the University of Northern Maine

Verdella Skillings: wife of Pete Skillings, town manager for Finney Junction

Diane Peligroso: lobbyist for Future Minerals and other companies

Lily Thornfoot: Diane Peligroso's twin sister, a lawyer and blackmailer

Future Minerals: a mining company owned by a private equity firm

Future Minerals Maine: its operating subsidiary in Maine

Dick Auger: Adams County district attorney

Nina Daigle: recent girlfriend of Tapia

Jacob "the Growler" Coffin: Maine woods hermit

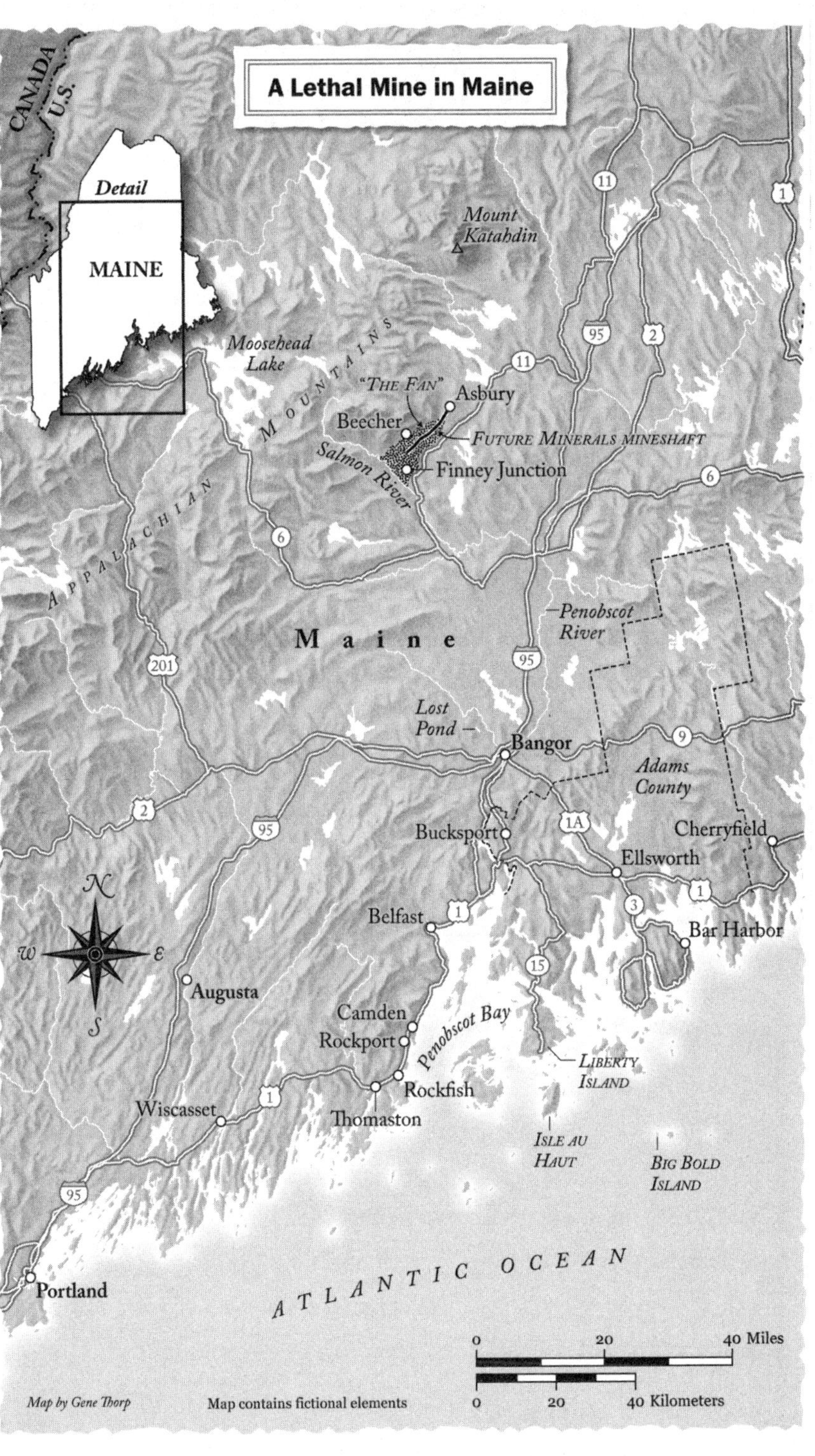
A Lethal Mine in Maine
CANADA
U.S.
Detail
MAINE
Mount Katahdin
Moosehead Lake
MOUNTAINS
"THE FAN"
Asbury
Beecher
FUTURE MINERALS MINESHAFT
Salmon River
Finney Junction
APPALACHIAN
Maine
Penobscot River
Lost Pond
Bangor
Adams County
Bucksport
Cherryfield
Ellsworth
Belfast
Bar Harbor
Augusta
Camden
Rockport
Penobscot Bay
Rockfish
Thomaston
Wiscasset
LIBERTY ISLAND
ISLE AU HAUT
BIG BOLD ISLAND
Portland
ATLANTIC OCEAN
N
S
W
E
11
1
95
2
11
6
6
201
95
9
2
95
1A
1
1
3
15
1
95
0
20
40 Miles
0
20
40 Kilometers
Map by Gene Thorp
Map contains fictional elements

“Money insulates, but power protects.”

—Lily Thornfoot

PROLOGUE

TOWN JAIL IN SALEM, MASSACHUSETTS BAY COLONY

JULY 1692

Martha Foot slumped on the side of her bed in the dank cell, leaning forward, her long, coal-black hair almost covering her face. In the other bed, just two feet away, her father, his face gaunt and livid with pain, rattled one last time. Then, mid-breath, he stopped. She leaned in to look closer. She had never seen a dead body before, but at that moment, she knew with certainty that he was gone. He was so absolutely still, and seemed slightly smaller.

At this moment, at the age of sixteen, she became entirely alone in the world. Her mother, his wife, had been hanged as a witch a month earlier. Meanwhile, Martha and her father had been jailed in a room in the stone-lined cellar of the Town Building, themselves awaiting trial on the same charge. She looked upward, trying to comprehend this hard life.

As she sat on the edge of her bed, she sensed she was not alone. There was an odor in the air. The jailer—really just the keeper of the Town Building—had been watching from the shadows.

"Who's there?" she asked, though she knew.

"Only I, girl," the jailer whispered. Unusually, he was trying to be pleasant, which made him all the more terrifying. He turned his key and opened the metal door of the cell, giving the fresh corpse just one quick glance of confirmation. "I will take care of you."

What did that mean, she wondered. She shook with fear.

"Lay back on your bed," he ordered, again in that soft, breathy voice.

She didn't know jail procedure. What did this have to do with the death of her father? She did as she was told.

He reached down with a second key to unlock the cold black shackles that held her ankles four inches apart. They dropped off.

"Now lift your skirts," he instructed. "And spread your legs."

Now she was certain this was wrong. She reached under the thin, damp mattress for the gift her father had left her, really the only object he had still possessed. It was a sharp-pointed, four-inch-long dirk. The jailer lay his belly upon hers. Supporting his bulk with his right elbow, he reached down with his left hand for his erect penis.

There is a feminine instinct for male vulnerability. At the moment men feel most in control, that is the moment to strike. As he moved his chest upward to guide his red penis into her, she inserted the little knife below his ribcage and then, with a hard push, thrust it up toward his heart.

She hadn't expected so much blood when she had rehearsed this move in her mind. She must have severed an artery, something her father, a self-trained physician, hadn't warned her about when he had made the gift of the knife to her. The bright red fluid arced over her. She lifted her two arms and pushed his still-warm body away. She covered it with her blanket. She closed the heavy door behind her and walked up the wooden steps and out the back door of the building. She put her hand up against the side of her neck and felt where the man's warm, sticky blood had splashed her.

She knew the town well, but her parents had warned her against going at night to these few rowdy blocks along the waterfront where sailors drank, whored, and gambled in three taverns, or "ordinaries," as they were called. She took a right and walked down to that area, taking alleys and side streets. At the first corner she came to the Black Horse but slipped by it. Next, she came to the Hole in the Wall, the smallest and priciest of the three, frequented more by skippers and others inclined to avoid rubbing shoulders with the regular seamen. These were the masters and commanders, as well as the merchants of the town who supplied them with their outgoing cargos. Lucrative deals were reached nightly at those tables, even if the details sometimes were difficult to remember in the foggy light of the subsequent dawn.

Standing in the shadows of the alley, she watched through the tavern's front window across the street at the drinkers inside. It was a muggy summer night, but she was shivering from the experience in the jail cell. After a few minutes, a man she vaguely recognized staggered out of the tavern. He was perhaps thirty-five years old, stout but strong. She had seen him around the town, but not like this—his face was red, and his black beard dripped with sweat or ale or both. His gait was uneven, one foot moving, then the other, then a pause.

She followed him for a few steps, then touched his sleeve. "I need your help," she whispered.

He blinked and peered at her. "One of the, uh, witches?" he said, squinting. He was not seeing well, but he could smell. He leaned in and sniffed her and her black frock. Suddenly his voice was clearer, a bit more sober. "And drenched in someone's blood, I'd say. And you need my help?"

"Please," she said.

"Very well," he said. He threw a heavy arm across her shoulder. She walked, half leading him down toward the lapping waters of the midnight tide.

"Your vessel, sir?"

"The *Sea Hawk*. Port side of the dock, third down."

She located the craft, which despite its lofty name was a slow-moving, broad-hulled fifty-five-foot-long sloop built for the donkey work of coastal freighting—rum and wood one day, cobblestones the next, hay and grain the third. And, always, in a corner of the hold, a pile of second-rate tools and cooking pots for sales along the coast. The upcountry rubes paid well for tools bought in Salem or Boston, even though their metals were cheap and brittle. She led him aboard. A Black man, sleeping on the foredeck, raised his head and stared at her and his captain for a moment, then dropped his head back down.

"We sail on the morning ebb," the skipper said to her. "Go below and stay there." He pointed at the hatch.

She went down, wrapped herself in canvas, and closed her eyes. When she awoke many hours later, she could hear the soft "shhhh" of water along its hull, just inches from her head. So we are at sea, she thought. Her black shift was stiff with dried blood. She climbed the three steps of the ladder to the deck and saw a rough-looking man—neither the skipper nor the Black man from the night before—holding the tiller. She said, "A bucket of water, if you please."

"Get it your own fucking self," the man at the tiller barked, barely looking down at her but pointing at a wooden bucket near the taffrail.

She did, then went below to wash the dress.

Late in the day, the skipper appeared below. "Now you'll pay your way," he said. He raped her and left. A while later, the Black hand appeared with a plate of black beans, rice, and boiled pork. Without a word, he handed it to her and left.

That became the routine of her life aboard the *Sea Hawk*. Cold biscuits and hot tea in the morning, a rape by the skipper in the afternoon, then, at the dog watch, an evening meal. On the third day the cook caught a big cod, and that became the substance of several meals that day and the next, first roasted and later in a chowder. The *Sea Hawk* was cutting north and east, she could tell by the locations of the sun.

She stayed below as the vessel put in at the lesser ports of the coast at the part of the Massachusetts colony called "Maine," trading barrels of rum, bolts of cloth, and sets of metal tools for salted cod, smoked venison, and pelts of bear, beaver, and otter.

On the fifth day after leaving Salem, the sloop edged up to the town dock at Castine. Sitting below, near the hatch, she heard an angry voice on the dock. "You're not to tie up here, you've got a witch aboard, we hear," a man was saying. "That Salem plague is not welcome here."

The skipper did not argue. The sloop cast off the one line that had been tied and its jib caught the wind to head back down Penobscot Bay. Once out of the harbor, its crew of three—the skipper, the mate, and the cook/carpenter/second mate—gathered around the tiller to mull the next step. She stood near the foot of the hatch, where she could hear them talking. "Throw her overboard right now," the mate counseled. "Finish the job that Salem began." The cook said nothing she could hear.

"That's like throwing away real silver," the skipper countered. "I know a gunkhole where we can land her." They sailed south and then east. He filled the dinghy with the tools of survival that he usually peddled in ports—axes, saws, knives, hammers, fishhooks, fishing line, rope, nails, two blankets. And to tide her through, a bag of kidney beans and a jar of olive oil.

They sailed up an uninhabited shore to a narrow cove bounded by two forty-foot cliffs but with a small beach at the end. He rowed her in, unloaded the dinghy, and then laid her down and raped her on the sand. She sat up and watched him row away. Then, when the *Sea Hawk* turned south, she slept.

She was handy with an axe and saw, and soon built a livable cabin. When she found an old sail on a beach she cleaned it and stuffed it with rabbit fur and pine needles that made for a luxurious mattress.

And so it went for years. From June through October, the *Sea Hawk* would appear once a month off her cove. The skipper would bring her a tool or other supplies and demand sex. In July of the third year, she asked for a big meat cleaver, "the better to butcher the deer," she said.

In August he brought it, a huge and heavy implement. She spent her evenings in the following weeks before the fire in the little cabin she'd built, honing the cleaver to a hair's-width sharpness. The edge of the blade shone like gold in the light of the flame. She never used it on the deer. She was reserving it for a special task, one she contemplated nightly.

He didn't come in September because of storms. In October, he fought the cold wind out of the northwest to return with woolen clothes she'd requested for the winter. He told her to lie down. She did. After he was finished atop her, he rolled over and closed his eyes to rest. She got up and picked up the razored cleaver. She raised it above his neck and swung down. His eyes flashed open and his left hand shot up to seize her right wrist. "I suspected you were too full of cheer today, you burnt-tail bitch," he snarled. He twisted his hand and forced her to drop the cleaver to the floor.

But she also had done some anticipating. At her side, in her left hand, she gripped the same dirk she had used in Salem years earlier. While he wrenched her right wrist, trying to break the bone, she jabbed the dirk in her left hand into his side. She hit him hard, but still was surprised that bubbles instantly shot out of the wound. She must have struck a lung. He gasped, wide-mouthed, and let go of her wrist. He writhed in pain on the mattress. She grabbed the cleaver and brought it down, slicing the side of his neck. Now there was a second surprise: He was a strong man, even twice wounded. He rose from the bed, clapped both his hands on his neck, and took one step, then a staggering second, toward the cabin door. Then he fell forward on his face, fainting from pain or loss of blood. As he lay there, she stood over him and brought the cleaver down again, faster and more accurately. This time she was surer of her swings. With the third long arc, his head came loose from his body.

She picked it up by its long black hair, finding it surprisingly heavy, perhaps sixteen pounds. She walked up the path she had cut through the blueberry bushes and ground cedars. At its end, at the top of the cliff, she flung the dripping head out at the *Sea Hawk*, anchored below in the cove. It landed on the deck, bounced twice, and rolled to a stop near the tiller. Soon the mate and the cook/carpenter weighed anchor and set sail.

She gave birth the following May. Her infant daughter had the black hair of both her parents, and the dead skipper's muscular build. She named the child Lily.

She carried her daughter in a wrap on her back when she went hunting. In later years, they roamed the island together. The girl grew up strong and, thanks to Martha's early schooling, literate. By this time, Martha had acquired a dory that the two rowed down the coast to sell salt and hides and to buy tools and seeds. When she was asked her name at a store in Castine, Martha said,

"Thornfoot." Thus she commemorated the thorn the town of Salem had placed forever in the Foot clan.

At the age of fifteen, out hunting by herself on another island, the girl Lily met a young man. The two fell in love, but when his parents heard of it, they rowed over to see Martha. In grave and slow words, they told her to keep Lily far away from their son. "We'll have no witches in our family," they said.

Lily decided that if the world thought she was a witch, she would indeed be one. She gave birth nine months later and named her child Martha. She never saw the young man again.

And so, mother and daughter and granddaughter lived for decades in what other islanders had come to call "Witch Island." Old Martha died. Young Martha grew up and, in some quiet way, unknown even to her own mother, also became pregnant and gave birth, to another Lily. The American Revolution, the War of 1812, the Civil War—all came and went. The Thornfoot women, a steady march of Marthas and Lilys, maintained their hold on their little island, despite holding no legal claim. People living on nearby islands in the bay steered clear of them.

The women came and went, burying the generations before them. Their graveyard, unmarked on the maps, and really lacking a recognizable path, lay undisturbed until three decades into the twentieth century. Then, on a hot morning in June 1934, a long-faced lawyer from Rockfish tied up at their dock. They walked down to ask what his business was on the island. He said he represented a banker from J.P. Morgan who summered on nearby North Haven. He told them that Witch Island, to which they never had held a formal title, had been purchased from the town. "You're to move off, of course," he said. He added that the purchaser had renamed the place "Lamont Island." He told them, "You're welcome to move your family graves, of course, but after that you're not to come back to this island." They quietly moved to a nearby cove on a smaller, uninhabited island.

A few weeks later that lawyer hanged himself. The following summer, the buyer from J.P. Morgan drowned, along with his wife and daughter, when a sudden squall capsized their catboat just outside Pulpit Harbor. The local talk was that these catastrophes were the entirely predictable consequences of messing with the Thornfoots. The islanders knew better than to do that. After those two deaths, the women returned to the island and were left alone there, unmolested, for many more decades. They fished, hunted, trapped and quilted. They rowed to Castine to sell their goods and purchase canned fruit, nails, and other essentials.

Another generation of Thornfoots came and went. And in 1990, nearly three hundred years after her ancestor had fled Salem, Martha Thornfoot gave birth to twins, a first for the family. Both were girls, of course. She named the one that came out first Lily, and the second Diane, introducing a new name into this singular, hard, rugged, isolated family of Maine island women. And thereby hangs this tale.

PART I

1

A DEATH IN THE WATER

PRESENT DAY, FINNEY JUNCTION, MAINE

The first person to notice a change in the water of the Salmon River was Dr. Ed Healey. It was a fine Maine morning in late October, so he was out fishing. The mornings were chilly, the breeze a bit brisk, but it was still pleasant if you dressed right and stayed in the direct sunlight. It was the end of the growing season for plants and animals alike. As the morning sun warmed the shallows, the fish were hungry, which was why the doctor was out just after dawn, looking to catch a trout or two before going to work at the hospital in Bangor. There was no finer lunch, he had found, than melting two tabs of Irish butter and sautéing the filets of the trout you caught that morning before work. Salt them, slap them on toasted artisan bread, and you were set.

He already had bagged two smaller trout and an errant togue. But today he was searching for a long rainbow trout he'd seen before. It was at least fourteen inches, maybe even sixteen. He waded out into the riffles of the clean, fast-running Salmon, casting into an eddy where he'd seen the big rainbow. He felt something float up against his right boot. He looked down and saw a dead brook trout bobbing there in the little eddy made by his legs. He stared, puzzled, at the smaller fish, a speckled brown specimen perhaps five inches long. It was upside down, showing its white and orange belly and bloated gills. He could tell it probably wasn't a victim of a botched "catch and release," because there was no blood evident around its mouth, nor any indication of a hook wound. Rather, there was a white foam bubbling out along the edges of its gills, just above the pectoral fins. Its dead eyes were bulging a bit. He'd never seen a fish in that condition before. Curious, he netted it up, slipped it into a plastic sandwich bag, and put it in his belt basket.

Healey cast his line again, but his mind kept drifting back to the odd little corpse of the brookie. What had killed it? After pondering that question, he reeled in, gave up on fishing for the day, and began walking against the current along the riverbank. Soon he came to the mouth of Spring Brook, a tributary stream that ran along the northwestern edge of his property. He had fished there hundreds of times. But on this fine morning he noticed that along its sides, many of the plants and rocks carried something he'd never seen there before, a kind of rust-colored fuzz. He also noticed that there were no tadpoles, frogs, or minnows in the water. Nor even any bird, who normally would be feeding ravenously in preparation for their fall migrations.

The doctor knew this cold little brook well. In the depths of winter, he had walked its frozen surface, contemplating likely fishing spots that the melt-out would bring along in a few months, in late spring. He knew there was no factory nearby, nor even a gas station that might have messed up and dumped some chemicals or oils. Indeed, there was not even a road crossing this little tributary.

And in just half a mile, bubbling out at the base of a small cliff, was the spring that was its source. The doctor followed the bank of the stream all the way to the spring. There, coming out of the base of a cliff in the green woods, he saw that the spring too had that unhealthy rust-colored fuzz all around its mouth. He looked at it, shook his head, and turned around to head for the hospital. All the way on the drive, he pondered what was happening to that spring and that stream—and that little brook trout.

2
A BOON FOR SOME TOWN MANAGERS

One of the hardest occupations in Maine is town manager. The most difficult time to do the job tends to be late winter, when funds for plowing, salting, and sanding the roads are running low. A good town manager needs to keep the plows rolling, and also make sure they stop by and clear the driveways of the old people who can't afford private plowing. That wasn't an official duty of the town, yet at the same time everyone considered it an essential service. What kind of town wouldn't take care of its elderly?

And when those driveways are plowed and open, a good town manager stops by and checks on those oldsters. Are they warm, eating, getting their prescriptions, staying in touch with people? And sometimes you find that even inside their houses they are wearing winter coats, woolen caps, and gloves, yet still are blue lipped from the cold. They explain that they have stopped buying heating oil because they have been forced to choose between paying for their prescription drugs or heating their houses. "Food, drugs, and heat—we get two of the three," Warren Blanchette, a retired schoolteacher, said to Pete Skillings during one visit. "This month, it's food and drugs, and whatever firewood I can drag in. Next month, maybe we go half rations on the expensive medicines."

So when a company comes by the town office and says that they want to run a horizontal mineshaft three-hundred feet down, well below the town, in lateral boring from elsewhere, and that no one on the surface will even feel the slow, steady drilling, and adds that the company will pay the town $100,000 a year for mineral rights, you listen, if you're a town manager in a small town in the northern interior of Maine. That money can pay for an awful lot of heating oil and plowing, and perhaps make it so the principal can offer a valued teacher or two a $1,000 bonus for turning down an attractive offer to move to a wealthier school down on the coast.

And if the company's representatives throw in an extra $5,000 in cash "for your troubles," maybe you turn it down the first time, even the second. But you know some kids in town are hungry. That money could make up some helpful grocery bags of chicken, milk, bread, peanut butter, potatoes, pasta, and peas for the families that really need it and are too proud to ask. Especially in Maine's traditional "starving time," early spring, when the deer have been shot and butchered and the canned vegetables consumed, and no grass or vegetables are growing yet.

"It's great," Pete Skillings, the manager of the town of Finney Junction, told his best friend, Marty Flurry, the town postmaster, over the cups of coffee they had together every weekday morning at ten. "We get the money, and we'll never see or hear the mine. The shaft's entrance is south of here, miles away. They'll just have a robot boring machine down there, chugging away, and a conveyor belt shipping out the rock and soil. And we get a hundred grand a year."

"What's the catch?" asked Flurry, his white hair cascading around his head in curls. Skillings thought Flurry looked a bit like a wizard.

"Ain't one," Skillings said happily. "The payment papers have a severance clause that explicitly states that the mining company maintains or asserts no claim on the land, underground or surface, other than extracting minerals." He drained off the last of the coffee in his heavy white cup.

"Dude. There's always a catch," countered Flurry, who thought of himself as more worldly, having labored in a fruit and vegetable distribution warehouse in Boston for several years after high school. In rural Maine, that was considered to have tasted a bit of the big outside world.

"Maybe so, but I haven't seen it yet," replied Skillings, always the more optimistic of the two. He looked at Flurry. "Don't be so glum, chum. In fact, it's almost too good to be true. They're prospecting for cobalt. And they say the only place in America where they've found it in large, commercially viable deposits, is right here"—he pointed downward—"under our feet in a vein running from the Salmon River up toward Mount Katahdin. Word to the wise, they've asked us to keep that hush-hush, at least until they have contracts signed with us and with Asbury and Beecher. They said, like, 'there are national security concerns at play here.'"

"What makes this company so special?" asked Flurry.

"I looked it up," he continued. "Cobalt is becoming like the oil of the twenty-first century. You can't make smartphones or electronic cars without it. Well, you could, but you'd have real problems. People don't pay a lot of attention to it, but it turns out that cobalt makes lithium batteries more stable, less prone to burst into flames, and able to hold a charge longer. The federal government has even designated the stuff a 'strategic mineral.' They're worried because almost all of it right now comes from vast mines way off in far southeastern Congo, where the cobalt is buried in huge nuggets. They mine it there, ship it off to China, where it gets refined and put into batteries. Uncle Sam worries that China could squeeze the market one day.

"The deposits hereabouts are different, the company's guy told me. Unusual for cobalt. High-grade, but found in one little old narrow thin vein that runs underground across north-central Maine, mixed with copper. And they say that as the first major domestic source, the Maine mine would be able to sell as much output as it wanted to the US government itself."

What the mining company hadn't shared with Skillings was that this new find thus enjoyed twin benefits: Politically, it would be difficult for environmental activists to challenge its existence—those activists wanted electric vehicles, but you couldn't have them without cobalt. And simply by coming into play, the mine here would have the market effect of tempering the price of cobalt exports from the Congo.

Postmaster Flurry remained skeptical. He was right to be so. In fact, as he suspected, the soft-talking executive from Future Minerals' subsidiary company hadn't been entirely candid in describing the mining operation to Town Manager Skillings. The mineshaft's surface entrance would indeed be, as the man had said, located miles to the southwest. There was just one problem, and it was a big one: The shaft the company already had begun excavating was damp, with a constant trickle of water running down its low walls. Much of that water, carrying leached acids and heavy metals, eventually was pumped out into a holding area called "a red dog pond" in the mining industry. Soon its bottom would be thick with a toxic sludge. And that outflow was handled according to all relevant environmental laws and regulations. And so on.

But there was indeed a catch, though it was invisible: The company only captured about 30 percent of the water flowing through its tunnel. Most of the rest seeped downward, pulled by gravity into layers of soil and rock. Some of that eventually trickled its way down into a water-bearing sedimentary level, labeled on geological maps as an aquifer. That tainted water ran inexorably through that gravelly level, and then, six miles southwest of the mineshaft entrance, it hit a layer of impermeable clay, which forced it to bubble up in the form of springs, either at the surface or in the beds of streams. And even before that water came to the surface, the aquifer was being tapped by wells. And at that point, every single molecule of water was laden with potent minerals, not all of them healthy for fish—or indeed for human beings.

3

LILY THORNFOOT'S BUSINESS

After law school, Lily Thornfoot had spent three long, hard, lonely years on the staff of a federal prosecutor in Newark, New Jersey, where she specialized, as did many in that state, in minor financial crimes—corporate kickbacks, bribery of officials, fraudulent tax schemes. But she hadn't thrived. She had felt bored with the work and stymied by bureaucracy. She didn't like having a boss. She hated working in a system that moved at a snail's pace. And she really didn't know how to make friends, especially among city people whose smiles always seemed false to her.

So she quit the federal job and drove back to Maine. She instantly felt at home, even living on the mainland. It was still on the coast, so she could smell the salt air most mornings and feel the breeze off the water in the afternoons. She set up a law practice in Ellsworth. She mainly handled wills and real estate transactions. But even at the start, while that routine drudgery paid the bills, she labored weekends and nights to develop a new niche business. It wasn't legal, but she knew it could soon be profitable. To wit: When she had been in the federal employ, she had noticed in every case of financial malfeasance that there almost always were people at the periphery who could have been indicted but weren't. They were enablers or people who knew or should have known. Also, she noticed, there tended to be parallel situations—when one company flourishes through illegal or corrupt practices, people at other companies often are doing the same. But there was usually no particular reason to go after those parallel cases, because the offending company had been caught, and that had the effect of stopping the practice across the board. Prosecutors would select the low-hanging fruit, the easier cases to prove, picking off the weakest in the herd.

Lily perceived a business opportunity in those murky situations at the shadowy fringe of such fraud cases. If the contracting officer at Company X had taken bribes or kickbacks, she calculated, there was a good chance that people holding similar positions at major competitors, Companies Y and Z, had been approached as well. To narrow down her target set, she focused on senior people who retired unexpectedly—say a guy who punched out at the age of fifty-two and in good health, without any hint of sexual harassment, substance abuse, or erratic behavior, from Company Y within a year of the case being brought against Company X. She found that about half the time, those people had gotten out one step ahead of the feds, having done the same things but done them more intelligently, or without pissing off someone who would turn them in. She narrowed her focus to those living in the northeastern United States. It took about a year, but this quiet sideline soon started turning a profit. It helped that she had brought with her from her federal job a bundle of backdoor entry codes to dozens of financial institutions. To be blunt, she knew how to hack into account statements from brokerage firms. And the more she did that, the better she got at it.

Soon, the most lucrative part of her law practice was blackmail. But she was careful, and had figured out how to make it have the appearance of legality. On paper, she simply was being paid retainers for her legal advice in certain specialized areas related to shady corporate dealings. And for appearances' sake, she kept active in working on real estate closings, even if it bored her to tears. It paid some bills, maintained some contacts, and provided good cover. In chitchat over signing closing documents, she often learned of a big new purchase of a coastal mansion or a hunting lodge.

The downside to the blackmail was the amount of time it took to put together the case before approaching a given target. At the outset, getting the business up and running had eaten up all her savings. Preparing a blackmail case against a target often involved multiple trips to courthouses and investigators and crime locations around the country, and it always involved countless hours with documents. The upside was that the cases she was delving into already had been compiled, in indictments, depositions, testimony, and plea agreements. You just had to have the patience to put them together, and the imagination to make them come alive. For example, if a document mentioned that unindicted executive Y met with the same prostitutes sent the previous day to executive X, and in the same hotel room, 972, then you got a photograph of that room and put it in the dossier. Such images tended to jog guilty memories. The target would see the couch in the photograph and remember the two Vietnamese prostitutes nicknamed "the Muppets" who had been sitting there. When shown the photo, the target's next question sometimes would be, "How much do I pay you?" And then visible relief that it was just a few thousand dollars a month.

Another advantage was that the targets came in bunches—perhaps two or three executives each at companies Y and Z, and another few at suppliers or joint venture partners.

She would build the cases slowly. Around the walls of her back office, she kept six card tables. Each new target got his own table. Cases that were related got adjoining tables. Little things would pop up that would spice up individual cases—for example, an executive having a little side hustle firm that was retained as a "consultant" by a foreign firm that was contemplating entering the field. The feds wouldn't worry about such a case, but it would spice up a dossier. The executive's former employer might not have been informed about such shady side pursuits, and might cut off retirement health care coverage if it found out.

Her favorite moment in preparing a case was deciding what her monthly fee would be. For standard, low-level, run-of-the-mill tax evasion, the charge was $1,000 a month. Her best type of target was the executive who had been a survivor and knew it, someone who hadn't been caught but knew he might have been. These men—and thus far they all had been males—prided themselves on keeping a low profile and acting discreetly. They valued their privacy. And in this case, that meant they would pay good money on a regular schedule. She especially liked that, with the scandal that took down a competitor or colleague now receded a few years into the past, these prematurely retired executives were just beginning to breathe easy, tucked away in rambling houses on the Maine coast, or in rural Connecticut, sailing their boats in the summer, spending winter vacations golfing in Florida or the Carolinas. But their respiratory systems tended to seize up soon after she knocked on their front doors.

So Lily Thornfoot was especially pleased on this sunny afternoon when she drove up a long driveway to find her newest target living in a pleasant but not ostentatious house on a lake in the Maine woods about a half hour north of Damariscotta. Perhaps the only giveaway was a four-car garage, an unusual structure in Maine. The owner of the place, named Charles Rappaport, had been a top executive at a data communications firm that had provided services to the Pentagon office that, among other things, performed the final legal review on all major defense contracts before they were awarded. His friend, the chief technology officer at the firm, had figured out on the q.t. that buying the stock of companies that were about to win major contracts could get him in trouble. But there was another, subtler stock play: No one seemed to notice when, a few times a year, he shorted the stocks of companies that had been expected to get contracts but did not. It was only when his friend left his wife for his young and alluring executive assistant that this clever insider trading scheme began to unravel. The scorned wife knew a woman in their Bethesda, Maryland, neighborhood who worked for the enforcement division of the Securities and Exchange Commission. They had a cup of coffee together. "Oh, honey," the SEC woman said. Later that day she went to work. The chief technology officer soon faced a bevy of SEC charges.

But the SEC did not go after the man who at the time was the executive IT architect, and who had piggybacked his friend's insider training, but more carefully, in several different small accounts. It was that man, Charles Rappaport, upon whose door she now knocked. It opened slowly.

"Mr. Rappaport?" she said. He looked older than she expected, and had an unhealthy pallor to him. He nodded but said nothing. He looked her up and down—in her mid-thirties, attractive, her coal-black hair done in a severe bowl cut, wearing her standard outfit of a fringed brown leather jacket, black jeans, and cowboy boots. It gave her a whiff of an Old West gunfighter, which indeed was how she liked to think of herself.

She hinted at why she was there. "I'm Lily Thornfoot, a lawyer."

He squinted at her. "You look more like a cowboy. Or cowgirl, I guess."

She ignored that assessment. "I've been looking at the mess a few years back at your old company, right after you left and the CTO was charged by the feds."

"That's all in the past," the man said, moving to close the front door.

"And that's my job, to keep it there," she said. She smelled Scotch on his breath. It was not even three in the afternoon, she noted to herself.

"What exactly is that job?" he said. He stopped closing the door.

"Mine?" she said. "Legal advice and financial consulting."

"I'm satisfied with the people I currently have for those." He kept his hand on the door.

"As you should be," she said, sliding the toe of her left boot forward. "They are first-class firms. Especially Cat Cove Financial." She watched as he registered the fact that she knew where much of his investment portfolio resided. He didn't seem very fast on the uptake, she thought, but perhaps that was his age or the glass of whisky already in him. "They're careful and honest. Not real imaginative, but you can't have everything."

"So why should I talk to you?"

"Because I offer an ancillary service. One you may not be aware of needing. There are facts that you need to keep quiet. And I can do that."

"Like what? I was never charged."

"And then you left the company very quickly, after that kerfuffle about shorting the stocks of companies that lost out on big federal contracts. That was interesting. And I think the IRS especially would be eager to know more about the taxes you didn't pay on the money you took in. By my count—which I know is far from complete—your profits ran into more than two million dollars." She paused. "You know, they tend to want not just disgorgement but also civil penalties. Which really are punitive fines. In cases like yours, even a stretch of prison time."

"Jail?" said the man, blanching a little. The prospect clearly had not occurred to him before.

Lily waved a hand dismissively. "Don't worry about that. That's almost always in a Club Fed, which isn't so bad. You could do it."

"Isn't there, like, a statute of limitations on tax evasion?"

He was asking the questions she wanted to hear. It was time to set the hook. "Funny you should ask," she said. "That's Title 26 stuff, in the seven thousands of the federal statutes. You're right, on the surface of it, at least. The statute of limitations is indeed three years."

"But?" he said cautiously, almost not wanting to hear the answer.

"But, and this is where it gets interesting, that limit can be waived if civil fraud can be established. And of course, there the burden of establishment is lower—not the criminal standard of being beyond a reasonable doubt. Instead, the civil burden is just the clear preponderance of evidence. So concealment, misstatements, subterfuge—that's pretty much all they need to overcome the statute of limitations. Bottom line, yes, they still can come after you. And they probably will, if I give them a hint or two." She paused. "Sorry to bore you with the details." He was, of course, anything but bored. Little shots of adrenaline were cutting through his stupor and jolting his heart and brain. He put a hand on the entryway wall to steady himself. He was growing alarmed and a little angry that his lawyer years ago hadn't been clearer. Of course, he had not been quite open with his lawyer back then, either. This woman clearly had the facts in hand, many more than he had seen fit to share with legal counsel back then.

Usually at this point, she would drop a heavy hint or two. Perhaps pull out a page from a deposition that named this executive.

In this situation, that wasn't required, because today's target cut to the chase. Rappaport stood thinking, and finally said, "What you are proposing is extortion."

"I am not threatening violence. So I prefer to think of it as profit-sharing." She cocked her thumbs into the belt loops of her jeans.

"Why don't I just call the police?"

"Because you didn't back then, did you? You had reasons not to, back then, and most of those reasons still exist." She squinted at him, taking his measure. He failed. "Nah, you're not gonna squeal, I'm sure of that." She moved on. "Would you like to see the account statements?"

He was curious. "How do you survive, carrying out this kind of operation?"

"That's a thoughtful question, even if it does possibly indicate homicidal thoughts on your part. How I survive is this: I'm careful." She looked him in the eye. "Real careful. More than you ever were." That remark hit home. He realized she was kind of playing with him. Toying with his fears.

Lily Thornfoot could see he was impressed. She continued. "As you've seen, I do my research. And I protect myself. I make multiple copies of each dossier, with instructions at several law firms about where to send them in the case of my death, accidental or not. So you better hope I don't cross paths with a drunk driver on my way home today."

"Those types of files can be located."

"But you'd never be certain that you had them all, would you? And simply locating them, on more than one continent, would be expensive and, in most cases, quite illegal. And the clock would be ticking. It could get real messy real fast. Which is why my business model works: It is cheaper to work with me than to try to stop me. A lot cheaper. Always."

"How do I know you're not bluffing?"

"I think you already understand I'm not. But this is how it works: When your first check clears, I will mail you a copy of the file on you, holding back only a few choice documents. You read it and decide whether I have you red-handed enough to retain my financial and legal services." She rocked back on the heels of her boots. She had made her case. His move. She waited.

"You bitch."

She winked at him. She enjoyed this. It was almost like winning a high-stakes poker hand. "Then I'm hired?"

"Yes." He sighed. He seemed almost impatient to agree, which surprised her. She wondered what else was going on in his life.

"First check is twenty-five thousand. It's like a renter's deposit. Thereafter five thousand a month, unless you give me any trouble, in which case the monthly fee doubles. I don't like difficult clients."

He nodded, albeit a little sleepily, she thought. Nevertheless. Charles Rappaport was signed up as one of Lily's more lucrative clients.

He closed the door and went off to take a morphine pill. That wasn't because a good day had just turned bad. All his waking hours nowadays were dark, and now, with the stage 4 cancer tightening its stabbing grip on his guts, they were getting even duskier.

4

AN UNUSUAL FORENSIC AUTOPSY

After he parked at the hospital, Doc Healey had gone directly to the basement cubbyhole of Walter LeDroit, the best lab technician in the building. LeDroit probably was too bright for his job, which meant, Healey had found, that he occasionally got bored and careless with routine work. But give him a solid challenge and he would rise to the occasion, concentrating his energy and imagination. Healey liked to bring him odd problems, tell Walter that he had his own theory but add that he wouldn't share it because he didn't want to influence Walter's analysis. Walter would dive in. Likewise, today Healey simply had said, "Found this little brookie floating in the Salmon this morning, near a tributary. Let me know what you think."

The tech had shrugged and reached out for the plastic bag, almost eagerly. "First time I've done an autopsy on a fish," he had said.

Early that afternoon, LeDroit came to Healey's office. The doctor was eating at his desk and reading the *Wall Street Journal*. "Sorry to interrupt your lunch," LeDroit began. "But I thought you'd want to know. Your poor little brookie is loaded with heavy metals and minerals, especially copper, nickel, and cobalt. That's weird, I mean, really weird. I would guess one of those things, or some combination of them, shut down its breathing. Hence the foam in the gills as it struggled for oxygen."

"Why's that so weird, Walter?"

"Because as far as I know, cobalt isn't found in Maine. Nor anywhere in the United States in commercially viable deposits. And Doc, these are glow-in-the-dark levels." LeDroit added, "I mean, that's what we call them down in the lab."

"That cobalt trace *is* weird," Healey said.

"Yep." LeDroit paused. He eyed the doctor's toasted sandwich, held in his meaty left hand. "I was you, I wouldn't eat any more fish out of that stream."

Healey slowly lowered his left hand and placed the sandwich back on its paper plate. In it were the two smaller trout he had caught that morning before the brookie bumped up against his leg. "Oh dear," he said, gazing at the filets in a new light. "I probably eat a couple hundred of these things a year. Most caught near that spot."

"Let's take a blood sample," LeDroit said. It wasn't a suggestion.

As LeDroit prepared the needle and swabbed Healey's forearm with isopropyl alcohol, Healey began wondering about his recent spells of deep fatigue, the occasional pangs of neuropathy in his right foot, and a stiff heaviness in his long leg muscles. He had guessed these were probably the consequences of knocks taken in his time decades earlier as a defensive lineman in college football at Dartmouth. But now he began to think that those might actually be symptoms of heavy metal toxicity.

The situation had energized LeDroit. He spoke quickly as he drew the blood. "This reminds me of a body I have down in the cooler," he said. "You ever heard of Jacob the Growler?"

"Don't think so," Healey said, hesitantly.

"I bet you have. Recluse who lived up near Coffin Spring?"

"Oh yeah, the hermit guy in the woods just north of town," Healey said, nodding in recognition. "Tall, skinny fellow. Black hair going every which way, beard the same."

"That's him. After his parents died, he stayed alone in their cabin by a spring. Basically a loner, but bicycled into town almost every night to fill up a growler at the Carcass Pile. Even in the winter. You'd see him out there pedaling through the snow and ice."

"Yeah, I'd seen him. I hadn't realized that's how he got his name. I thought it came from the way he talked."

"Could be both. Also his dad, Preston Coffin, was known as 'Preston the Prowler.' So Jacob's name came naturally."

"Why 'prowler'?"

"Kinda funny. Preston Coffin wasn't a thief. He was a borrower. People appreciated the distinction. He was shy, almost never spoke. Didn't like to ask for things. So if he needed a ladder to cut a limb or patch a roof, he'd just slip one out of someone's garage, return it later when the job was done. Once he borrowed a whole gas-powered pump, I think when he wanted to deepen the spring pool. I don't know how he carried it up there, and back down, but he did.

"Anyway, Jacob was like his dad, never said much. Like I said, he'd walk into the Pile, plop the jug down on the counter, put a fistful of ones and change next to it, and say in a low grumble, 'Fill 'er up.' Then he'd bike home with the growler on a sling around his back."

"Where'd he get the money?"

"Typical hardworking Mainer. This and that. Trapped and sold beaver pelts. Sometimes had a bearskin. In the fall, shot enough deer to feed himself through the winter. Got a moose in the swamps sometimes. In December, made Christmas wreaths from cuttings around his property, sold them by the side of the road, probably along with little bags of marijuana for Christmas cheer. Rest of the winter, sat in front of his fire and built rustic chairs and small tables. In the spring, when the snowbanks melted, he walked the roadside and picked up bottles and cans so he could redeem the deposits. In the summer, sold blueberries, raspberries, and blackberries by the highway. The furniture too. He got by, as Mainers do.

"Anyway, other day, he staggers into the town hall, limping, wincing, white faced. Slowly says to Albion at the desk, 'Lock . . . me . . . up.' Albie is used to running the front desk, figures Jacob is just drunk, puts him in the holding cell, leaves a bucket next to him, you know, just in case. Hears a shriek or two. Then quiet. Goes back to check on him an hour later, and Jacob is stiff and white, not breathing.

"Jacob doesn't have any living relatives, so they just trucked him over to the hospital. I put him in the cooler. Didn't think of it as a priority, because I assumed we knew the cause of death—booze. But now, seeing this poor fish, I'm not so sure."

"What's changing your mind?"

"I was up to Coffin Spring a few weeks ago, hunting. Jacob pretty much lived off that spring. His water was piped from the little pool at the top. He grew fish in the bigger lower pool. Watered his garden with it. Ate the deer and turkeys that lived around it. His ducks swam in it, and he fertilized the garden from their muck. He ate the eggs from them and his chickens."

"And?"

"The ferns had died. Even the plants farther back were kinda brown-red. And I am guessing that every bite he took was toxic."

The blood drained from Healey's face. Had he just had his future foretold? "That's a terrible thing to do, poison a spring," he said softly. "A spring is a gift from creation."

Two hours later, as the day was ending, a young doctor Healey had never met knocked, poked her head in, and then walked into his office. "Walter LeDroit, down in the lab, called me," she began.

"That's not good," Healey said, rising to greet her.

"I'm Doctor Warshinski," she said. "Hematology. Started last month."

"Uh-oh," he said, and sat down. She remained standing. She had a small pad in her hand and was taking notes.

"How far did you find the dead fish from your house?" she asked.

"Maybe one hundred yards." He was getting more worried. This woman is half my age and far smarter than me, he was thinking. He was seasoned enough to make that judgment and wise enough that it didn't bother him. She had his undivided attention.

"And you live downstream from that tributary you mentioned to Walter?"

"Yes," he said.

She clicked her tongue as she absorbed that bit of data. Then she said, "I am guessing your house, out there in the country, relies on well water."

"Yes," he said.

"Well, first thing, stop drinking it. Throw out anything made with water from the well, like lemonade, orange juice, or cooked pasta. Get the well capped."

"And?"

"You're married, right? Call your wife and tell her all that. And tell her you're going into hemodialysis in one hour. I want to start cleaning the metals out of your blood ASAP. After that, we'll keep you here for observation tonight, maybe longer. It will take a day or two for your organs to feel any relief—if they do. Could be weeks."

"This is all happening pretty fast," Healey said.

"I hope fast enough," Warshinski said. "Tell your wife to bring one overnight bag for you and another for herself."

"Anything else?"

"Just one thing. I've texted a nephrologist I know. She's in Boston but is flying up tonight. She's an old friend. She'll examine you and your wife in the morning."

After she left, he sat in his office chair and absorbed the day's changes. He could feel his life being turned upside down. His health was in jeopardy. His house seemed to have become a toxic waste site. Yesterday he had been the Marcus Welby of north-central Maine, a well-liked and widely respected doctor on the verge of a well-deserved retirement. Today he was—what? A walking toxicology exhibit?

The next morning the young nephrologist poked and prodded him, frowning again and again. She examined each finger on each of his hands, turning them over, squeezing them, looking grim all the while.

After that, Healey lay in his hospital bed, taking notes on a legal pad and talking to his wife, in the adjacent bed. It was a way of steadying himself, of reasserting control over his world. And also of figuring out a way forward.

If he were no longer a practicing doctor, what would he become? He decided that instead of being a victim, he would become an activist. He thought about how to proceed. He wrote out a list of people to call. First on it was Lincoln Addison, the editor of the *North Country Times*, and someone he had known since he had come to Maine twenty years earlier. He called Linc and filled him in, suggesting that a reporter look into the situation.

At the end of their conversation, Addison suggested that Healey also contact Ryan Tapia, a former FBI agent who lived on Lost Pond, near Bangor. Healey added Tapia to the list. "If I recall correctly," Addison said, "the man left the Bureau after a noisy run-in where he had sided with a band of protesting Penobscots or Micmacs two years ago. Remember the bombing down in Wiscasset that hit the Indian march?"

"Yeah," said Healey, who had been on the receiving end of some of the medevac flights that day. "I think I actually met Tapia once, when he needed a fast checkup."

"So I'd say the man isn't afraid of being in a minority, or of controversy," Addison said. "You'll need that here. I've heard some worrisome things about the mining company."

Healey telephoned down to his office and got Tapia's number. He called him and told him everything he had told Addison. Then he called his own lawyer, Ted French. After that he was exhausted and slept for several hours.

5

BETTY GROLEAU ON THE CASE

Betty Groleau was gazing out the big bay window next to her desk at her newspaper job, mulling how she had done on her first month on the job. When she told friends at her college newspaper that she would be joining a weekly newspaper in a small town in rural Maine with a sagging economy and an aging population, they had shaken their heads. The group was having a few beers after closing the college paper's weekly edition. "Aren't you climbing aboard a sinking ship?" asked the features editor, who had been accepted by a decent second-rate law school.

The sports editor, who was kind of a jerk, had been even snarkier. "I hope you like writing obituaries," he jibed. He was going to a company where all the news would be written by AI, with humans only needed to oversee the operation. He had been interviewed for the job remotely and still wasn't even sure that his new boss was a human or a machine. Still, he told Betty, "Hey, I'm getting on the gravy train, not the steam train."

And her first day at the *North Country Times* had indeed left her a bit wary. Lincoln Addison, the editor and owner, was clearly old school. "We don't have a lot of rules, but two are ironclad," Addison had told her over her welcoming mug of coffee. "First is, we don't use anonymous sources. Mainers hate that kind of sly hiding."

"Got it," Betty said.

"Second, each week, before you go out to cover your beat, you have to write and turn in an obit. Robin at the front desk keeps a list of ones to be done."

"How long does that rule last?" Groleau asked. To her ear, it sounded a bit like hazing the new kid.

"Oh, it's not just for you," Lincoln said. "That rule applies to the whole staff, all of us, including me. Obits may seem dead to you, but they help keep this paper alive. Families buy multiple copies."

Betty thought back to the warnings of college friends. Had she made a mistake in going to this small-town outpost of the old school? Maybe the smug sports editor had been right.

Addison read her face. "Don't worry, you learn the formula pretty fast: Every obit needs to state the basic facts of job, family, schooling, any military service. Fraternal organizations, VFW, volunteer fireman, anything like that. Recreation, which is almost always going to be hunting, fishing, and snowmobiling. Drinking, too, but we don't put that in. Then a quote from a boss or friend about what a great person the dead person was. List the surviving family members. Location and time of services.

"Just remember that someone loved the person you're writing about. And don't make mistakes. People get real insulted by those in obituaries. Double check the spellings of all names."

"Cause of death?" she had asked.

He looked a little harder at her. This new kid was sharp. She had noticed he hadn't mentioned it. "No, we don't put it in, because a lot of families are shy about it. And honestly, it is just too depressing. Cancer, cirrhosis of the liver, heart attack, suicide, car crash—who needs to have that thrown at them every week?"

That night, back home, she started a blog to record her life as a young journalist in rural Maine. "I share a house with three other women, one of them sleeps in the laundry room in the basement. I drive a sixteen-year-old Toyota, and I do my clothes shopping at Goodwill. And I love it." She decided to call the online diary *Tales of a Cub Reporter.*

And now, after a month on the job, Betty Groleau was beginning to feel at home. She had written four obits and filed six stories about minor local events. She looked again out the bay window. There was a reason the new reporter had that location. The view of the main street of Beecher was pleasant, from the library to the bank to the Congregational and Baptist churches, buildings of wood painted white that had been facing each other for two centuries. The Baptists thought the "Congos," as they called them, were stiff-necked snobs, while the Congregationalists privately viewed the Baptists as undereducated and overemotional. But this fine vista of small-town Maine was given to the newest reporter on the newspaper's staff of five for quite another reason: It was by far the coldest part of the room. The old window had grown loose in its big wooden frame. Her predecessor in this spot had jimmied the window against the frame with four pencil stubs. That had stopped its rattling when the wind blew heavy from the northwest, as it was wont to do in winter. But the stubs did not block the steady creep of cold air around the frame. That other reporter had moved up to a job covering high school sports for the Bangor paper. Betty had added packing tape to his work, but when the wind blew down the street, she not only heard it, she felt it seep in and tickle the hairs on the back of her neck.

She was on deadline, typing up her article on last night's North Country Consolidated School District Board meeting, so she didn't notice Mr. Addison standing next to her desk. Finally, to get her attention, he said, "Hey, Betty."

With her hands hovering over the keyboard, she looked up at the editor and owner of their little country newspaper. Lincoln Addison was only fifty-six, but to her young eyes he looked ancient, standing there bald and bespectacled, a bit stooped, in his customary white Oxford shirt mail-ordered from Land's End years ago, almost worn through at the elbows, a red bowtie, and a blue sweater vest over his little potbelly. Everyone on the staff wore some kind of outerwear—sweater or vest or even light coats—because Addison had locked the thermostat at 61 degrees, to save money on heating bills.

They understood the logic of that move. Like many other newspapers, the *North Country Times* was built on a business model that had eroded over the previous two decades. Before then, it had thrived on several dependable sources of income, with page upon page of classified ads for boats and hunting rifles and snowmobiles. It also had made good money from a regular schedule of lucrative full-page advertisements from car dealers, department stores, and grocery stores.

Now much of that cash flow had dried up. Classified advertising had been destroyed by Craigslist and other outlets on the internet. All the local car dealers had folded. Department stores, with their big full-page ads, had gone away as well, seemingly overnight. There was still some advertising for groceries, but even that was dwindling. There was just one big grocery store remaining in the area, which meant it didn't need to ask people to drop by. They had no alternative, except a long drive south to Bangor that took time and gas and could be dangerous in winter when the roads iced over after the sun set at four in the afternoon.

All this meant, among other things, that the newspaper was operating on a thin profit margin. Lately heating oil had become a bit of a luxury. The reporters were young, but even for them, it could take a while to warm up in the chilly newsroom after being out reporting in the cold. Even Steno, Addison's aging golden retriever, had pulled his little round bed to the warmest spot in the newsroom, directly under a heating vent, and in the middle of an aisle. When Betty had tried to move the dog bed one day so it didn't block the way, Steno, usually quite friendly, had curled his lip and issued a low growl. She had backed off the notion of relocating his bed.

"Possible story for you," Addison told Groleau, who herself was wearing a fleece jacket, with a woolen ski hat atop her pony-tailed brown hair. "It'll take some legwork. Tomorrow, I want you to go up to the area north of the Salmon River, the Pushaw County towns, and talk to people about their water problems."

She grabbed a notebook. "Which towns in particular?"

"Here in Beecher, down in Asbury, up in Finney Junction."

She considered that list for a moment. "How could they have water problems? It felt like it rained at least a couple, three times a week the last few weeks."

Again, he was impressed by her ability to quickly sort out where the story was. "Not quantity. Quality. Some bad stuff in it, apparently. First thing to do is call Doctor Ed Healey. He practices in Bangor but lives in Finney Junction. He'll give you the basic facts. Then go up there. Take two, even three days if you need it."

Her eyes got big. This was the first time since she'd come to the paper that he'd given her more than a day to report a story. He was taking this seriously.

"Call me at the end of every day of reporting, let me know what you're seeing."

"You think this could be big?"

"Maybe. I've never heard Doc Healey so vexed. And the guy knows his stuff."

6

AN AWKWARD FIRST DATE

Ryan Tapia, at the age of thirty-five, was no longer lost in grief or dominated by constant mourning. His wife and two children had been killed in an awful car crash four years earlier. He still thought about them every day, but now was able to do so without his back knotting up and a headache inching down the right side of his forehead along to the eye socket. And his ability to think had slowly become clearer. He also had recovered the thirty pounds he had lost during his time of mourning, and now looked healthy and fit. His eyes were no longer sunken and haunted. He looked like someone at home in the world, ready and eager for each day.

He was meeting with his grief counselor, Dot Williams. "I don't usually do this," she said to him at the end of their biweekly session at her office in Hallowell. She was in her sixties, and time told on her face. From the deep creases in it, Ryan guessed she was a recovering alcoholic, or perhaps had suffered through a long and painful illness. She was large, slow-moving, and wise. She used a cane when she walked around, which she often did as she talked, keeping off the stiffness. "But there's someone I'd like you to meet,"

Dot said. "I don't know quite why, but I think you and another client of mine, Nina, might hit it off."

"Why are you making an exception?" Ryan asked, curious.

"I think you probably would be good for each other," Dot said.

"What makes you say that?" Ryan asked.

"You two seem to be in similar places, emotionally, coming out of times of deep and wrenching grief. Her husband was in law enforcement, as you were. He was a game warden. Died violently—shot by a drunk hunter. She's reserved, but you strike me as someone who doesn't mind that. You're about the same age as her." Dot gave him an email address. "Just keep in mind that she isn't quite as far along in the process of loss as you, okay?"

Ryan's first date with Nina Daigle may have set a record for awkwardness, if such accounts were kept. They met for lunch on a Saturday at the Quarry Tap Room in Halloway. Nina was almost the opposite of Solid Harrison, Ryan's former lover. Solid was tall, outgoing, and eager to take on the world with both fists. Nina was not just shorter than him, she was shy and often looked like she wanted to withdraw back into her shell. Ryan sensed that she just wanted someone to curl up in her cave with her. Solid wore her hair long, down her back, or piled high in a Gibson Girl. Nina had a short, neat pixie cut of solid black hair. Her face was dominated by eyes that conveyed both intelligence and quiet sadness. Underneath them, she had a receding chin. Her skin was very white—not pale, more like porcelain.

He had prepared for the date by thinking up questions to ask. He asked them, one by one. He thought he had composed enough to last through the meal, but he ran through them in just ten minutes.

"What do you do for a living?"

"Tax preparation." She sipped her white wine.

"In Bangor?"

"At home. Don't get out much since Dave died."

"Do you have any hobbies, distractions, things you do for fun?"

"Fun?" she said, as if it were a word new to her. She seemed puzzled that he would even ask. She gave a small shake of her head.

Ryan tried again. "I mean, you must have some distractions, hobbies, recreation."

"I work, I cook while listening to music, I read books, mainly novels. Elizabeth Strout, Richard Russo, stuff like that. And I go for long walks. Once a week I clean the house and then go grocery shopping."

"Doesn't it get lonely?"

"Not if I don't think about it." She paused. "Now I'm thinking about it."

Oof, Ryan thought to himself, you're not making this easy. She had mentioned music, so he decided to go with that. "What kinds of music do you like?"

"Oh, it's stuff most people have never heard of." With that, she lapsed back into silence.

"You don't talk much, do you?" he finally said.

"I'm sorry," she said. "I've talked more in the last ten minutes to you than I have in a year, except to Dot"—that is, their mutual grief counselor.

"You know what?" he said. "I think this date is a mistake."

She looked stricken. She had hesitated while dressing for this meeting. She had stopped at the door for two full minutes. Once in her car, she even had picked up the phone preparing to say she couldn't make it. But she didn't want to disappoint Dot. And now, after that effort, it was over?

He saw the crumpling look on her face. "I don't mean that us meeting up was a mistake," he said. "But us sitting down across a table from each other, trying to talk. I know you've been through a lot. Maybe this is just too much. I think it puts you in an uncomfortable situation. You said you enjoy walks. So, have you ever walked Vaughan Woods?"

"No, but I've heard good things about it, especially the trail along the brook."

"Shall we go now? I've got my dog in the truck and he'd love a walk in the woods."

"Yes," she said, the tension draining from her face. They stood. He left twenty-five dollars on the table for two drinks.

It was a lovely, clear, early November day, the end of an exuberant Maine autumn. Winter was just around the corner, with its screaming winds and blizzards. With the sun not far above the horizon at three in the afternoon, you could sense that malevolent cold hovering just over the hill, building up, preparing to come over and settle in for five or so months of ice, snow, slush, biting winds, and darkness. That knowledge made the bright, pleasant day all the more one to savor.

Ryan lifted Moolsem out of the cab of the pickup. The dog hobbled ahead of them, happy to be out, even if he could hardly run.

"Is your dog okay?" Nina asked.

"Yeah," Ryan said. "But still kind of recovering from some bad injuries."

"Hit by a car?"

"Worse. Remember that Indian march a couple of years ago?"

"The one that got bombed?"

"Yeah," Ryan said, closing his eyes inadvertently as the memories of that day in Wiscasset came back. "The blast blew Moolsem off the road and into the water. Shattered his front legs. I looked down and saw he was half out of the water, head on the sand. A state trooper was standing over him with his pistol out, going to put the dog out of its misery. I got him to stop, took the dog to a vet. He's been living with me ever since."

Nina said nothing, just blinked. After a long moment, she said, "What a vale of tears we live in. The most infinite thing in the universe is its ability to inflict pain."

Ryan silently agreed. That was, he thought, the kind of thing people said when they no longer believed in God, or at least a benevolent one. They walked the trail along the brook and then kept going up to a pond and stood on a little arched bridge made of stone. They admired the small waterfall below it. Just its gurgling sound was soothing. They walked another mile, through an open meadow where seven deer were grazing, perhaps taking refuge in the preserve, where no hunting was allowed, that being the season. Ryan and Nina ambled south to the sporting fields of the town high school and then curved back to the bridge, where they stood again to watch the rush of water over the rocks. "Thank you for this," she said, "for sensing my unease at the restaurant and doing something about it."

"Of course," he said. "I feel like I am beginning to see why Dot thought we should meet."

"Me too," she said.

Later, as she stood next to her Subaru, she added, "Let's do this again soon." He was surprised by that, and so was she. They shook on it. She leaned over and patted Moolsem's big brown head.

7

A TALK WITH THE SICK DOC

In the morning Ryan drove over to see Dr. Healey in the Bangor hospital. At the front desk he was directed to the fourth floor of the main building. At the ward desk, a man directed him to the "third room on the right."

Ryan walked down the hallway and knocked, then opened the door a quarter of the way. The lights were out. He could just make out in the semi-darkness an old woman in one of the beds, her hair gray, skin yellow, wearing a nose-and-mouth oxygen mask. Her eyes were closed. Ryan said, "Sorry," and turned to go back to the ward desk to say there had been a misunderstanding. But then he heard a muffled voice. He poked his head back into the room and saw, lying in the second bed, a man in a mask saying something unintelligible through his own breathing apparatus. Ryan took another step into the room. The patient was waving a feeble hand to beckon him closer. Ryan did so and realized that this was indeed Doc Healey in the further bed.

Healey talked with his head sideways on his pillow. Ryan had to lean in to hear him. Healey's breath was a stench, like something was dying inside him.

"Can't pay you much," Healey said.

"Don't worry about the money. I have some, and I also have time. And I'm a Mainer now. So call it my civic duty."

"Okay," Healey said, taking the charity. "I'm thankful." He had given plenty in his own time and had seen that there could be as much grace in accepting help as in offering it.

"So what do you want to know?" Ryan asked.

"Who is this mining company that poisoned my water, killed the fish?" Healey paused, then added, "Who are they? How can they get away with this?" He closed his eyes, took another deep, ragged breath, then opened his eyes and said, "What can we do about it?"

"Those are good questions," Ryan said. "I'll start on them today. You look tired. I will be in touch."

Healey nodded wearily and closed his eyes again.

Ryan thought over the doctor's three questions: *Who are they? How do they get away with it? And what, if anything, can we do about it?* Ryan had learned during previous investigations that everything has a history. So the first step in any situation is to find it. You can save yourself and others a lot of time by learning it. If there's an instruction manual involved, read it. And every trade has its own language. Once you've got the basic lingo down, people often will assume you know more than you do and tell you things that can be very helpful.

Once back home, he began searching the internet. He found only one news story, from a site that tracked new mining operations in the United States. It said that a company named Future Minerals had placed a major order for robotized boring gear, and speculated that the company might be opening a new operation in the eastern United States. He also found a press release about a geologist at the University of Northern Maine who was planning to study the effects of mining on water supplies in north-central Maine.

He spent over an hour trying to dig up more on Future Minerals, the company doing the cobalt mining, but found precious little. He decided they probably were one of those outfits that paid "reputation management" consultants to delete information and commentary about them or bury that material beneath mountains of online trivia. But he gleaned enough to understand that cobalt was an essential ingredient in most batteries for electronic cars, smartphones, and other electronic devices nowadays. Without it, they would have to be recharged far more often. Every smartphone contains a few grains of high-grade refined cobalt. But, he learned, it is electric cars that are hungriest for the stuff. If you want to reduce the heating of the planet, you need to cut back on gasoline-powered vehicles. And the electric ones require cobalt for their batteries. Right now, he learned, most of the cobalt came from mines in the southeastern Congo. But not all. The Maine mine was already producing.

He called the office of his onetime lover Solid Harrison, now the governor of Maine, but only for a few more months, as she was term limited. She called him back later that day. "Future Minerals?" she said with an unusual caution in her voice. "Ryan, I know about that company. And I've heard the stakes are huge. This is bigger than Maine. It's Wall Street money, private equity funds. They're in a different arena than you and me, where the rules are different. If there are any."

"What does that mean?" he asked. "I've never known you to shy away from a challenge. Are you warning me away from looking into this?"

"I know you won't be deterred. But prepare to be surprised. And expect to be disappointed. Be careful, Ryan," she said, her voice unusually tight. It was the first time he'd ever gotten that buzz of worry from the ever-confident Solid Harrison. At the same time, she had a well-developed sense of self-preservation. A natural politician, she instinctually understood the need to pick your battles. And the message Ryan got was this was a fight she was not going to take on, even if people were getting sick. Something about Future Minerals had given her pause.

"Did they get to you somehow?" he asked. He wondered to himself if she had hinted to the Department of Environmental Protection that it should sidestep or slow-roll the cobalt-poisoning problem. His question came out harsher than he intended.

Solid sighed. "Like I said, be careful," she repeated, and hung up.

Ryan put down the phone and thought. He was not sure what he was getting into. But it was interesting. He felt invigorated, alive in a way he hadn't since his early days in the FBI. If you were going to get into trouble, it might as well be high-stakes trouble, something that merited taking a few risks. It was better than getting shot by an adulterous husband caught red-handed.

Something was different about this situation that engaged him. In most investigations, the task was to figure out who did it. But in this case, he knew pretty damn well who was doing it, or at least the name of the company. But who was behind that name? And what could be done to stop them? Anything?

He felt he was venturing onto very thin ice. But he was ready to try.

8

WANDERING IN THE ORONO BOG

Ryan and Nina had learned their lesson. For their second date, they met not at a bar or restaurant, but at the Orono Bog, an eerie place just north of Bangor. It was a genuine piece of tundra, about three miles long and a mile across, that had remained behind when the glaciers receded northward from Maine some twelve thousand years ago. Nothing grew in its highly acidic soil but weird outliers of plants—scrag moss, low bushes, pitcher plants, and dwarf black spruce. Its edges were marked by larch and red maple—two other anomalous trees. It felt like an asylum for stunted flora willing to eke out a meager existence on infertile soil with a short growing season. The pitcher plants pulled their sustenance from the rain and air, there being no nutrients available in the soil of the bog. Ryan and Nina walked out on the boardwalk through this unusual and edgy but beautiful landscape. Moolsem trotted behind them, sniffing the new smells of this strange place.

Ryan told her about his conversation with Doc Healey. She listened intently. A shadow crossed her face. "Do you know what you are getting into?" she asked.

"I think so. I know it's big." But as he said it, he sensed that she was so rattled by the killing of her husband that she didn't trust anything in the world anymore. "But I don't think I'm being foolish."

"Well, be careful," she admonished.

They walked on in silence. Nina took his hand for a spell. He sensed that she needed to tell him something.

As the boardwalk curved back toward the more normal Maine forest of spruce and fir, she began talking about herself in a way she hadn't before. "My husband was shot in the chest by a drunk hunter firing through a closed cabin door. When you lose someone far too soon, and it happens violently, and stupidly, you can't be sure of what has happened to you. All you know is that the world doesn't make sense to you anymore. There's a hole in the heart of my world.

"Even more than that, my whole life feels off-balance. I've stopped trusting my senses. Had I been a fool for all those years? I didn't know. What else am I fooling myself about? For example, I didn't know if I had the capacity of happiness anymore."

"I've walked that road," Ryan said sympathetically.

"That's why I'm telling you about this. Today, now, I feel that I might be able to feel some happiness again." She squeezed his hand in thanks. "That's not a small thing."

"It's huge," he agreed. "Like maybe a little balance coming back into your world."

"Exactly," she said. "The axis tilting back."

At the end of their bog walk, she stood on tiptoe to give him a quick but soft kiss, a peck of gratitude. "Do you want to come to dinner at my place?" she asked.

"Big step," he teased.

"No joke," she said. "I surprised myself by asking."

"Yes," he said. He put his arms around her head and drew her toward him. Looking down on her head, he noticed that here and there were gray hairs, much premature, amid the black ones. They both had been through a lot. They had a longer, slower, pleasant kiss. When it was over, they stayed in each other's arms, her head resting against his neck. Moolsem sat contentedly next to them. He liked this female addition to their little pack.

"Most of the time when I'm with other people these days, I feel a kind of nervous jangling," Nina said in the quietest of voices, as if she were talking to herself. "Not now. I haven't felt this comfortable, this calm, in a long time. I didn't know if I ever would again."

"Yes," he said.

They separated in the parking lot. On his drive home, Ryan played the "what if" game: What if this investigation goes wrong? What if it lands me in trouble? What's the worst that can happen? He didn't have any answers, but these were questions he knew he needed to keep in mind as each new fact unfolded. Moolsem stared at him, wondering where the nice woman had gone.

9

A DOCTOR LUNCHES WITH A LAWYER

A week later, Doc Healey was discharged from the hospital. He arrived home to step into a life that had utterly changed. He had suspended his practice. Using a walker, he moved around his house, looking at it through new, sadder eyes. Then he sat in his rocking chair by the window to rest and contemplate his next steps.

A man walked up to the front door and knocked. "Mr. Healey?" he said.

"That's me," Healey said.

"This is for you." The process server handed him a subpoena. Healey stood in place and opened it. It was a notice that he and his employer, the nonprofit organization that owned the hospital, were the target of a class action lawsuit purporting to represent the estates of everyone Healey had seen in the last two years who had gone on to die. There were fifteen of them—not surprising in a state that had the oldest population in the country, and from that population, these were people who had come to him seriously ill. The suit, he would learn, alleged that Healey, as an experienced physician, knew or should have known that he himself was growing ill from cobalt poisoning, that this had thrown off his judgment, and thus had been negligent in ignoring his symptoms.

He called his lawyer Ted French, also one of his oldest friends and occasional fishing and hunting buddy. The man had handled his will and house closing. He kept his practice small and routine, intentionally. French came by to pick up the papers. A few hours later, he called and suggested lunch the next day at the Ice Hole, their wood-paneled local bar and grill. The name was reference to the cook's favorite wintertime activity, fishing out on the frozen lakes. It was considered slightly higher class than the Carcass Pile.

"You ever looked at a totem pole?" Ted asked, after they ordered.

"Yes," Healey said. "Why?"

"Because you are the low man on that pole, that little guy at the bottom who always looks squished."

Healey wasn't following. "What are you saying?"

"My guess is that the people suing are not really after you. The suit is designed to put pressure on you to agree to settle. So I'm saying that your goal, in the months that come, should be to stay out of the way. When the elephants dance, the mice in the grass get squashed. The lawyers for the hospital and their insurance company will begin dancing soon."

Mabel, the waitress, delivered their tuna sandwiches. Looking at the fish, Healey instantly regretted the choice. But he hadn't really been hungry anyway. He nibbled on a potato chip.

"Let me tell you a legal secret," Ted continued. "This is just preliminary maneuvering, the prelude to the bigger suits that will come down the road. I wouldn't be surprised if the mining company is funding the lawsuit in order to do some discovery on the sly."

"That sounds kind of conspiracy minded to me," Healey said.

Ted French nodded. "I know it does now, but you'll see. There is one thing that I will guarantee you in all this. And that is, when there is this much money involved—several hundred million, perhaps a billion, if the cobalt holds its value and the mining continues—justice will not be done."

Healey frowned. "Doesn't sound like the country I was raised in."

"It's not," French said. "That's why I've stayed small. A lawyer can still seek justice in small ways. Most of the time, when I go into court, I'm seeing lawyers I've faced before and will again. Implicitly, we are working for good, livable outcomes. We all have to work with each other, time and again. To do that, you have to operate in good faith, and keep it. And the people we are representing, they're all neighbors, people we see in the grocery store, at church, and at the high school games. We got into court to try to make things right, not to score points.

"But," French continued, "this is different. The guys behind this suit, they have never met me or you before, and never will see us again in their lifetimes. All they are looking for is a win. When they look at us, all they see are scalps waiting to be nailed to the wall." French put down his sandwich. "What I am saying is that in the big arena, you get up into the tens of millions of dollars, especially the hundreds, the rich will always win. Sometimes one guy, sometimes another, but always the big guys. Not us."

"Is the system really that rigged?"

"I don't think it was when you and I were coming up. But since the 1980s, the whole Reagan thing, money has taken over. It runs national politics. Across the country, the rich call the shots as never before. Extremist billionaires have installed the majority of the Supreme Court, stuffing it with right-wing nuts. We have the worst chief justice since Roger Taney. He oversees a court wildly out of touch with the people of this country, really attacking our history. Effectively, the game is over."

"What do you mean by that, 'game over'?" Healey asked.

"It means that you and I, we now live in an oligarchy. We don't see it here much where we live, until something like this cobalt situation comes along, because we are not in the big money arena here in rural Maine. But believe me, the super-rich run this country. Dollars are more important than votes."

"Hasn't that always been the case?"

"At times. But the situation now, it hasn't been this bad since the Gilded Age, when the railroads and then Standard Oil bought and sold members of Congress."

"What does that mean for my case? Can't I be Maine's Erin Brockovich?" he said in a weak attempt at humor, but genuinely trying to suss out a silver lining amid French's bleakness.

"Only in Hollywood. Your case will be a matter of money, in both courts and politics."

"So what do I do?'

French chewed on his tuna sub. He was thinking. Finally, he said, "I'll tell you what I do. I seek peace in small ways. I listen to my wife. I try to help my friends and neighbors. I go to church on Sundays and recite the Lord's Prayer. I walk the dog. I take consolation in nature, just the trees, the wind, the sun, the sky, the flow of seasons."

"And no hope beyond that??"

The old lawyer shook his gray-haired head. When he lifted his chin, Doc Healey saw that his eyes were watering. "And sometimes," he said a bit more harshly, "I think we need to tear this country down, take it back from the rich." He let that sink in. "But, being a simple country lawyer, I keep that to myself." He put down his sandwich. He was no longer hungry either.

Back home that afternoon, Doc Healey had another visitor: Mrs. Healey's sister. She had driven up to take his wife away. She took the fragile woman by the elbow, walked her to the car, buckled her seatbelt, and then drove away to New Hampshire, away from the poisons of Pushaw County. After his wife left, Doc Healey sat in his rocking chair and wept. His life had been blasted to pieces. He opened a new bottle of scotch whisky.

10

THE WOES OF ROGER ROBICHAUX

Ryan drove to Moody's Diner in Waldoboro. Coming down the highway, he saw at the junction of Route 220 and Route 1 a warm red sign atop the roof glowing through the gray morning fog like a hearth fire. He walked in and looked around. The old restaurant was basically in the middle of nowhere, but that very location had made it Maine's favorite meeting spot, because it was roughly equidistant from Augusta, Bangor, Ellsworth, and Brunswick. It was even reachable for breakfast from Portland, provided that you got an early start and there were no fog delays and crashes on I-295.

The place was packed, as usual, with six waitresses trotting through the narrow aisles toting oval platters of eggs, bacon, sausages, and blueberry pancakes. Ryan looked over the sprawling place and saw a hand wave from a beefy man, white haired, who looked to be in his late fifties. He had called Ryan and asked him to meet there, in the back booth on the left. He had said over the phone that a mutual friend from Liberty Island had recommended Ryan as a solid, honest investigator.

"Is that a friend of ours temporarily living in Thomaston?" Ryan had replied.

"You got it," the man had said in that phone call. "I went to see Caleb the other day." Years earlier, back when he was still employed by the FBI, Ryan had solved a murder case in which Caleb Goodwin, a respected lobsterman from Liberty Island, had been convicted after Ryan's investigation of a homicide seen by many on that island as justifiable. Despite the crime, Ryan had come away with respect for Caleb, even admiration—just as many native Mainers did. Caleb currently was serving time in the state prison in Thomaston, but in the curious ways of Maine, also was serving on the Liberty Island school board. He had run for office from his cell, been elected, and faithfully attended the board's meetings by Zoom. With time on his hands, he almost always was the best prepared member of the board, the one who read the background papers and legal opinions and even think tank studies. It had become a joke among them that at some point in each meeting, someone would turn to his Zoom image and say, "Caleb, what do the experts say?"

He also was a sensible man whose opinions were respected generally, which is why Roger Robichaux had gone to see him. Caleb was a natural problem solver.

Ryan sized up Robichaux as he made his way to the booth in the back. The man, half standing to greet him, was wearing a green khaki shirt and blue jeans, his feet clad in scuffed steel-toed work boots. He had a big square head with white hair, but despite the latter attribute he looked like he was still doing physical labor every day.

"Ryan Tapia," Ryan said.

The man extended his right hand. Ryan saw a bit of engine oil under the nails and lining the deeper creases of his palms. This was a man who still worked with his hands, at least part of the time. Ryan sat down on the booth's other bench.

"Mr. Tapia, I'm a pretty simple guy," Robichaux began. "I'm good with small engines. I can safely drop a tall pine, spruce, or fir, and make it land where I want, most of the time. I'm not as good with hardwoods, which are heavier and broader, because I don't deal with them much. I know how to plow a field. I've picked more than a few potatoes in my day."

Ryan nodded. "But that's not why you called me."

Robichaux nodded but continued on in the same vein. He had a point to make. "I learned, the hard way, how to make money. And then I found out, on my own, how to keep it and invest it. I dropped out of high school to work as a truck mechanic. By the time I was twenty-five I owned my own repair garage. As my business grew, I started to understand how money works."

"What do you mean by that?" Ryan said.

"I mean, if you have money, you can make more. As it piles up, making money gets easier and easier. You put it in the bank, they pay interest. Then you have more. So you invest in stocks and bonds, and they usually go up. I did all that.

"But I found the best place to put money, at least for me, is in land. I knew the area, who might own some acres but needed some money, and I'd go offer them cash. I kept my ear to the ground. I got lucky a few times as the town expanded. I made me some real money. I mean, a few times I made more in one day on real estate than I ever made in a year of fixing blown transmissions."

After the waitress poured their coffee and left, Ryan asked, "May I ask how much?"

Robichaux gulped and gave a small shake of his head. "We don't talk about that in Maine," he said quietly. Indeed, like most prosperous people who lived in the state, he did not show his wealth. He lived frugally. He drove an aging pickup truck. He still believed that a sweater wasn't truly his possession until it had a hole in it.

The man was, in socioeconomic terms, a landed peasant, though that isn't a term Americans tended to use.

"So where do I come in?" Ryan asked.

"I'm getting to that," Robichaux said. Ryan realized that this was the hardest part for the man. He leaned back, closed his eyes, took a deep breath, opened his eyes, and then got to "that." "Unfortunately, someone has been digging around in my financial records."

"The IRS?"

He shook his big head. "Worse. Much worse. Two months ago, a woman comes to my office in the back of my garage. Not from around here. Her name is Lily Thornfoot, has an office up in Ellsworth. She said that if I don't pay her, she'd tell the IRS that I owed them a whole lot of back taxes on income."

"How much did she say you owed?"

"She said at least fifty thousand in income taxes, maybe double that." Robichaux gulped again, then took a roll of Tums antacid tablets out of his pocket and popped two in his mouth.

"You can afford that. So what's the problem?"

"Well, plus substantial penalties, she said. And maybe prison time."

"Or what?"

He stared at his mug of coffee. "She said or I could pay her one thousand dollars a month. She had a deal set up where nothing would happen if I paid her a small, and continuing, amount of money. She called it 'legal consulting.' I call it blackmail or extortion." He looked up at Ryan as a question occurred to him. "I don't know—is there a difference between the two?"

"Yes, generally," Ryan said, reaching back in his mind to his classes years ago at the FBI Academy in Quantico, Virginia. "Extortion is someone threatening violence against you or someone close to you, or against your property, if they don't get paid or get some favor from you. Blackmail goes in the opposite direction—it is threatening to disclose information that likely would harm you somehow if it were known publicly."

"Then this is blackmail, I guess," Robichaux said. He looked at Ryan with his big fists balled. He had been squeezed by her for two months and was embarrassed by it. Nothing like this had ever happened to him. He felt humiliated. He needed help and he hated asking for it, especially from a stranger. His big head reddened as he began. He said words that tend to be difficult for a proud, self-reliant man to say: "Caleb Goodwin said you might be able to help me. Can you?"

"That depends. What outcome are you looking for?"

"I want her off my back. I don't want nothing violent. I just want her to stop and go away. And I don't want to get the law, or the IRS, involved."

"Let me think on it," Ryan said. "First question: How much money do you have, total? I need to know the score."

Robichaux leaned forward and almost whispered. "For real? Business, stocks, bank accounts, land?" He looked around, scratched his bushy hair, and then said, in a very quiet way, "I'd say total of about seven to nine million, depending on where land and stock prices go in the next year, and I guess that kinda depends on the Fed and interest rates."

Ryan knew from his time in the FBI that dealing with blackmailers was like handling a live bomb. You needed either to defuse the situation or get well out of the way. Generally, a lawyer would tell you there were only two ways to handle it: Get the information out, which made their threat harmless. Or blackmail the blackmailer—say you would turn them over to the authorities if they didn't stop. That ran the risk of becoming a lethal standoff, where both sides had their hands on the triggers of loaded guns, facing each other.

But seasoned investigators with forensic financial expertise knew there was a third way, which is where Ryan knew he would come in. That is, find out who else the blackmailer is doing this to, then threaten to disclose that fact. Make it someone else's problem. This is the course that Ryan knew he would pursue. "First thing I'll need is all the information you have on her," he told Robichaux. "Any contact information, any emails, any phone numbers, any documents she has shared. Copies of any checks you sent to her."

The waitress brought Roger a big platter of two fried eggs, buttered toast, home-made pork sausage with sage and fennel seeds, and fragrant, hot home fries. To Ryan's eye, it looked great, if not entirely healthy. Robichaux was not in the mood. He stared at it for a moment, wondering why he had ordered it, and then pushed it away miserably. "That's my usual, for sure, but I got no fucking appetite since this started," he said unhappily.

Ryan felt sorry for the guy. "I'll take this on," he said.

"How much is it gonna cost me?"

"Generally I charge a thousand a day," Ryan said. "But we can agree on the fee when we both feel the situation is resolved." That was the Maine way to do it, Ryan had learned. They shook hands. In this part of Maine, that action was as good as a contract.

"That's reasonable," Robichaux said. "I'll email you copies of all the checks. And Mr. Tapia, thank you." Ryan pulled a napkin from the dispenser and wrote out his email address.

That afternoon, the emails arrived from Robichaux. His checks to the blackmailing woman had all been deposited in the same place, a branch of the Gulf of Maine Bank. The account name was "Witch Island Money Management." Ryan sat back in his truck and pondered that. He checked Google maps. There was such a landmass near Bristol, Maine, but it was uninhabited, so the name did not lead him easily to an address. A Google search turned up not a single reference to such a company. Ryan's first conclusion was that this was a careful blackmailer, someone who knew what they were doing. This wasn't being done by someone who had tripped across Roger Robichaux's secret and decided to cash in on it. This was a more sophisticated operation, one that took planning and research. Ryan realized that in turn it would take some work to figure out what that operation was—and even more to stop it from blackmailing Roger Robichaux. To obtain the needed information about the workings of this blackmailer, he would need to follow the money, of course. But how? Somehow he had to get inside the workings of the Gulf of Maine Bank.

11

GROLEAU GOES REPORTING

Betty Groleau dove into her new assignment probing the water quality situation in the Pushaw County towns. She was delighted with the confidence her editor had shown in her. She, of course, had no clue that this assignment, this "story," in the parlance of journalism, would change her life altogether.

Each of the towns she was to examine—Asbury, Beecher, and Finney Junction—still possessed the four establishments it takes to stay on the map in Maine: a gas station, a convenience store with a liquor license, an elementary school, and a library. In the summer, the trees and fresh air disguised the essential dreariness of these places. But when icy winds out of the northwest tore away the last of the leaves, the disguises blew away. All that was left was the bare essentials, enough to fuel the pickup trucks, keep their drivers well fed and lightly inebriated, books to help the readers get through the five months of winter, and enough schooling for the children of those drivers so they could grow up and sign mortgages and take out loans for their own pickups.

Betty parked her battered Tercel near the town's main intersection, marked by a single blinking red light. None of the buildings were more than two stories—no reason to stick your head up out here. There were only a few paved roads. Except for the two lanes leading south to Bangor and north to Jackman, most of the asphalt, going east and west, petered out within a mile of the stoplight.

She got out and began buttonholing passersby on the cracked sidewalk. It seemed that in the last day or two, everybody she asked had become worried about the water. People were puzzled and confused. She got all those standard quotes down in her notebook. "I'm very nervous," said Wanda Hennigar, fifty-six, of Finney Junction. "My dog died and I think the water did it."

"Usually, I'm the rock of the family," commented Fran Primm, forty-nine, of Asbury. "I like to charge into a mess and clean it up. But not now. I'm taking it hard. I think because I've never tried to handle a problem that's, like, invisible and three hundred feet below my feet." She had a question for Betty: "What do you call a problem like this. Is it an 'unnatural disaster'?"

Lois Burdette, seventy-eight, who said she was from "far western Beecher, really out in the boonies" said that one of her cats had gone spastic, "I think from drinking the water and eating mice and birds that had this toxic crap in them. Do you know anything about that, how it gets passed along?"

A thin old man in Beecher with greasy white hair said to her, "You don't recognize how important water is in your life until you can't rely on it." He said his name was Gary Rath. Asked his age, he said, "Old." He pointed at his foot. "I had a circulation issue, from Type 2 diabetes, and the docs said the water thing probably made it worse. Now they want to chop off some of my toes. Even worse, my granddaughter was pregnant, lost the baby the other day. The docs say they don't know why, but my guess is . . ." He choked up, tears streaming down his cheeks. She leaned forward and gave him a sympathetic hug. He said, "I'm sorry, I just don't feel worth a damn anymore. If a man can't protect his family, what good is he?" Finishing the hug, Betty quickly developed the suspicion that because of the water problem, Mr. Rath had stopped bathing. She shivered, not sure why. Something about the guy haunted her.

She walked into the area's sole grocery store, the IGA Food Mart, where she noticed that the shelves where drinking water was sold were empty. "Gone as soon as I put it up," Charlie Pierce, a stocker, told her.

She saw Lorenzo Dow, the Baptist minister in Asbury, whom she had interviewed two weeks earlier for a story about a funeral for a well-loved retired teacher. He was staring at the piles of cabbages and potatoes.

"What do you think of this mining company?" she asked.

His dark eyes seemed to burn. "They are wolves and ravens," he said loudly, waving his index finger in the air. She wrote that down but she wasn't sure that quotation would work in her article. It rang true, but it just didn't sound newspaper-ish to her.

The one odd note in her reporting was struck by Verdella Skillings, fifty-eight, of Finney Junction. "I think there are a lot of rumors flying around and folks are just being irresponsible going on about it without knowing what they are talking about," she told Groleau, who didn't know that Verdella was married to Pete Skillings, the town manager of Finney Junction.

In fact, Groleau found as she made calls from her car, not one of the three town managers would give her much help. Did the towns get any money from the mining company? "Can't talk about town business without a green light from the selectmen," said the town manager in Beecher. The two selectmen she called said they'd heard there were water problems and were planning at their next meeting to discuss the issue. Until then, one told her, "it would be premature to comment, even kind of irresponsible."

Schools are the lifeblood of rural communities, Betty knew, so she dropped by the high school to see the school nurse, Kay Lake. "Can't talk," Lake said. But as she did, she wrote down her cell phone number and handed it to Betty, who took it as a suggestion that the nurse could be more open if she could speak in private away from the school.

That night, Betty called her. "There's some problem, some crap in the water," Lake said. "I'm seeing a lot of dermatitis on the kids."

"Derma-what?" Betty asked.

"That means skin rashes. Maybe twenty or thirty percent. More among the girls, I don't know why. And I really don't know why the town governments, the town managers really, have been so slow to react. People say it's connected somehow to some mining that's going on. I don't know anything about that. But I have a card here from a guy from the university who was looking around. Name was Bap Salim, S-A-L-I-M." She gave Groleau the number. "He came by, said he was studying the effects of the mine on the drinking water."

Next, Betty dialed that number. "Professor Salim?" she asked.

"Please," he said, objecting politely. "I am as yet merely a small graduate student. Call me Bob, like everyone else here does. I have grown accustomed to that usage. I am studying for a doctorate degree in geology. The specialty I have taken on for my dissertation research is sedimentary formations in Maine. The subject has little commercial potential, hence it has not been deeply examined, heretofore. But I find it interesting, especially in the glaciated valleys."

Betty thought to herself that this Salim guy was one of those people who will always tell you twice as much as you need to know. This wasn't a bad person for a reporter to encounter, except that a reporter's most precious commodity is time.

Bap Salim said he had been looking at the groundwater flowing in the gravelly formations under the three towns, just inventorying the elements the flow carried in different spots. "The water was close to toxic, which is entirely new to me, I must tell you," he said. "It gave me quite a fright. Now, when I go to research in that area, I bring my own bottle of water from home."

"What concerned you?"

"There was much I simply could not fathom. Most of all, I recorded high levels of nickel, copper, and cobalt. This is what we might call levels that bring to mind lethality."

"Wow." Betty was genuinely taken aback.

"Yes. I fear the people residing there are ingesting poisons. Yet, much to my puzzlement, I have not been able to awaken the interest of state officials. I confess I do not know how government works in this country. It is just two years that I have resided on this continent, so I have much still to learn. Perhaps you know of some sort of study you could recommend? Something about how American politics works in practice? I read the theory but that is not what I am seeing in the quotidian flow of events."

Betty steered the conversation back to the subject at hand. "Have you tried the Maine Department of Environmental Protection?"

"They said they need a request from a town government."

"State attorney general's office?"

"I called and they never called back."

"This is great stuff you're giving me," she said with gratitude as she wrote all this down in her reporter's notebook.

"Oh!" he said with sudden alarm. "Heavens, no! Please, miss, do not put my name or affiliation in your newspaper account. I worry that there could be grave consequences, misfortunes of many worrisome kinds, were I quoted by name. I could lose my green card or be ejected from the university. I was merely trying to be well-mannered with you and tell you what I have gleaned in my field studies, which I see as my scholarly duty. But I implore you most deeply, do not quote me!"

Betty was flummoxed. "But something needs to be done," she protested.

"I have seen in the movie accounts of the workings of newspapers that reporters sometimes use the words of someone without a name. Can you call me 'an observer who has grown greatly concerned'?"

"I'll ask my editor."

"If you put my name in the newspaper, I won't be able to talk to you anymore."

She called Mr. Addison, her editor, who reminded her he had never allowed what he called "blind quotes" in his newspaper, and said he wasn't going to change that policy now. "Aside from that, good work," he said.

The next day he put her article across the top of the front page. Even without Salim's name, and with his concerns paraphrased and also attributed without quotation marks to "an expert who has done preliminary research who declined to be identified," Betty Groleau's article was powerful. In the middle of the article was a big, black "pull quote" box highlighting Healey's words that, "They have just about killed my wife—Dr. Ed Healey."

The article was boosted by a short, pungent lead editorial that Addison wrote at the last moment. It read, in full:

> *The Mining and the Salmon River*
>
> *Who are the stewards of the land and water here? Where are they?*

On the morning that the article and editorial appeared, the chief of staff of the state legislature's Committee on the Environment and Natural Resources called Betty Groleau to inform her that two hearings would be held. The first two would be closed, for information gathering, to get the members up to speed. Next, they would hold an open hearing.

Later that day, Betty heard that several people in the three towns of Asbury, Beecher, and Finney Junction had announced that they were forming a new organization called the "Afflicted Citizens' Group." They hoped to help the populace deal with the water problem, and especially to prod their governments, state and local, to move faster.

Betty was flattered. It was the first time she felt her journalism really was having an impact.

The two-pronged attack was received less enthusiastically by Diane Peligroso, a political consultant in Augusta. She spent much of the day taking notes and then writing a memo for the executives of Future Minerals about the way forward. Among other things, she needed to figure out how to neutralize this "Betty Groleau" reporter. It likely would take a lot of money, but that was the company's strength. It had deeper pockets than anyone.

12

RYAN SNIFFS AROUND

On the same day that Betty Groleau's article appeared, Ryan drove up to Finney Junction, Moolsem in the cab with him. He stopped first at the post office. In rural Maine, he had learned, the postmaster is like an old-time telephone switchboard operator, talking to townspeople all day long and hearing a lot.

Ryan introduced himself. "Doctor Healey asked me to poke around on the water issue," he said. "First, I'm trying to get a sense of the town, how it's doing, how it's reacting to the water issue."

"I'm Marty Flurry. How's the doc doing?" said the postmaster, standing at the counter. "Haven't seen him lately."

Ryan shook his head. "Pretty bad," he said. "Wife is worse."

Flurry nodded, his white curls bouncing around his head. "Yeah, I've been hearing it aged her about thirty years. They're good people. They've helped out a lot of folks around here."

"I guess you know most of the people here?"

"Pretty much here in Finney Junction, except for a few recluses out in the woods," Flurry said. He knew what was up, who was ill, who was struggling.

"How are they handling this water problem?" Ryan asked.

"People are getting hit pretty hard," Flurry said. He stuck out his right arm and rotated the wrist to show Ryan the angry red skin streaking upward toward the inside of his elbow. "We call this the Pushaw County rash. Mine isn't as bad as a lot of people got."

"I was thinking of going to see Senator Tweedy," Ryan said. "Do you know his views on the water thing?" Tweedy was the man who represented Pushaw County in the upper body of the state legislature.

"Beats the hell out of me," Flurry said. "Between us, Tweedy doesn't like taking stands." He frowned in disapproval.

"Who should I see, then?" Ryan asked.

Flurry took a piece of yellow lined scrap paper and began writing names. "Start with these four. Solid people," he said. "Not the talkers, like Tweedy. You don't want them. Some people are good at talking. I know, I'm one of them. But these I'm writing down are doers. My list is good for Finney Junction. The other towns, I don't know so well. So in Beecher, see Rick Trexler. He is one of the organizers of this new outfit, the ACG. I put him on the list, fourth."

"What's that?"

"The Afflicted Citizens' Group. Locals who are getting rashes and worse. Older people who already had lung problems seem to be having more, too. Some bad respiratory shit going on. He also can direct you to some people up in Asbury. That's kind of back of the beyond to me."

The first two weren't in. The third told Ryan to come back later. So, half an hour later, Rick Trexler, a neat, well-trimmed accountant who believed in knowing the rules and following them, walked him through what he knew, which wasn't much. "There's something up with the town managers," he said. "I don't know what it is. But they seem to be real jumpy about this mining situation.

One of them, probably the best of them, told me on the down-low that he wished I would just drop this ACG thing."

"Which one was that?"

"Pete Skillings, down in Finney Junction," Trexler said. "Surprised me, 'cuz I've always thought of him as a stand-up guy. Real solid."

He also had a recommendation for Ryan's foray northward into Asbury: "Go see Ned Meddybemps. He's out in the boonies. I'll give you directions." He drew a map for Ryan to show how to get to the man's remote location, in a protected little valley in the foothills on the remote western side of town.

"Why him?" Ryan asked.

"Just some talk I've heard, that Meddybemps and some of his backwoods friends have been carrying on a little campaign against Future Minerals, like letting the air out of the tires of company trucks when they were parked outside the diner down on the Bangor Road. I heard that once when some company guys were drinking at the Ice Hole, they poured sugar into the gas tank of three company vehicles, and ice-picked their tires. Even some rumors that they want to drop power lines running to the company's tipple or flood the mineshaft."

Trexler's handwritten map led Ryan from the town's main road to a graveled one with a hand-painted sign that said BACK SWAMP ROAD. When the bed changed to dirt, he saw the "white mailbox" on Trexler's map and turned down a driveway that led, after a half mile through spruce and fir woods, to a mobile home in a clearing. Out front was an aging red Datsun pickup truck. Next to it stood a double deer hanger, looking a bit like a gallows. Dozens of sheaves of freshly harvested marijuana plants hung from the deer hanger, drying in the brisk wind out of the northwest.

When Ryan got out of his truck, the front door of the mobile home opened. A man who looked like a Native American, with a copper-colored face and long black hair, his face elongated by a wispy black beard, and wearing dark brown overalls, looked him up and down. "I'm guessing you're that guy that's poking around," the man said.

"I am," Ryan said. "You're Ned Meddybemps?"

"I am. Glad you came. We don't get many visitors up here, and I was curious," Meddybemps said.

"About what?"

"About what kind of stupid motherfucker would take on the mining company directly." He grinned at his own blunt wit. "Those company people, they're a bunch of bear plugs"—a reference to the hard, dry core of fecal matter that accumulates in bears while they hibernate in winter.

Ryan was surprised. What had he done to deserve a rural Maine raspberry as a welcome? He looked questioningly at Meddybemps. The man's face softened a bit as he said, "Look, mister, I don't know a lot. I hunt, fish, cut some wood, fix small engines, grow some dope."

"But?" Ryan asked.

"But one thing I know is that in the United States these days, Big Money talks. If you get in their way, they'll knock you on your ass every time. Hard."

"So you're giving up?"

"No, but I'm not gonna try to take on an eight-hundred-pound gorilla alone."

"Well, what do you think me and the ACG should be doing?"

"Come out on the back porch, why don't you?" Cutting through the mobile home, Ned stopped at the refrigerator and took out two Bud Lights, handing Ryan one. Sitting down out back, on a homemade deck made out of split cedar logs, Ned filled a bong, lit it up, and took a big draw. He kept his mouth closed for about fifteen seconds, then let out a stream of smoke.

He handed the bong to Ryan, who took a big puff.

"You look like a nice guy," Ned said.

Ryan had lived in Maine long enough to understand that Ned wasn't giving him a compliment.

"Meaning?" asked Ryan.

"I'm saying you're probably too nice for what we need to do about the fuckers at the mining company." He stopped to puff and then expelled another cloud of smoke.

"So what do I do?" Ryan said, as he took another hit.

"Stand back and let me and my friends do our work against the company."

"Which is?" Ryan asked.

Ned shook his head as he held in the smoke. Then he puffed it out and said in a half-choked voice, "Better you don't know." There was a long history in the back country of turning to violence in response to intrusions by Boston bankers and big paper companies. They came in like they owned the place, and often they held documents that backed up that claim—even if the locals had lived on the land for decades, clearing out the rocks, draining the swamps, and pulling a living from the soil.

The dope hit the center of Ryan's brain, sending numbing but tingling messages down his legs and arms. He had the odd sense, new to him, that purple light was flowing out of his fingernails. "That's strong stuff," Ryan observed.

"Thank you," said Meddybemps. "Been working on it for months." He reached down and passed Ryan the ounce bag he had used to fill the bowl of his bong. "Take this with you, why don't you?" That was, Ryan recognized, a friendly signal that their discussion was ending.

At the door, Meddybemps noticed Ryan admiring the old Datsun pickup. "It's a 1972 King Cab," he said. "Has over three hundred thousand miles. Had it twenty years now. Put in two replacement engines."

"That's a long time for a truck to live in Maine, what with the winters," Ryan said.

"I gotta keep it going. I understand old engines. These new ones, with the software, I got nothing." Meddybemps looked at him again as another question occurred to him. "Hey, do you happen to know anyone handy with dynamite? Maybe some fish poachers—they always seem to have some around. You know, drop a half stick down some deep hole in a lake, get a few hundred fish?"

Ryan was puzzled, and said so. "I thought you'd know any of them around here."

"Only one left that I know was Donut Michaud, and he blowed himself up."

"What kind of name is 'Donut'?"

"Oh, his real name was French, 'D-O-N-A-T,'" Meddybemps said, spelling it out. "He told me once that it was real popular among French fishing families who worked the English Channel. But people around here, they didn't know that word, so they kind of made a Dunkin's out of him." He snorted with amusement at that outcome.

"How did he blow himself up?"

"Well, he wasn't real organized."

"Why does that matter?"

"Flicked a cigarette butt out his pickup's window. They say it landed in the bed of the truck, where he'd put an old propane tank. Tank must have been leaking. The butt lit off the propane, and that exploded the dang powder box next to it, which blew him and the truck clear off the highway. He never knew what hit him. Old days, he used to sell the trout he dynamited from a big ice cooler side of the Bangor Road."

"You're right," Ryan replied. "It's better I don't know what you're up to." He climbed into his truck and slid the bag of marijuana under the passenger seat, where he forgot about it. Moolsem hopped down to sniff it.

13

THE STUDIED IDLENESS OF SENATOR TWEEDY

On his way back south, Ryan got a call from Senator Tweedy saying he could see him in a few minutes in the senator's office in Beecher.

Bud Tweedy—"Bud" was his given name—proved to be a plump, old, pink-faced man. His modest success in life came from an insight he had developed early on when term limits became the law of the state. A careful politician, he realized, could work the new restrictions to his advantage. The trick was to find a partner who was willing to alternate with him. So Tweedy served one or two terms, stepped down, made money while he waited to run again, and then went back into the state senate.

Ostensibly, he and his political partner, Bill Dunn, belonged to opposing parties. In practice, they belonged to one of the oldest political groupings of all time, the Don't-Rock-the-Boat party. While in office, both neglected ideology in favor of patronage—highway contracts, state usage of federal subsidies, and such. And each reserved for the other the choicest patronage plums. When Tweedy was in office, he appointed Dunn to slots on the Turnpike Authority, the Resources Advisory Council, the Liquor and Lottery Commission, the Gambling Control Board, the Maine-New Hampshire Bridge Authority, and the Public Utilities panel. And when Dunn was in power, he did similar favors for Tweedy. Over the years they had learned to keep a close eye out for openings on panels offering that ideal combination of hefty per diem allowances, generous annual compensation, and light work. By themselves, each of these board slots didn't amount to much. But taken altogether, they provided a small but dependable income, especially if combined with "consulting fees" that some industries offered. Tweedy and Dunn were, in short, small but hardy barnacles on the slow-moving hull of the ship of state.

Tweedy sat looking at Ryan from behind the desk in his office. He was wearing an old black blazer, shiny from age, flecked with dandruff on the shoulders. His hands were folded over his ample stomach. His eyes looked over the top of his eyeglasses, which rested on the tip of his nose. He had been reading the new edition of the *North Country Times,* which now lay on the desk before him. "Where do you live, young man?" he asked, affably enough.

"Lost Pond," Ryan said.

"Down near Bangor?" he said, his voice suddenly less warm. He sat forward, ready to end this conversation. "That's out of my district. I recommend you contact your own senator."

"But I'm here about your district," Ryan protested. "I've been talking to some people today who are upset by what's been happening with the water as a result of the mining."

"That's not been proven," Tweedy stated. He leaned back in his chair.

"But it's pretty certain. How else is cobalt and nickel going to get into the aquifer in the amounts we're seeing?"

"I see you've been talking to Trexler at his, uh, A-C-G," Tweedy said, leaning back even farther. By this point, his head was near horizontal, his face looking upward. Ryan could see straight up the man's nose and so noticed both the man's nostrils could use a trim. Tweedy said more slowly, "I wonder if you all are getting out ahead of your headlights, making some pretty wild accusations. Even slanderous, some might say."

"What do you mean by that?"

Tweedy didn't answer the question. Instead, he lifted a pack of Winston cigarettes from a desk drawer, located a match, examined a cigarette, lit it, took a long draw, and then blew a column of smoke about two feet over Ryan's head. Then he posed a question of his own. "You're not from around here, are you?" Few things are ruder to say in Maine than that. In rural parts of the state, it carries the same aggressive emotional weight that a New Yorker would convey by saying *fuck off.*

The blast of contempt was not lost on Ryan. "No, I am not," he said. "But that shouldn't matter. This is a real problem, right here in Beecher and Finney Junction."

"Ah," Tweedy said, as if suddenly seeing the light. He leaned the chair forward and pointed a finger at Ryan. "I recognize you now! Another out-of-stater come to educate us simple backwoods folk on how to run our lives." As the man talked, Ryan thought he detected an odor coming from him. It was like a whiff of onions, swirling through the toasty smell of cigarette smoke. It was, Ryan realized, coming from Tweedy's body. In torrid climates, people showered every day, even twice a day, to cool down and stay clean. But in Maine, in the winter, there was little reason to be so fastidious. When the weather stayed cold, most rooms were heated to somewhere in the range of 60 degrees, with 68 the ceiling. And most people went through their days swathed in layers of cotton and wool. Ryan decided that Tweedy's clothes must be saturated with his body's exhalations. And when Tweedy angered, it was almost as if that residue ignited.

"Well—" Ryan began to respond.

The senator cut him off. He lifted an arm to point at Ryan, and another wave of odor emerged from him. "What burns my ass is this: First, you from-aways mess up the places where you live. Then you visit here, you realize the place is beautiful, and a lot of you buy a house and settle down. And next, an amazing number of you then start telling us how to live. You know what I think? I think, why the hell should we listen to you? We kept the place beautiful long before you all ever got here. So a little humility would be in order, I say."

Ryan knew better than to speak. But he was mulling what this small-time politician was saying. There's a lot to be humble about in this situation, Ryan thought to himself. Lots of rubble to go around. And, in the long run, we are all from away.

"I won't take any more of your time, sir," Ryan said, and stood. Tweedy waved a hand at him as if shooing away a fly and ostentatiously resumed reading the *North Country Times*. Had to keep an eye on whatever mischief that Lincoln Addison, the editor fellow, might be stirring up.

Ryan looked on as Tweedy crushed out the remains of the cigarette. It was rare to see people smoke these days. He had noticed that the practice really only existed anymore among the rural poor, and in America, mainly in the South. For Tweedy to persist in the habit evidenced a kind of peculiar insouciance, a way of telling the world he just didn't give a damn. He had made a niche for himself in his part of the world and would stay in it, not unlike a little crab in an abandoned snail shell. There wasn't a great amount of money in it, but it was his. And there he would stay.

After Ryan was gone, Tweedy laid down the newspaper, lit another cigarette, and poured himself a shot glass of coffee brandy. The nerve of that guy coming in and bothering him, he thought, as he sipped the harsh liquid.

14

RYAN ENCOUNTERS DIANE PELIGROSO

After that dismaying meeting, Ryan got back in his truck. Moolsem sniffed hard at him, as if it was now Ryan who needed the shower. Ryan realized that his clothing must have absorbed the rank odors of Tweedy's office.

It was just mid-afternoon but the sun already was going down, its pallid rays slanting over the ridges from the southwest. Ryan turned left to drive down to Doc Healey's house on the south side of Finney Junction. Passing the county high school, he saw a sign out front: GIRLS BASKETBALL, TOMORROW AT 5. He decided he would attend it.

He knocked on Healey's front door. There was no answer. Healey either was out or, more likely, asleep. Ryan turned around on the front steps and looked over the yard and, beyond it, to a U-shaped bend in the Salmon River. Though wounded, the river was still lovely, with riffles and even one small rapid. Ryan could see up and down the river about three hundred yards. Between them, in the middle of the river's curve, stood a sharp ridge that was covered with spruce and fir on its lower slopes but tapered to bare rock along its spine. This had been Healey's paradise, the place where he planned to live out his old age. Now it was where the doctor's dreams were dying.

He was walking back to his pickup when his phone rang. He didn't recognize the number, but it wasn't flagged as spam, so he answered.

"Mr. Tapia, I'm Diane Peligroso, down in Augusta. Do you have a moment?"

"Sure. Can you tell me what this is about?"

"I represent a client with an interest in the mining operation up where you are today," she said.

"How do you know where I am?" he asked.

"Just part of my job," she said.

"Which is?" he asked.

"I can explain that all when we talk."

"And you want to talk to me about?"

"About your getting the whole story, not just one side. I think we should meet. But, to help me prepare for that, can you tell me if you have been retained as an investigator for someone?"

"We can talk about that when we meet," he parried. She struck Ryan as pretty nosy.

"How about tomorrow morning? Coffee in my office?"

And so, early the next day, Ryan knocked on the polished wooden door in an Augusta office building that said "Peligroso Consulting." A woman opened it. "I'm Diane," she said. "You must be Ryan Tapia."

She struck Ryan as sharp-featured, slender, and elegant. She was wearing a light gray wool women's suit with a royal blue cotton blouse and a gold and white Hermès scarf. She was terribly overdressed for Maine but carried it off somehow. In fact, she was not particularly interested in clothing, but she liked to project an image. She tended to wear expensive women's suits—Belgian linen in the summer, merino wool in the winter. Her business was to make other people do what she wanted them to do while leaving them with the notion that that had been their goal all along. She had found that well-made clothing seemed to help her achieve her aims.

She had a remarkably placid voice. She usually spoke with the slow, warm tone of an old friend, familiar and helpful, happy to see you. Some people who wield power can be brittle about it, but there was no anxiety in Diane's soothing voice, which tended to make the listener think there was nothing to worry about. However, this absence of anxiety in her speech was the result of her being a dominant predator in the political world of Maine. She was a powerful shark in a small pool, which made her useful to companies such as Future Minerals that valued discretion and privacy. Indeed, Future Minerals paid good money to "reputation management" companies to keep its name off the internet. "We operate in stealth mode as much as possible," the company's head of security, Will Payne, had told her. She knew what that meant: No social media, nondisclosure agreements for all employees, and all private money, which meant no stock sales and so no filings with the Securities and Exchange Commission.

Her small plush office conveyed the feel of the interior of an expensive European sports car—black leather seats edged with burnished steel, dark green walls, a polished dark brown wooden desk, dim yellow recessed lighting overhead. In the corner, atop a small refrigerator, stood a shiny new Rancilio Silvia Pro espresso machine. They talked as she fiddled with the high-end Italian coffee maker. "I'm still getting used to it," she said. She leaned over the machine, conscious that she was showing off her terrific figure.

"Take your time," he said, speaking to her back and noticing that figure as intended.

"I don't mind if you're just gathering information," she replied over her shoulder. "That's really a lot of what I do. We're not so different, you and I."

Ryan was struck by that phrase of hers, *I don't mind*. He asked, "So, what *would* you mind?"

She turned around and looked directly into his eyes. "I would mind if you got in my way." She turned back to foam some milk in a steel cup. But in that moment, Ryan was struck by her eyes, which were black, rapt, and unyielding, devoid of empathy. He had seen those eyes before. During his college years, while hiking alone in the Sierra Nevada in California, he had come around a bend in the trail and surprised a red-shouldered hawk sitting on a low branch. It had just stared at him, measuring him as a fellow predator. Then, leisurely, it had flown away. Ryan had stood there, frozen by the hard look of the hawk.

"That's not my intention," Ryan said. "What I want to do is help out the Afflicted Citizens' Group."

Suddenly all the soothing calm drained from her voice. "Then we may have a problem," she said with a new curtness. "Because the ACG is out to put a stake through the heart of my client."

"That seems an extreme way of putting it. I mean, they're just a group of worried people, locals with water problems."

"Not if you're me," she said, handing him his coffee. "The ACG is getting in my way."

"And that's exactly what you do mind," he said. He looked at the foam in the small blue porcelain cup, which brought to mind the white bubbles on the gills of a dead brook trout that Doc Healey had shown him. He took a sip anyway. "Talking about stakes in the heart, that doesn't sound like the nice 'information gathering' you just mentioned."

"No, but I'm giving you information you can use—if you're smart about it," she said, blandly. She ran her left hand through her hair. When she did it again, he remembered that he had been taught at the FBI Academy that such a gesture was a sign of anxiety, especially when it was repeated. Despite her calm façade, something about him was making her nervous.

He stood up. "Thanks for the joe," he said, ignoring the implied threat in her comment, and for some reason reaching back to Navy slang for coffee. "But I must be going."

"My sister told me about you," Diane said, assessing him. She wasn't finished with him.

"Who's that?" he asked, remaining standing.

"She's a lawyer down in Ellsworth, in Adams County. Her name is Lily Thornfoot."

"I don't know any—" he began. Then it occurred to him. That was the woman whose name had come up in connection with the blackmailing of Roger Robichaux. "Oh, I guess I do. I just didn't think of her as a lawyer. I haven't met her." Ryan looked at Diane, puzzling through the connection between the two sisters. He chided himself for not seeing it on his own.

"Well, she's been looking into you," Diane said. "She got wind that you were poking around her business."

Ryan remained where he was standing, lost in thought.

"What's the question you have on your mind?" Diane asked.

"Well, I have a couple. I was wondering if you know how she makes her money. But on second thought"—he shook his head—"it is pretty clear that you would. I mean, you make it your business to know things like that. Also, you have different last names. But all that means is that one of you is married."

"I was. But no longer."

He said goodbye and headed out the door.

Ryan didn't see the grimace on her face as she shut the door behind him and turned a key to lock it. Then she sat behind her desk, unconsciously glaring at the closed door. She was wondering whether Ryan couldn't take a hint or was just being mulishly stubborn. In either event, he was creating problems she didn't need. He was trouble from away, and that set off alarms in her head. She picked up a legal pad from her desk and wrote, at the top, in block letters, "R.T.—OPTIONS?"

Meanwhile, Ryan drove a few blocks north to a spot overlooking the Kennebec River. He sat in the cab and stared at the chunks of white ice floating southward on the river's surface. What did it mean that he was simultaneously entering into confrontations with Lily Thornfoot and Diane Peligroso—and that they were sisters? He considered that it made the situation more dangerous. The two sisters could cooperate with each other in parrying his moves. He wouldn't necessarily be able to figure out where an attack was coming from. He would need to be on his toes even more. He had the uneasy feeling that the two women, joining forces against him, could be quite dangerous.

15

AN EDITOR'S CONCERNS

Betty Groleau was working at her desk, answering the flood of emails that had come in about water quality problems in central Maine. She knew that most of them would lead nowhere, but that a good reporter would read them all, because you never knew where a story would go next.

Lincoln Addison pulled up a chair next to her desk. This was the signal that he wanted to have a serious talk, not just a quick editorial conference. By sitting down, he could speak more softly and so not be overheard by everyone coming in and out of the newsroom.

"Good work on the water story," he said. "Stay on it, okay?"

"Will do." She nodded. She was pleased by the praise but he clearly had something else on his mind.

"What's next?"

"Hearings in Augusta."

"Be all over them, okay?"

"Like white on rice," she assured him.

He paused. "One other thing," he said, speaking even more softly. "I hear there is an online thing called a 'blog' about being a reporter on a small paper in Maine. It's called *Cub Reporter*."

"And?"

"Is that you?"

Betty knew never to lie to an editor. She swallowed and said, "Yes."

"Hmm," he said.

"Am I in trouble?"

"I don't know. I haven't read it. What is it?"

"Kind of an online diary."

"Why?"

"Just to help me figure out things."

"Couldn't you do it in private? I thought that's what diaries are supposed to be."

"There is no privacy anymore," she said.

That was a new concept to him. "This is a new world for me. But I am a true-blue believer in free speech, so I am not going to tell you what to write in your private life." Privately, he was impressed. This kid had potential. She was learning old media and exploring the new at the same time. That was a lot to tackle, and she seemed to be handling it.

16

A CORPSE GOES AWOL

When Bap Salim came to see Healey, who was back in the hospital for a second round of tests, Salim began by saying, "If only we had a concentrated specimen," using the technical term for an organism subjected to all the poisons present in a given spot. "Such a body would be most helpful."

"You've got me," Healey replied. "What more do you need?"

"You did not live entirely in the compromised environment, all the time," Salim said. "That would be helpful to have. It is quite rare in real life, but useful as a construct."

"So, a worst-case scenario, you mean?" Healey said. "I think they have one of those downstairs here. Go see Walter LeDroit, and tell him I sent you."

Salim took the elevator to the basement. LeDroit nodded. "I think I have just that in my cooler." He explained the history of the corpse of Jacob "the Growler" Coffin.

Salim's brown eyes widened. He clearly had never seen such a specimen. "Please, let us go look."

In the morgue, the assistant, a round-faced quiet man with the technical title of "Diener," nodded to LeDroit and slid open a steel drawer. It came out far too quickly. The reason soon became clear: It was vacant. The assistant rechecked the number on the door. "That's funny." He frowned. "Was here this morning when I did inventory."

He walked out to the clerk at the front desk, then returned, holding some yellow forms. "Guys from the funeral home took him an hour ago," the diener said, clearly unhappy. "Had paperwork signed by the family." He held up the forms, signed in triplicate.

"That's pretty unlikely, given that there is no record of any living relative," LeDroit said. He reached for the paperwork. It all looked absolutely correct—but also felt entirely phony. A few minutes of checking by phone and internet determined that there was indeed a "Greene Funeral Home" in Portland. But the woman at the other end of the line insisted they had no corpse received that day, or any day, by the name of Jacob Coffin. And there was no one at the funeral home of the name "William Fournier," which was the name given on the form.

LeDroit and Salim went up to Healey's room. He listened, then said, "I'm calling Ryan Tapia about this."

17

A BASKETBALL FIZZLE

There are many winter activities in Maine—downhill and cross-country skiing, deer hunting into early December, and when that season is over, hiking for the hardy, snowmobiling and ice-fishing for the rest. But most of those activities require daylight, which is in very short supply from Thanksgiving until daylight saving time returns in early March. Around Christmas, the sun sets at about 3:45, and if the skies are overcast, the darkness begins to close in even earlier.

So any entertainment at night, especially a chance to gather in a warm space with other people, is more than welcome, especially in remote towns. During those dark months, town librarians can schedule lectures on relatively obscure subjects—"The Secret Lives of Crows," for example—with confidence they will get a packed crowd. People just need to get out of their houses.

The Pushaw High School student body of just ninety-eight students was too small to field baseball or football teams, but the girls' high school basketball squad was strong this year. People thought they might make it to the regional championships, and even beyond that to the statewide Class D game. They were proud of these kids, and they came out to the games with enthusiasm.

Ryan followed the crowd into the dusty, aging gym, with its old, slightly warped wooden floor and a latticework of steel rafters overhead, holding up the curved metal roof, designed to shed the snow. After the slushy cold of the parking lot, the place was a warm bubble of light, chatter, and excitement. A few old banners of yellowing white felt hung from the rafters—VOLLEYBALL CLASS D CHAMPION, 1936, was the one closest to Ryan. He couldn't find a seat until he saw Rick Trexler waving him over and making room for him in the retractable stands, pushing a pile of winter coats farther down the bench.

"Smart of you to come," Trexler said. "I can point out some people to you."

"Who's the guy with the big beard talking to the ref?" Ryan asked. "He looks unhappy."

"John Skratsbud, assistant principal and athletic director. Hard-working guy, well-liked. The students' nickname for him of course is 'Scratchbutt.'"

"Why is it that principals so often have funny names?" Ryan asked, half to himself. He remembered the principal of his junior high in the San Diego suburbs, Phil Mayness. The nice kids called him "Mr. Mayonnaise." The precociously mean-spirited dubbed him "Fill My Anus."

"My guess is that they got bullied in high school and grew up determined to do something about it," Trexler said. Ryan was impressed by that quick answer. He nodded in agreement.

"And the woman over there, oval-faced, sitting apart from everybody else?" Ryan said, pointing at a woman in a metal chair alone at the end of the stands. Her arms were crossed and she looked like she was spoiling for a fight. Her big lower jaw thrust out. "The one with the broad forehead," he added.

"That's Verdella Skillings," Trexler said. He lowered his voice, though there was small chance of being overheard in the hubbub of the expectant crowd. "Kind of a sad case. Wife of the Finney Junction town manager. Thinks people blame him too much for the whole mess with the water. And yeah, she has a big forehead, never thought of that before."

"Speaking of unusual names," Ryan commented, "I've never heard of a 'Verdella' before."

"Runs in their family," Trexler said.

"And the tired old guy taking notes down behind the home team bench?"

"Johnny Boyle," Trexler said. "Covers sports for the *North Country Times*. Been there forever. He's at just about every game the high school has. Even when track and field has just one kid."

The two teams came walking out of the locker rooms, not running, as is the custom at important games, done partly to loosen up but mainly from excitement. On this evening, the visitors, from Bridgton, looked particularly morose, dragging their feet and moving slowly, more like they were going to a funeral than vying for an important win.

The reason for the sluggishness of the Bridgton girls was the dermatitis they had noticed on the home team players during warmups. Indeed, one of Pushaw's shorter girls was scratching red rashes on both forearms and her neck. The lanky center had a long red and purple welt on the back of her left calf. Another girl had been digging at a small, hard patch on her cheek so hard that a trickle of blood was running down it. The Pushaw fans looked similarly afflicted, but Ryan also noticed that the older ones—parents and grandparents, mainly—also were wheezing and coughing, which Doc Healey had said was a respiratory symptom of cobalt poisoning.

The Bridgton coach went to the referee, who in turn waved over Pushaw's assistant principal to join him. All three looked upset.

The ref's shrill whistle cut through the noise of the players and spectators. He held his arms out flat on both sides and waited for them to hush. "The visitors choose not to play," he announced. "I therefore declare this game a forfeit. According to the rules and regulations of the Maine Athletic Association, this match is declared a victory for Pushaw over Bridgton by a score of two to nothing."

The disappointed crowd stood, discussing this turn of events and looking to round up wandering children. When people learned the reason for the forfeit was that the Bridgton team was afraid they would get infected by the home team's rashes, they began to boo and jeer a bit. But it was clear their hearts weren't in it and their minds were elsewhere. They mainly headed for the exits, put the seat belts on their kids, turned on their headlights, and drove home to warmed-up macaroni and cheese or hamburger casserole.

Ryan noticed that Verdella Skillings remained sitting alone in her chair. He was intrigued by this woman who seemed to be on the outs with everyone. He went over to introduce himself. She stared at him, the teeth in her big square jaw clenched. "I know who you are—you're the guy talking to people who got cobalted," she said coldly. "Not interested in discussing it." She stood and turned away from him.

18

DIANE PELIGROSO'S MAGICAL MYSTERY TOUR

Before the legislative hearings got rolling, Diane Peligroso circulated an offer to take state legislators on a "half-day tour of the affected area" in the three towns. Sixteen signed up, so she rented a luxury minibus.

Her luck held with the weather. It was a brilliantly sunny winter day, the kind that makes people think that the season in Maine really isn't so punishing after all. The first stop was in the pasture of a farm in the rolling snow-covered hills of western Asbury. Herefords stood together in a corral, enjoying the day's strong sunlight, steam flowing from their nostrils as they grazed on a bale of hay. On the far side of a red barn, four big workhorses wearing blankets stood and watched the visitors. Ducks and chickens wandered around the edge of the half-frozen cow pond squawking and looking for pellets to eat. In the tack room of the barn, a long table made of broad pine planks had been set up, holding a lovely lunch spread—a creamy buffalo mozzarella, the last tomatoes of the season from a well-run greenhouse, basil from the same, and artisan sourdough baguettes from a good local bakery run by a commune of aging hippies in the woods. An array of German cold cuts from Morse's Sauerkraut in Waldoboro was complemented by a spread of craft pilsners and IPAs from a brewer near Lake St. George. After they made their sandwiches and sipped their drinks and got comfortable, Diane spread out her hands to indicate the beautiful, old eighteenth-century farm outside the barn. "Ladies and gentlemen, let me introduce you to the supposed environmental disaster you've read about in the papers. Three hundred feet directly below you"—she pointed downward—"runs the supposedly dastardly mine tunnel you have heard about. There are no ventilation shafts connecting it to the surface."

"How's that possible? Doesn't the machinery need air?"

Nice to begin with an easy question, Diane thought. "The driller at the vein face runs on electric batteries, so it doesn't. Same with the little robot cars that roll in and out, getting loads from the conveyor belt behind the digger." Diane waved her arm toward the window. "As you can see, the cows look contented. Frankly, this whole place looks pretty happy to me." She had planned to have the farmer and his wife come out and greet the visitors, but she had nixed that idea after seeing the rashes on their hands and necks.

After lunch, the next stop was similarly enticing. The little luxury bus drove up a back road in the woods along an extended ridge and pulled over at an overlook. "Below you, about as far as the eye can see, is the so-called Fan that you might have heard some talk about," she said. Behind her, the ridge fell away to a dormant apple orchard, and behind it, a long valley crowded with spruce and firs. The open fields of cattle farms dotted the distance. It was a peaceful, pastoral site. "I know, I know," Diane chuckled to the onlookers. "Pure Grandma Moses, no? This would be a great place to build a house. I might just put in a bid."

Next the minibus pulled into the parking lot of Future Minerals. "This area is what miners call 'the tipple,' mainly for reasons of mining traditions. Because of safety and insurance regulations, we have to stay here on the bus," she said. She had made that up, but she was sure that it was probably true, and it kept people from nosing around. "Anyway, it's a pretty small setup. The operations center, where the company's people monitor the machinery inside the shaft, is in that mobile home there. Usually, one technician monitors the state of the Ripper and its drilling work, and also the state of the battery cars that power the drill. Another is running the robot car operations, the hoppers that carry out the excavated ore and deliver it here.

"Over there, two company officials work at the opening of the shaft. One is a mining analyst, checking the quality of the dig—what's coming out, how much of it is copper ore, and where the seam is going. He knows where each hopper load was dug. Depending on what he finds, he may ask that the Ripper be directed to reach a little higher or lower, or turn several degrees in one direction or another, to stay in the middle of that all-important cobalt-bearing copper vein.

"The other guy, there, is overseeing the human trucking, making sure they are loaded well and safely, and meeting schedules. The trucking contractor manages the actual truck drivers and such. About five full truckloads a day."

"I don't see an environmental office," said the state rep from Falmouth Foreside, one of Portland's most prosperous suburbs.

"Good question," she said. "It used to be out here, but Future Minerals found it more convenient to have it down in Dover-Foxcroft, the county seat, where they can easily meet with state and local officials, file their reports, and go to governmental meetings," Diane said. She didn't mention another major reason, which was that it made everyone at Future Minerals more comfortable not to have environmental officers, even those on the company's payroll, hovering constantly around the tipple.

Diane wanted to appear candid, so she went on. "Truth be told, dust churned up by the human trucks as they come and go is a real environmental issue, because it might contain minerals and metals. If you water it down, you get runoff. If you oil it, which is what miners did in the old days, you get long-term problems. Lately we've been using a vacuum machine on wheels, like an industrial Roomba, to go back and forth across the lot when the trucks aren't here. It makes bricks out of the dust, which we then ship to a special facility. Expensive, but worth it for the environmental benefits."

"Why do that if it's expensive?" asked a state rep from Houlton.

"Future Minerals tries to be a good corporate citizen," said Diane, hoping she wasn't laying it on too thick.

"What's that bigger building over there?" asked a state senator from Aroostook, pointing at a cement structure painted green.

"I'm glad you asked," Diane said, and indeed she was. "That's the mechanical shop, where they do routine maintenance on the drilling equipment, the battery cars, and the hoppers. Swapping out parts, changing tires, checking batteries, and so on. That shop is actually our single largest employer, paying thirty Mainers good corporate wages year-round." In front of the building, a man in the company's trademark green overalls was working in the sunshine, putting new tires on a hopper car.

"That many jobs means a lot in this part of Maine," said another legislator. "Especially if the pay is good and steady."

"You bet," Diane agreed, happy to have the point underscored. "Last, but not least, that little metal shed over there, that's the star of the show—the covering of the shaft itself." The bus pulled out.

Finally came the last stop, ten miles south, at a rest stop on the road overlooking a scenic view of the Salmon River. This is where the Fan ended, its toxins trickling from the north bank of the river into the water. When the lawmakers had piled out and were standing around her, Diane pointed down at the rushing water. It looked normal, its fast, cold, clear water tumbling around rocks and over small white waterfalls. A fly fisherman wearing green overall waders stood in sunny riffles near the far bank, framed by the spruce behind him, his favorite flies decorating his khaki hat, his filament of line rising and lofting with ballet-like grace. "This is the Salmon River," she began.

She paused and cleared her throat. "I want to be frank here." She took out some typed notes. "Yes, the mining project has caused some problems here. Brook trout have been especially affected, according to some preliminary research. We are seeing some indications, especially in its tributaries, that we need to do a better job of collecting the water that flows through the mined areas. We are studying that right now. Let me tell you, we are just as concerned as you are. Perhaps even more. This is our livelihood, after all."

She looked at her notes again. "But in fairness, we also need to keep in mind that cobalt is a strategic mineral. We need it for our smartphones and electric cars, especially if we are going to do anything to curtail global overheating. And we shouldn't allow foreign concerns to maintain a stranglehold on the cobalt supply. If we can produce just a little here, and keep it in a strategic stockpile, that prevents those overseas suppliers from charging American companies ridiculous prices, or even cutting off the stuff, which would be an economic disaster."

She turned and pointed at the fisherman across the water. "But, as you can see, the Salmon is hardly the environmental catastrophe some are describing." The distant angler waved lazily to Diane's little group, as he had been instructed, and then turned back to his artful casting. He was a guide from Bangor. He knew damn well that there were no trout still living in this stretch of the river, but this lady had offered him $600, double his usual daily rate, cash up front, to drive up and stand there and practice his casting for just two hours, so why not? She seemed to be showing around a group of tourists or something, so what was the harm?

The little bus headed south, back to Augusta. After it rolled onto the smoother pavement of Interstate 95, Diane's assistant went down the aisle offering plastic glasses of sparkling rosé wine. When the bus got back to the parking lot in Augusta, the legislators thanked Diane for the most wonderful tour. "I feel much better after seeing it all with my own eyes," said a representative from Kittery. "It's a big state, and it's hard to keep track of everything that's going on, especially in these backward areas."

"We're here to help," Diane said, handing out her business card. "Call me anytime."

When she got back to her car, Diane found an email from Payne, the security chief, with the subject line, "Just a heads-up." It stated that his people had found on surveillance tapes an old red Datsun pickup truck being used by someone who was vandalizing company equipment. "We're gonna put a tracker on it," he said, meaning a hidden emitter that would give them the GPS location of that old truck at all times. "Also, of course, we are following the location of his phone."

She wrote back, "You might also want to put a tracker on the vehicle of this ex-FBI guy, Ryan Tapia. He's been nosing around."

19

PUSHAW VS. FORT KENT

On this night, the crowd from Fort Kent was loaded for bear. Their team had heard about the debacle at the previous match and had formally asked that the Pushaw players be required to wear full-length pants and shirts. The state athletic association had convened by phone to consider the request. Pushaw's coach and assistant principal Skratsbud argued that they were giving in to fear without any evidence that his team's skin problems were contagious. But the association voted to grant Fort Kent's request, persuaded by the idea that there was no harm in having the girls cover up.

The Pushaw team walked out of their locker room wearing baggy sweatpants and sweatshirts, which had been picked up by the assistant principal's wife that afternoon at the Bangor Mall. They looked miserable. The ill-fitting attire made them uneasy. So did the chant they heard from the Fort Kent stands cascading over their heads. The taunts were sung to the tune of "Farmer in the Dell":

Pushaw has a rash
Pushaw has a rash

Scratch and itch and scratch and itch
Pushaw has a rash

What the chant lacked in imagination it made up in sheer callousness. It was aimed not just at the Pushaw County team but also at their fans, the friends and families of the players. Several of Pushaw's players teared up. The ball went up and play began. A pushing match broke out in the end zone stands, where the Pushaw fans were mixed in with the Fort Kenters.

Within five minutes, the team's best forward walked off the court, ripped off the baggy sweatshirt, and said to her coach, "I can't play like this." She continued out the door of the gym. Pushaw lost 61 to 33, a crushing defeat. Their chances of making it to the Class D quarter finals were dwindling rapidly.

Ryan sat in the stands, taking it all in. This basketball game had brought home to the community the fix that it was in with the cobalt pollution. How would the towns react now?

20

NINA'S SONGS

The next night Ryan was at Nina's house for dinner. After eating—just a salad, bread, and a cup of homemade chicken noodle soup—they moved to the sofa, which was nearer the woodstove. Her Amazon Echo was playing music, which made her frequent silences easier.

"I've been thinking about the long-term grief, how it works," she finally said. "We know that scar tissue lacks feeling. You can prick it with a needle, and if that is done right, you won't feel it. Yet the flesh of the scar isn't strong. People who lack vitamin C, their scars can reopen."

"And you're thinking that emotional scar tissue may be the same way?" Ryan said.

"Exactly," she said, pleased he saw the analogy so quickly. "Just because you're not feeling doesn't mean you're strong. In fact, it may be the opposite. And developing feeling again, even if it aches, that might be a sign of strength."

Ryan was pleased. "That's an optimistic way of viewing pain," he said.

"I'm trying," she said, with a wan smile.

"No one should have to carry knowledge like that," he replied. "But we both do."

"It's just life," she said. "For weeks, I couldn't get that phrase out of my head, 'a vale of tears.' It sounds like a cliché, but it is pretty spot on. It is where we now live, people like you and me. We can perceive there is a world beyond, but we see it through that mist of pain."

He thought she had something more to say. She didn't. So after waiting a minute, he asked, "Is there something you need to tell me?"

Again, she appreciated that he was in tune with her emotions. "Yes," she said. But she said nothing more.

"How can I help?" he asked. He reached out his hand for hers. She allowed him to take it. It felt cold to Ryan's touch.

"Sometimes I think about leaving this vale of tears. Just moving on. Like I've had enough."

He moved over and put his arm over her shoulder. "I am so sorry," he said. There was nothing more to say. She knew that he understood how she felt.

They sat and listened to her Spotify list. After an hour, he stood to go. "I don't know a lot of these songs," he said, "but I like them—their tone, their thoughtful words, their care."

The next day, Nina emailed him the list. The sole song he recognized was "I'm So Lonesome I Could Cry," by Hank Williams, an old favorite of his. He'd heard of Bob Dylan, but didn't know the song of his she included, "Not Dark Yet (But It's Getting There)." The others were a revelation: Elliott Smith, Leonard Cohen, Aimee Mann, Son House, Etta James, Billie Holiday, Townes Van Zandt, and Cat Power. All were new to him, and all were powerful. There were two entire albums on the list by the last artist—*The Greatest* and *Covers*.

In the following days, he listened to those two Cat Power albums incessantly. The whole Spotify list was excellent, he thought, but also dark and depressing. It was music for someone in mourning, but not for getting beyond that phase. Especially Tom Waits singing "Cold Cold Ground," a song that Nina told him she "played every morning for a month after Dave's funeral." From the title, he expected it to be somber, but found its rhythm and Waits's voicing to be oddly jocular. She reported that eventually she replaced it with "Way Down in the Hole," a somber Waits tune about wrestling with the devil. "You gotta keep the devil way down in the hole," Waits counseled in a howling growl.

One day while driving home from Hannaford's grocery in his truck and listening to the list, he realized he was falling for Nina. She was different, thoughtful, intriguing. Solid Harrison had been colorful and powerful. Nina was an intense black and white; in many ways she challenged him more. After putting away the groceries, he sat out back in the afternoon chill and warmed himself with a big mug of black coffee, looking out over Lost Pond and meditating on these two women who had come into his new life after losing Marta. Moolsem leaned against his knee. A kingfisher was darting along the trees on the bank, diving in favorite spots, then going to the next branch to dry its bushy black head feathers and prepare for its next shot. It cast a glance at Ryan. Looking back, Ryan thought the bird's head feathers had a punk rock look to them.

He opened his laptop and went to the site of the *Bangor Daily News*. One article in particular caught his eye. A fisherman had been busted down in Minnow Harbor for catching tens of thousands of pounds of herring and not reporting it, as federal fishing regulations require. This made Ryan's investigative senses tingle a bit. He made a quick calculation: Commercial fishing throws off a cash flow. And there weren't a lot of places to put money in Maine. So in this herring case, there might exist a nugget of possibility in dealing with Roger Robichaux's problem.

21

BETTY GROLEAU MEETS TWO VERY DIFFERENT WOMEN

Betty Groleau, the young reporter from the *North Country Times*, was sitting on a brown metal folding chair in the chilly hallway outside where the environmental committee was holding a closed meeting to prepare for the open hearings that would be held in a few days.

She could have gone back to the press room to write and file, but she had decided the walk would take time that would be better spent writing and then revising her story. She had a small laptop perched on her knees. Also, by staying in the chair in the hall, she could keep an eye on who was coming and going from the committee's session, and perhaps glean some nuggets of information from them.

She glanced out the hallway window at the lowering sun. It was about to kiss the horizon. She knew she had until about sunset to file, which gave her about five more minutes to finish the day's article. A young woman with hair, freckles, and eyes all in shades of brown took the empty chair next to Betty Groleau. As reporters tend to do, they looked at each other's credentials hanging on lanyards. Betty was surprised that the woman's press pass identified her as being from Radio One of the Canadian Broadcasting Corporation. "Why is the CBC interested in this?" she asked.

"Partly because mining is a quite significant Canadian industry. The Toronto exchange is driven by mining and mining finance stocks. And partly because this is more interesting than anything happening in New Brunswick today," the woman said in English that carried a distinctive light French accent. "I've been on this job six months, since I got my master's at Laval, and the biggest story I have covered all year was when a lobster truck collided with a moose and ran into a potato field. It was picked for national play and introduced as, they said, 'an event that captures the essence of the maritime provinces.' It was the only time I was congratulated by my boss.

"By the way, I have read your articles on the water problem, all of them. Good work!" She stuck out her hand and said, "I am Monique Bouchard, as you can see." She tapped her press credentials.

"Betty," Betty responded, shaking her hand. She instantly liked this spunky Canadian who was ready for bigger things. And she admired her chic but low-key combination of designer jeans, a black turtleneck shirt, and a necklace of polished topaz the same color as her warm brown eyes.

"I think that all this, the hearing which they are going to present, is happening because of your articles," Monique said. "I see you have to file your report. I will let you be." She handed Betty her business card. "Let's stay in touch." As Betty watched Monique walk away, she felt a stirring inside that she didn't understand.

Just as the Canadian left, Diane Peligroso emerged from the committee room. The lobbyist was dressed in an expensive black suit with a white silk blouse and a colorful golden neckerchief. Her shoes were sensible but pricey hand-made black flats by Italeau.

Betty took out a pen and jabbed it against the "O" key on the laptop's keyboard as Diane watched her. A moment later she did it again, and sighed. "Computer trouble?" Diane asked.

"The 'O' key is stuck, and there's no budget to get a new laptop this year," Groleau muttered. Then she reverted to her professional journalistic mien. "How come you can go in there and I can't?" she asked, still sitting, nodding at the closed committee door.

The lobbyist looked down at her. "I can only talk to you off the record. Anything for quoting has to come from corporate. They're pretty strict about that."

"But the corporate people don't know anything about what's going on here in the legislature. You do."

"That's right. So, I can give you guidance, but only on an off-the-record basis. Which is the same thing I was just doing in there."

"Which, off the record, was?"

"I can go into the committee room because I am a former staffer. I can give them legislative history. I can direct them to relevant studies and other documents. I can tell them what issues were considered when. None of them know that stuff because they're term limited—two terms of two years each, and you're out. So I was acting as kind of their institutional history."

"Oh." Her head was spinning a bit. This is not how she had expected government to work. Term limits seemed to have made such sense when she first heard about them—get fresh faces in, people who haven't sold out to the system, people with new approaches. Like the average voter, she hadn't realized that limiting the amount of time someone could serve in the legislature inevitably would shift power from elected legislators to unelected staff and even to lobbyists, who generally were themselves former staff. What's more, current staffers knew that their most likely career path was to leave the public payroll and go work for trade associations and big corporations, the two major lobbying groups. So term limits, while sounding like a way of cleaning up politics, simply had increased the influence of corporations and others who could afford to have lobbyists overseeing the workings of the state legislature.

"I'm Betty Groleau," the young reporter said, sticking out her hand.

Peligroso took it. "I know who you are. I read all your stories." Peligroso handed Groleau her business card.

Groleau studied it. "Doesn't 'peligroso' mean 'dangerous' in Spanish?" the reporter said, reaching back to her high school language classes.

"Nah, my ex-husband was Italian, and he told me it meant 'thick-skinned.' But I already knew he was super-sensitive. Still, it's better than my maiden name."

"What's that?"

"Thornfoot. In some parts of Maine, that name still spooks people," Peligroso said. She looked at the time on her cell phone. "Have you had dinner?" she asked.

"No, and I'm hungry. But I'm not allowed to let you pay for my meal."

"That's okay. You pay for yours. And if you have a sip or two of my wine, that's okay."

"Just let me file this story," she said. She hit "send" and closed the laptop, slipping it into her blue cotton Land's End bag.

They walked down the street three blocks to the steakhouse. Peligroso had an account there, an open tab she settled monthly. But she also tipped generously, in cash. They were seated instantly at her regular table in the corner, where serious conversations could be held, but also where she could see the front door, and so keep informed on who was in the place and who was talking to whom.

Without any direction from her, a bottle of her favorite brand of California cabernet appeared on the table a moment later.

As they sat, Peligroso said, "Look, I know we're not on the same side."

"I'm not on any side," Groleau protested.

"That's what you think." Peligroso smiled. "But my point is, at least we can treat each other like human beings." She poured out two glasses of the rich red wine.

"This is the best wine I've ever had," Groleau said after one sip. It kind of astonished her. It wasn't sweet. It was smooth but full of sensations. It first tasted like a bountiful flower, and then it blossomed across her tongue into a full feel of grapes on their way to becoming perfume.

Peligroso asked, "How did you wind up at a county paper up in the wilds of Maine?"

"First job out of school," she said. "I always wanted to be a journalist. And to me, even the *North Country Times* feels sophisticated. I'm from the County." This was a reference to Aroostook County, the sprawling district at the northern top of the state that was so big—indeed, larger than several states—that Mainers referred to it that way, as if it were the sole county.

"Where in the County?"

"Ashland. My dad was a pulp cutter, at least until a fir top fell and broke his back. After that, with three of his discs fused, he started driving a truck for the same contractor. Less money but at least he can do it without much pain. We were grateful for the job. My mother is the town librarian."

"Why become a reporter?"

"I'm naturally kind of shy. But being a reporter, you get to ask questions and get paid for it. So it's kind of like permission for an introvert to act like an extrovert, a license to talk to people."

"Do you like it?"

"I love it. I mean, it pays nothing."

Peligroso poured Groleau another glass of wine.

"It's peanuts. Twenty-eight thousand." She was surprised that she was being so open. But why not? She had nothing to hide.

Groleau's burger arrived, along with Peligroso's rare filet mignon sliced and served over chopped romaine and blue cheese crumbles, a dish Betty hadn't seen on the menu.

Hearing the number, Peligroso winced in sympathy. "And you're probably still carrying some college loans." She jabbed her fork into a piece of the filet.

"You bet," Groleau said. "But they'll be paid off in, what, about ten or fifteen years." She laughed, but with a sad edge to it. She was surprised at how much she liked Peligroso. They both had more wine.

Later, as she walked alone back to her worn-out Tercel, Groleau thought to herself that it had been like talking to an older sister, something she'd never had. The rust holes above the rear tires of her car were getting bigger, she noticed. As a native Mainer, she knew that those spots were where salt on the roads got trapped inside the car's body.

22

RYAN COOKS FOR NINA

Ryan invited Nina to dinner at his place. "Okay," she said. "But, uh, no closeness yet. I'll tell you when I am ready."

He was happy to take it slow. He was enjoying getting to know this elusive woman, and was in no hurry.

He pulled out all culinary stops for dinner. The main dish was a venison filet he'd been saving, a gift from a neighbor. He served it with a sauce of creamed caramelized onions, on a bed of jasmine rice cooked in chicken broth. On the side were roasted brussels sprouts in a reduced balsamic dressing.

Over dinner he talked, a bit relentlessly, about the cobalt situation. What the company was doing. How it manipulated people. How a lot of people felt helpless, and how he thought he might be able to give them a needed hand. Then he talked about how it was changing his view of the world, of how the country worked. "I grew up a true believer in free markets, free people, free minds. But now I think that we have lost balance, that big money is running everything."

Eventually she said, "I think you're getting obsessed with this mining situation." She stood. "This was nice," she said, "but I have to go. We're getting into my busy season for work. April fifteenth looms on the horizon." There was a distance in her manner that he didn't understand. She pecked him on the cheek and left quickly. As he watched her car's red taillights head down the driveway, he realized he should have gotten the message she was sending. Moolsem stared at him. Sometimes dogs pick up signals that people don't.

23

RYAN CHATS WITH A SMALL-TOWN BANKER

Down at Minnow Harbor, the banker's trouble began as small fry. That's often the situation, metaphorically. But in this instance, it was literal "fry," meaning infant fish.

It began like this: An officer of the Maine Marine Patrol who worked occasionally in Minnow Harbor had heard rumors there that *Western Wind*, a fishing boat out of Massachusetts, was seining small herring illegally. That caught the Marine Patrol investigator's attention because he knew, as did pretty much everyone on the Maine coast, that the small, oily fish known as the Atlantic herring is the primary bait used by lobstermen in their traps. A bit of investigation provided some evidence that the skipper of *Western Wind* was cleaning out entire remote coves of baby herring, pulling in close to a million pounds a year, but not reporting any of the catch. The skipper's method was simple: He never "landed" his catch. Instead, he stashed the herring in big plastic barrels aboard his vessel, which he then transferred directly to the boats of Maine lobstermen on a strictly cash-and-carry basis—$100 a barrel, or eleven barrels for $1,000. He usually sold thirty or forty barrels a day.

The Marine Patrol investigator cared a lot about the unreported fish. He didn't care at all about the money, even though the skipper's reason for not reporting the fish was that he didn't want to report the income from them. The Marine Patrol busted the skipper and announced the case, hoping that it would send a message to others who were hauling herring illegally. A few guys doing that could wipe out the stock entirely, by not leaving enough fish to replace those caught.

On his back porch, Ryan had read over the news article about the herring bust, then called the Marine Patrol office down in Minnow Harbor. A "Sergeant Merlin" answered. "Lucky you caught me here," the sergeant said. "Only work down here one or two days a week."

"I have a client whose interests may be involved here," Ryan said vaguely. "Do you have time for me to learn more about the case?"

"Okay," said Merlin. "Come on down."

Ryan drove down to Minnow Harbor, a very minor Maine port. It didn't have enough space to be any bigger. There was one strip of a main street overlooking a narrow cove with one dock. There was room in the harbor for only about ten working boats to moor. The street overlooking the dock offered the bare minimum for a town in rural Maine: a convenience store, a two-pump gas station, a tiny town library, and a little bank branch with an ATM. Ryan parked his Ford F-150 next to another one, and noticed the license plate on that other one: "4FKSAKE." Only in Maine, Ryan thought.

He met Sgt. Merlin at the office of the harbormaster, which was a hut about the size of a garden shed, out at the end of the town dock. The sergeant looked to be barely twenty-five—and, Ryan surmised, probably was on his first tour of duty in the Patrol. "Our office here is just an extra desk in the harbormaster's hut," Merlin said. "We work more up in Rockfish and Camden, the bigger landing ports. Which is probably why the herring guys picked this little spot to do their business." He was fiddling with a toothpick in his mouth. "What's your interest?"

"I'm a financial analyst and investigator," Ryan said.

"Like what?" Merlin said, though he wasn't particularly interested. If it didn't swim in the sea, it wasn't his problem.

"Mortgage fraud, Medicare fraud, banking compliance, other regulations."

Merlin looked even less interested. "Sounds kind of boring," he said with characteristic Maine frankness.

"It's a living." Ryan shrugged. "Look," he said, moving the conversation along, "I know a little about lobstering, from a case I had when I was with the FBI."

That caught the Marine patrolman's attention. It told him this guy was a major leaguer, or at least had been. He began to pay a little closer attention.

"But I'm no fisheries expert," Ryan said. "Can you walk me through this herring case?"

"Better than that," Merlin said. "I can show you the video of the act." He turned his laptop forty-five degrees so that Ryan could see it. "This is the day we taped them doing business on the dock here. We had set up the evening before over on the far shore, hiding the camera in the lee of a fishing shack." Looking at the computer's screen, he pointed at the image of a rusty old fifty-foot trawler tied up on one side of the dock. "That's the *Western Wind.* Now, the three lobster boats, they're over to the right, other side of the dock. Two are tied up, the third is idling, waiting his turn." In the video, a man from the trawler, who looked to be the skipper, walked over to talk to the two lobstermen on the dock. He accepted piles of dollar bills from each of them and tucked them into his coat pockets. At his signal, two crewmen on the trawler winched a fifty-five-gallon blue barrel, heavily loaded, from their deck to the dock. They were clearly practiced at this, moving a barrel or two a minute. A lobsterman rolled the first barrel over to his boat, where his sternman helped him wrestle it aboard. And so on. All in all, twenty-one barrels crossed the dock.

The video went dark. "That's about it," Merlin said. "Did that help?"

"Could you back it up to about barrel eight?" Ryan asked. "Just after minute ten."

"Sure. Why?"

"The guy behind them who gets off the *Western Wind* with the green duffel bag and walks to the ramp up to the shore."

"You're thinking he's carrying the cash?"

"Well," Ryan said, "he could be going to the laundromat, of course. But I think he's going to the bank." This made basic seagoing sense: A smart skipper doesn't leave cash aboard a boat any longer than he has to. No reason to tempt the crew or others, especially while in port—you never knew who might wander down the dock, see a "from-away" boat, notice a bag, and walk off with it. "What banks have offices around here?"

"Two out on the Route 1A bypass around town," Merlin said. "But Gulf of Maine, they have a small office just down the street, over there. If you're on foot, that's your only choice. And *Western Wind* is out of Gloucester, so they're not going to have a vehicle here."

"Can you zoom in on the duffel bag guy?"

"For an ID? No need," Merlin said. "I can tell you that's Randy Brown, the first mate. He handles the business end of things, does the bills, calls ahead for fuel, gets the groceries, while the skipper focuses on boat handling, navigating, and fishing. We charged Brown and the skipper with violating fishing regulations. But they're also facing time for perjury. Their sworn statements were just a pack of lies, even after we showed them this video."

"What do you know about the pattern of deposits?"

"Probably two or three a week," Merlin said. "From the fishing records and the numbers of barrels recorded, that would work out to maybe twelve thousand a week."

"But never that big, as far as you can tell?"

"Yeah. I think they didn't even pay off the crew until they got home. So, you're right, their practice has been to get the cash off the boat and into the bank."

That night, Ryan researched the Gulf of Maine branch in Minnow Harbor. The branch manager was Marshall Mayo. "Who would name their kid that?" Ryan wondered aloud. A few Google searches turned up some press releases from the bank. Mayo had graduated from the University of Southern Maine five years earlier. He had worked as a teller at Gulf of Maine while getting an online MBA. With that degree in hand, he was promoted to become the executive assistant to the bank's chief information officer. A year later he was made an assistant branch manager in Boothbay Harbor. And a year after that, he was promoted to run the Minnow branch. Ryan gathered that this little outlet was an operation that Gulf of Maine used as a kind of beginners' tryout for people on its management track.

In the morning, Ryan called Mayo's office. "Mr. Mayo, please. It's, uh, a regulatory issue," he told the woman who answered the phone. "Not a problem, not yet, really just a question—but one that I think Mr. Mayo would want to handle with alacrity."

"'Alaca-what,' what does that mean?" the woman asked.

"It means I need to see him today."

As Ryan had guessed, the phrase "regulatory issue" got the branch manager's attention. Two hours later, Ryan stood in the tiny lobby of the bank. Mayo came out of his office with a plump hand extended. He reminded Ryan of every officious Young Republican he had ever met at college. They all seemed to be overstuffed mediocrities bulging out of their clothes. Mayo's brown hair, a bit longish for a banker, was swept across his forehead. He also had a bushy mustache. "Mr. Tapia?" he said. "I'm Marsh Mayo." Ryan thought this man looked uncomfortable with the physical world, with working with his hands, or moving amid objects, which was unusual for a Mainer. That probably was why he had chosen to move into the world of banking, governed by numbers and regulations.

They sat in his office, Mayo behind an ostentatious brown wooden desk, a bit too big for the small dimensions of this two-teller branch. Ryan's chair was scrunched up into the opposite corner, its back touching the wallpapered wall.

"How can I help you?" Marsh said, opening his hands in a gesture he likely had been taught as part of Customer Care 101.

"The *Western Wind* deposits," Ryan said. "We're seeing a worrisome pattern there. Lots of deposits of five, seven, and nine thousand. But not a one over ten." He was guessing about those amounts, but it was an informed guess, based on what Sergeant Merlin had told him. "Why is that, do you think?"

"May I ask, when you say 'we,' whom do you mean?" Mayo parried.

"Me and my client," Ryan said.

"Why do you care? People can make deposits in any size they like."

"Sure. But never one of ten thousand dollars or more, eh? And no eighty-three hundreds?" Ryan said, referring to the bureaucratic title of the mandatory federal form used to report cash deposits of that amount or more.

Mayo began to talk, but Ryan held up a hand. "Before you say anything more, I'll let you in on an interesting secret: The skipper and mate of the *Western Wind* are facing federal criminal charges, not just the fishing violations you might have seen in the paper. What does that tell you?"

"I am sure I don't know," Marsh said, a bit stuffily. "I'm a banker, not a detective."

"Well, I am a former law enforcement investigator. It tells me that their lawyers are probably going to be looking to trade information to get them off the hook. And a branch manager from a well-known bank with a major presence in the state is, you know, a bigger fish than the skipper of a beat-down trawler peddling bait. They'll be all too happy to flip on you."

"I don't follow," Mayo said, though his ashen face made it clear that he had a pretty good idea of Ryan's point.

"Well, then, I will spell it out for you," Ryan said agreeably. "If it develops that you counseled them to keep their deposits under the amount of ten thousand, well, as I am confident you are aware, that's flat-out conspiracy to violate the Currency Transaction Reporting requirements. A good prosecutor probably could make a money-laundering charge stick."

"You needn't tell me my business, Mr. Tapia," said Mayo, looking a bit more uneasy. He leaned back and placed his hand over his mustache. In Ryan's experience, a person did that when he was afraid of what was about to come out of his mouth.

Tapia waited. Sometimes the essence of a good interrogation was patience. He said nothing for a moment to let it sink in. The jig was up. The question was, which direction would Mayo jump? Would he cave, or would he puff up and try to get rid of Tapia? Ryan gave him the time he needed.

Unwisely, Mayo chose the latter course. He drew in his breath, as if to inflate himself. He stood and said, "Well, this has all been very interesting, but now I must get back to the job. Busy day here. Monthly reports due." He began to walk around his big wooden desk to give Ryan the bum's rush. He even moved out his right hand to place on Ryan's back.

But Ryan did not join him in standing. He looked up and snarled, "Oh, sit down, you fat fuck."

Marsh blushed. "Or what?" But even as he said it, he reversed course and sat, deflated. Some people are said to be unflappable, but Marsh was eminently the opposite, the most flappable of men.

Drops of sweat appeared on his forehead. He wriggled a bit in his big office chair and then loosened his tie.

It was almost too easy, Ryan thought. He suspected he was getting meaner with age or, at least, less tolerant of pompous young people. He said, "Do you happen to have the phone number of your compliance officer at headquarters?" Marsh's eyes bulged at the thought of a meeting with the bank's internal police. Ryan added a prod, "That's a Mr. Mercier, I believe?"

Mayo looked stricken. He stared at Ryan. In his mind, he could see his fledgling banking career going down in flames. Finally, and with evident resentment, he muttered, "What do you want? Or your so-called client?"

This was the moment to back off. Let Marsh's internal adrenaline rush zoom through him for a while, bounce through his synapses and clang the internal alarm bells. "Tell you what," Ryan said easily. "I've put a lot on your plate, said a lot that you need to consider. You probably need a spell to think through all this. I'll be back tomorrow at the same time. We can decide then how to proceed." This guy would have an entire night to stew in his own juices, to think the worst. Everything looked terrible at four in the morning after a sleepless night, Ryan knew from grim experience.

The next morning, Ryan appeared at the bank and told Mayo's wide-eyed assistant, "He's expecting me." He walked by her to see Mayo behind the desk. Ryan closed the door behind himself.

The banker was red-faced, his lips thin. "How much do you want?" the banker asked, as if he were cutting to the chase. The skin around his eyes was puffy. He was acting as if he were taking the tough-minded course—and also putting Ryan in his place as a small-time squeeze artist.

Ryan waved a hand and gave a little laugh. "Oh, no, I'm not here for money," he said.

"What?" The banker's forehead wrinkled. "Well. Well. Then what do you want?" He was puzzled. And now a little scared. He had thought he had figured out Ryan. He had planned how he would handle the problem and dispose of this interloper. But now he didn't know where this was going. He thought he had gained the upper hand, only to find that he was back on the emotional roller coaster that he had been on since yesterday.

"Not much. Just some names," Ryan said easily. "I need a list of people who have written checks to one of the bank's accounts. Not in this branch."

"You know I can't do that," Mayo said. But his voice was uncertain.

Ryan said mildly, "I think you can. No one will know."

"I don't want to," Mayo said. He was almost crying as he regressed to that last line of defense.

"But we're adults," Ryan said sharply. "And sometimes we have to do things we don't wish to do. So, I think you will." Ryan knew that at this point, Marsh's brain would be flooded with relief at learning how little Ryan really wanted from him. Yesterday, violating a banking privacy provision would have seemed to him like the gravest of sins. This morning, a few little crossings of the line seemed like a minor worry compared to the dank jail cells in which his imagination had spent the previous night. He had seen *The Shawshank Redemption*, that classic movie about the jailing of a small-time Maine banker, more than once.

They sat in silence for a full two minutes as the addled branch manager adjusted to these new realities before him. "Okay," he finally said. "What is the account name?" There was more sweat on his forehead.

"Witch Island Money Management."

"What do you need to know about it?"

"I want the names of the people authorized to access that account."

Marsh typed for a moment. "Only one," he said, looking up, "A person named Lily Thornfoot. I've heard of her—she's a lawyer up in Ellsworth."

"Good," Ryan said. "Now, I want to see every check that has gone into the Witch Island account in the last twelve months."

The banker frowned, but typed on his keyboard, calling up the list of deposits. "I have to step out of the room for about five minutes," he said. "That's it. You'll get no more from me." He left his office and closed the door behind him. He acted as if he were drawing a line—albeit a bit late. He already had stepped back across that line twice.

When Marsh was outside, Ryan moved around the desk and used his cell phone to take several photographs of the screen the banker had left up. Then, for backup, he jotted down the names with the amounts of the checks beside them. There were nineteen individuals who were regular monthly depositors. Most were paying $1,000 or $2,000 each month, including the regular payments from Roger Robichaux, but three men repeatedly had paid $5,000. Those especially interested him. Up to this point, he had not touched the screen or the keyboard. Now he donned thin latex medical gloves and toggled across the screens to see what else the banker was looking at. Better to leave no fingerprints. One was a google search of "Ryan Tapia Maine."

Mayo had left open the top middle drawer of the desk a crack. Ryan eased it open and found what he expected: A phone set to record. He deleted the recording, put the phone back in the drawer, pulled off the gloves, placed them in his pants pocket, and left.

That night, he googled eighteen of the nineteen names, figuring he already knew Roger Robichaux. Most of them had led obscure but well-paid lives. Mainly what the internet yielded was a series of retirement notices from trade publications. A commodities trader. A plastic surgeon. A commercial real estate developer specializing in turning aging strip malls into higher density commercial and residential sites. A highway construction executive. A medical malpractice attorney. "The Corrugated Cardboard King of Akron." And so on. Most had retired within the last several years. Many of them were in their late fifties, which was premature for stopping work in America these days, he thought to himself. What had made them leave early? He created daily google searches on each of them to help him track them, should any make news again.

In the morning, Ryan talked to his dead wife, Marta, at the altar he had set up for her and for their two dead children. He had created it at the behest of Dot Williams. It was in a corner of his kitchen, next to the coffee machine. He tried on most mornings to spend a few moments conversing with them while his cup brewed. Marta was represented by her wedding ring, the two kids by two of their toys, and the dead dog by its collar. He lit the altar candle, updated them on his work, and then blew out the candle. This ritual always left him feeling settled, or centered. Whereas the mere thought of any of them was once crippling, he now found talking to them a reassuring way to begin each day.

After drinking his coffee and making sure he was thinking relatively clearly, he called Lily Thornfoot and set up a meeting with her in Ellsworth. There was a chance that simply telling her he knew what she was doing would scare her into stopping. Not a big chance, but one worth taking, he thought.

24

A SECOND CITIZENS GROUP EMERGES

It was at this time that a second citizens association emerged in the three towns. This new one called itself the Concerned Citizens of the North Country, or the "CCNC." It was led by a guy who had mainly kept to himself in the area he lived, which was in the ridges on the western side of Asbury. He popped up suddenly on several social media outlets, followed two days later by a half-page advertisement in the *North Country Times*. Despite coming from a previously unknown amateur, the graphics were surprisingly sophisticated. WE'RE PRO-ENVIRONMENT, BUT WE'RE ALSO PRO-JOBS, ran the headline on the ad that introduced the group. AND WE WANT CLEAN WATER IN PUSHAW COUNTY!

What Diane Peligroso and only a few others knew was that this new organization was funded almost entirely by a check for $10,000 sent to the Asbury man by a law firm in Portland. This law firm, not by chance, also did work for Peligroso. The new group was independent in the sense that its views were not dictated by Peligroso or the company. That wasn't her aim. A puppet group would be too obvious.

One of the few people who knew the origins of this new Concerned Citizens group was the chief of security at Future Minerals, Will Payne. He was perplexed. He called Peligroso and asked, "Why would we want to subsidize a group that sometimes will be criticizing us?"

Peligroso knew from experience that part of her job was to explain to company executives how political power works. If they understood her approach, they'd be more comfortable with it. "It's Politics 101," she told him. "When you're on the defensive, with people coming together to oppose you, you benefit by muddying the waters. Confusion is our friend, and clarity is our foe. For example, the existence of this new group ensures that the Afflicted Citizens isn't the only organization that reporters will call for comment. And after they talk to the new group, some stories will state things like, 'Locals are divided on how to respond to this situation.'"

In her design, the CCNC would characterize itself as centrist. "CCNC is designed to stake out the middle ground, calling for lowering temperatures, seeking out compromises."

"Why do we care?"

"Because that will make the other group, the ACG, look like the lefties. At least, we can paint them like that—a bunch of tree-hugging extremists who care about nature more than they do jobs, and who hate free enterprise."

"I like that," Payne said. "No fingerprints?"

"No, that's why we fund them through a law firm—the relationship is covered by the lawyer-client privilege."

That night, a Future Minerals truck ran over Ned Meddybemps on the paved road leading to the company's tipple. A state trooper told a reporter that it wasn't clear what Meddybemps had been doing there on company property. Meddybemps died that night while in surgery in Bangor.

25

TAPIA VS. THORNFOOT

Ryan walked into Flynn's and asked the bartender for Lily Thornfoot. She looked up, gestured rightward with her thumb, and said, "Back room, back table," then returned to her thick paperback copy of *War and Peace.*

"Miss Thornfoot?" he asked.

She looked up from her coffee. "Yes. Are you Mr. Tapia?"

"Yes."

"What do you want?" she said. Her eyes were black and unblinking, the look of a woman who long had expected most men to behave badly and had not been surprised very much.

"May I sit?" he asked.

"If you must," she said. After he did, she asked again, "What do you want?"

"Just to get you to back off my guy."

"And who is that?"

Ryan shook his head slightly. "I'm not ready to tell you. One of the nineteen you are blackmailing. I want to wait until I have a better sense of your operation."

"So I guess you're not going to turn me in?"

"Not my role," he said. "I'm no longer with the government, you know."

"Oh, believe me, I know." She wasn't smiling. "You got chucked out on your ass. FBI would like to see you in jail."

"We both know that federal employment isn't for everyone," he parried.

She wasn't buying it. "Difference is, I didn't get fired and nearly charged, like you did."

"I have no regrets," he said.

She shrugged. "I don't care. Anyway, Mr. Tapia, what game are you playing?"

Ryan was taken aback by that word. "It's no game, Miss Thornfoot."

"I don't think you understood my question. So I'll tell you: I think you are playing checkers."

"Okay." Ryan shrugged at the insult. "Nothing wrong with that."

"But I'm playing chess," she said. "So I'll ask again: Where do we stand?"

"I don't know."

"You're not being a lot of help," she said. "You ask me to meet you, you tell me nothing. I mean, it's your move, little grasshopper."

"I think I told you a lot," Ryan countered. "I told you I know what you are doing. I have a pretty good sense of your revenue from it. By my calculation, it comes to nearly $45,000 a month, which is pretty good income for doing nothing." My move here, he thought to himself, is to see how she reacts to that disclosure.

She took that in. He had just told her something else. "You seem to know a lot about my finances," she conceded.

He had expected her to be reeling at this point, or at least rattled. But she didn't seem to be.

"But," she continued, "my work is hardly 'nothing,' as you assert. You're forgetting my initial investment, which was substantial. The cost of research. The endless hours reading court filings and depositions. Of putting things together and connecting the dots. Building each case."

"Yes, you seem to do thorough preliminary work. Very thorough."

"And then there's the risk involved. Dealing with cranky old men. There has to be a premium for that."

"Yes," he said. "But then you got sloppy."

She closed her eyes briefly and leaned back slightly. That word hit home. She didn't mind being called names. She almost liked it when someone called her "bitch"—that meant she was on target. But having her work criticized as lacking, that hurt. Finally, she said, "What makes you think I've been 'sloppy,' as you say?"

"I'm here, aren't I?" Ryan said. "And I know more about your operation than you'd like. More than is healthy for you."

"So why don't I just have you eliminated, for the sake of my health and peace of mind?"

"Because you're too smart for that. I know you inform people that you have left letters to be opened in the case of your death, accidental or otherwise. The contents of those letters likely would do great damage to certain people."

"Yes," she said. "That's right. Standard procedure."

"Well, don't you think I did the same before coming here today?"

"You sound like you're in the same business as I am."

"I'm not," Ryan said emphatically. "You get people into trouble. I try to get them out."

She sat forward and issued a correction. "That's not accurate," she said. "The beauty of my operation is that I discover people who are in trouble that they've already made. I just point it out to them. I didn't make them cheat on their taxes, you know."

"Point taken," he said.

"So I take it you're not looking for a cut?"

"No, I'm not," he said. "But, truth be told, I'm still figuring out what to do with the information I have."

"I can't stand indecisive people," she muttered.

"Sorry," he said. "It's more a matter of developing a full understanding of the situation here. Once I feel I have a good handle on it, I'll get back in touch. So, I'd say, not indecisive, just deliberative."

"You're more complicated than I expected," she said.

He stood up. "And you're spunkier than I thought. I have to say that in an odd way, I like your attitude, even if I don't like what you do."

She rolled her eyes. "Oh, go fuck yourself," she said. "When you get your shit together, give me a call." She took out her phone, the twenty-first century's form of the curt dismissal.

Coming away from the meeting, it was clear to him that she was not going to stop requiring the monthly payments from the nineteen men. It had been worth a shot, he thought. Don't make it complicated, unless you need to. And then, take your time. Slow and steady almost always beats fast and easy.

26

WHAT KILLED NED MEDDYBEMPS?

Rick Trexler, the head of the Afflicted Citizens' Group, called Ryan. "Have you heard about Ned Meddybemps?"

"No," Ryan said. "What'd he do?"

"More, what got done to him. He got run over a couple of nights ago."

"Is he okay?"

"Nope, he's dead," Trexler said.

"That's too bad," Ryan said. "I liked him."

"On company property. Future Minerals."

Ryan suddenly was more alert. "Whoa. That is very interesting," he said. "Was anyone with him?"

"Dunno," the accountant said. "The company reported it."

Ryan thanked Trexler and called Lieutenant D'Agostino, a detective for the State Patrol, which handled homicide cases in most parts of Maine. They'd met years earlier, back when Ryan was still with the FBI.

"Hey, Ryan, you old hound dog," D'Agostino said, surprisingly friendly for an aging homicide cop on a cold, gray winter morning in central Maine.

"You guys looking at the death on Future Minerals property the other night?" Ryan asked.

"Nah. The incident was mentioned in the morning update. Looks like a routine traffic accident. A pedestrian at night in dark clothes. On someone else's property, too. No reason for the driver to be on the lookout. The deceased shouldn't have been there."

"I think it may be more than that," Ryan said.

"Why?"

"The victim was a guy named Ned Meddybemps. I met him once. He was against the whole mining thing up in Pushaw County. And he had found destructive ways of expressing that. First it was small harassment stuff like flat tires. But I think he had bigger ambitions."

"So what do you think he was doing on company property?"

"I don't know," Ryan said. "I have suspicions. And I think his death might not have been, you know, entirely an accident."

"I'll look into it," D'Agostino said. "Let me poke around. See if the company's surveillance cameras picked up anything."

Ryan didn't hear back that day, or the next. On the third day he called. He got no answer but left a message.

Ryan's old landline phone rang a few minutes later. "Hey, D'Agostino," he said.

"No," the caller said. "I'm not that."

"Sorry," Ryan said. "I was expecting a call from a guy I know."

"Well, you don't know me," the caller said. "And I want to keep it that way." The caller coughed, a long hacking sound.

"So why are you calling?"

"About that guy who got run over the other night at Future Minerals."

"Go ahead," Ryan said, reaching for a pen.

"You might find it interesting to talk to the ambulance guys who responded to the call. The EMTs, I mean."

"What might I learn?"

"Ask them." He coughed again.

"Any one of them in particular?"

"You're an investigator."

"Are you one of them?"

The caller hung up.

27

A CALL TO LILY THORNFOOT

In the morning, after having his coffee and reviewing the day's news, Ryan called Lily Thornfoot. "Out of the nineteen names," he told her, "these are the four I want you to back off." He read them aloud: "Charles Rappaport, Roger Robichaux, Mickey Slipp, and Bill Spriggs." He had picked a mix, varying them by geography and how much they were paying her.

"These four, they all hired you?" she asked.

"No need to get into that," he said.

"If I tell them they can stop paying me, will you get out of my life entirely?"

"I don't know. Personally, I think you should drop the whole blackmail business."

"When I want the advice of a broken-down ex-FBI man, I'll ask for it."

"Well, for the moment, just drop the four from your blackmail roster," he said.

"That's gonna cost me, like, twelve thousand a month," she protested.

"Bye," he said.

Lily thought for a minute, then called her sister Diane Peligroso. "You know this Ryan Tapia guy, used to be FBI?"

"Yes," Diane said. "He's been nosing around Pushaw County, the water thing up there."

"Well, he's getting on my nerves too," Lily said.

They talked it through. And they began making plans. Diane picked up that yellow legal pad and added a couple of new possibilities to her list of "R.T.—OPTIONS?"

Meanwhile, Ryan called Roger Robichaux. "You're probably going to be hearing from that lawyer who is blackmailing you, Lily Thornfoot. If you don't, let me know. If you do, don't tell her I was working for you. In fact, don't answer any questions she poses to you—like whether you know me. She won't be happy, and she'll be trying to figure out how I did it."

"So what's the bottom line?" Robichaux asked.

Ryan thought he had made it clear. "The bottom line is, you don't need to pay her anymore."

"I got that, and I'm grateful. But I was trying to ask how much I owe you for your help."

Ryan had considered that. He didn't need the money. He had $4 million in the bank from the settlement from the insurer for the construction company whose truck had killed his wife and children. But he had done a good, clean job for Robichaux, and competent professionalism called for payment of some sort. He thought for a moment. "There's a good animal sanctuary north of Belfast called Peace Ridge. How about sending them five thousand?"

"You're a funny guy," Robichaux mused. "But if that's what you want, I will do it."

"And you should visit the place sometime," Ryan added. "Happiest animals I've ever seen. I was over there last year and the horses looked me straight in the eye, and a donkey rested its head on my shoulder."

"I'll send them a check today."

28

DIANE MOVES ON GROLEAU

Groleau was sitting in her gray metal folding chair outside the room of the Natural Resources Committee. When Peligroso saw her, the reporter was wiping tears from her eyes.

"Something wrong?" the lobbyist asked. "Mean editor?"

Groleau looked up and smiled wanly. "No, it's just my parents. They're getting old, and the winters up in the County are getting harder on them. Especially my dad, with his back. He can't shovel and so my mom is out there doing it right now, in the dark and in the snow. I feel bad for them. I wish I could help."

This is the moment to strike, Peligroso thought. Work that guilt. "Have they ever tried a winter vacation in Florida? That warm sun can help those old bones. The sunshine just eases the joints somehow."

Groleau looked up sharply. "Are you making fun of them? They can't afford that."

"Not in your present job," Peligroso replied.

"Do you know of any better?"

That was exactly the question she had hoped to hear. "What good is a job you love if you can't take care of the people you love?" the lobbyist asked.

It was a line Peligroso had used before. And she watched it hit home now. Groleau took a tissue from her purse and wiped her eyes.

Peligroso pressed on. "And the answer to your question is: Yes, in fact, I do know of a better job."

"What's that?" Groleau asked, still a bit distracted.

"Come work with me."

Groleau shook her head in apparent disbelief. "Are you serious?"

"As a heart attack."

"Doing what?"

"What I do—tracking legislation, keeping clients informed about issues that might touch them, making sure that members understand those issues." This was a polite way of describing the tasks, which also included arm-twisting and making it clear that a vote against her client would make getting re-elected a lot harder.

"Nah," the reporter shook her head slightly. "I don't think my heart would be in that." She had always believed to do a job right, you had to be entirely committed to it. Even in college, when she had a part-time job as a short-order cook in the cafeteria, she tried to be the best hamburger flipper she could be. At the end of her shift, she would shower and try to rid her hair of beef grease. And then she would do it again the next day. It paid for her textbooks, which were surprisingly expensive.

"Doesn't have to be," Peligroso said. "Not every job is made for love. But the work is intellectually engaging. From what I've seen, you have the mind and energy needed to do it well. If your heart isn't in it, your wallet would be. And then you'll be able to help the people you hold in your heart."

"I never dreamed when I was a kid of being a lobbyist," Groleau countered. "I fantasized about being a reporter. My mom gave me a notebook and I even put out a few issues of a *My Neighborhood News* one year."

"But now, I am betting, you have other dreams," Peligroso said. "Maybe owning a house. Maybe some kids one day. Dreams change as people grow up. You're maturing. It happens. This job I'm offering can help that process—and even make some dreams come true. And they're not gonna happen on your newspaper pay." Peligroso could see that Groleau was intrigued. No reason to push it. "Look, we can pick this up another day," Diane told her. "You look worn out."

"I am," Groleau admitted. She was commuting an hour each way down to Augusta to put in a twelve-hour day reporting and writing. The drive took longer in the winter when it was dark and there was snow and ice on the back roads. When she got home, it was all she could do to throw together some food—scrambled eggs with cheese on toast if she had the energy, microwaved leftovers or potatoes or some other inexpensive starch if she didn't—and then collapse into bed. She looked up from her metal folding chair. "How much?"

"I like your spirit, striking while the iron is hot," Peligroso said. "That can serve you well. The money? Well, you're making twenty-eight now, right?"

Groleau nodded.

"Let's start by doubling that."

Groleau's eyes widened. That was fifty-six thousand, almost as much as her editor, Mr. Addison, probably was making after thirty years in the small-town newspaper business.

"Plus," Peligroso said, kneeling down next to the reporter to speak softly, "I think I can find you a ten thousand dollar signing bonus. That is, if you promise to use some of it to send your folks to Florida."

Groleau grinned. She teared up again, this time at the prospect of being able to treat her parents to that. They had worked hard all their lives. They deserved it.

"Tell you what," Peligroso said, reeling her in. "You join up with me, do the job for a year. If you don't like it, you leave. No harm done. You decide you want out, I could even introduce you to someone at the Portland paper. But if you choose then to stay on, at that point your pay goes up another twenty-eight, to eighty-four."

Groleau already was dreaming. "Shit, I might even buy a new car," she said, half to herself.

"No need," Peligroso said, standing. "One comes with the job. Audi or Benz, your pick. We don't represent labor unions, so no need to buy American."

It would be impossible to go back to the grind of reporting after entertaining such thoughts, Groleau realized. "I'm in," she said. She felt her world changing even as she spoke. She was half happy, half disappointed with herself. But maybe that feeling was what it was like to be a real adult, she thought.

29

COFFEE WITH LIEUTENANT D'AGOSTINO

On the fourth day after their conversation about the death of Ned Meddybemps, Ryan once again called D'Agostino at the State Patrol headquarters. He let the phone ring and ring. When his call was shunted to voicemail, he hung up and immediately called again. This time D'Agostino picked up. "Tapia, that you?" No greeting.

"Yes." Ryan waited. Let him explain the cold shoulder.

Finally, D'Agostino said, "I got nothing for you."

It was the first time Ryan had heard the state police detective so dismissive, even a bit hostile. "What's up?"

"Nothing I can talk about right now."

"Cup of coffee?"

"Kinda busy."

"I need this."

After a bit more of going around, D'Agostino agreed to meet, but didn't sound pleased about it. "The Dysart's on Broadway, half an hour from now. I haven't got a lot of time, so it'll be fast. You know the place?"

"Only joint I know that serves haddock chowder as a breakfast special," Ryan said.

"You got it," D'Agostino said.

When Ryan walked into Dysart's thirty-five minutes later, the aging state police detective was standing at a chairless high-top table. He was wearing one of those knee-length topcoats for men that were popular in the 1950s and '60s, and remain so even today with cops because they are long enough to conceal a hip holster but unlike an overcoat are short enough that they don't impede the knees when running or quickly climbing stairs. For some reason these things, also known as car coats, always reminded Ryan of Walter Matthau, a dog-faced actor popular in the 1960s.

"Tapia, you're bad news these days," D'Agostino said in greeting. He wasn't smiling.

"Been talking to my successor at the FBI, huh?"

"No, but I think I know what he'd say. He would say, 'Stay the fuck away from that guy.'"

"And then he'd go back to sleep," Ryan said. "So who do you know who is awake enough to be upset with me?"

D'Agostino leaned forward and lowered his voice. "The other afternoon, Chuck Wolchok, lieutenant colonel, head of my office, stops by. Asks why homicide is looking into the Meddybemps traffic case. I tell him. Chuck tells me to stop wasting my time. I explain that I've heard a couple of things, just want to check them out. He gets red in the face and asks if I didn't hear him the first time. I start to say something more, he waves his hand and says, 'Just fucking drop it. That's an order.' I say, 'What do you mean?' Like, I've known this guy for, what, twenty years, and he's never talked to me like that before. I've driven him home when he was drunk and puking out the side window. Got him to the couch, put a blanket over him, and then went out and hosed off the side of my car. I've sat with him when his son OD'd."

"The kid die?"

"Nah, but it was nip and tuck for a while. Kid got through it, joined the Marines. Doing okay now. Fighting in Syria, Pakistan, I dunno, one of them sandy places."

"So what was making the guy bounce off the walls over the Meddybemps thing?"

"That's what I'm wondering about as he gets all shirty with me. He goes kind of quiet and says, 'Patsy, I am trying to help you out here. Word to the wise.'"

Ryan realized that was why D'Agostino had agreed to see him: He was curious about why there was so much negative energy floating around the Meddybemps thing. But he needed a minute to think. "Your first name is Patsy?" Ryan asked, mildly interested but also buying a little time with the diversion. He'd never heard the guy's first name mentioned before.

"Not really, it's Pasquale. But when I was growing up in Boston, the Irish kids kinda squeezed it down into 'Patsy,' and that stuck."

"So, what was his word to the wise?"

"Chuck says, and he points his finger at my chest, 'The state police are not investigating Future Minerals. Got that?'" D'Agostino paused. "I say I understand, hear you loud and clear, will do. And I walk out of his office and go sit at my desk.

"But he can see I'm peeved, what with him talking to me like I'm a new recruit. After a while, he gets kind of apologetic, you know like people do after they've flown off the handle some. He comes back to my cubbyhole and says, 'Look, this didn't come from me, or from the colonel. This is way above our heads. There is real pressure coming down. You may not know it, but I'm doing you a favor.'"

"Bosses always say that when they act like assholes," Ryan observed. "Any word on the company's security video?"

"They say there isn't one," D'Agostino said, gulping the last of his coffee. "Gotta go." He pocketed his phone and picked up his paper cup of coffee. "I don't need to tell you, Tapia, there is some weird shit out there with Future Minerals. You best be careful." He turned and headed for the restaurant's front door.

30

A MESSAGE FROM LILY?

Checking his email, Ryan saw a familiar name in his daily Google News alerts: Charles Rappaport, the retired data communications executive who had been one of Lily Thornfoot's more lucrative monthly contributors. The headline from the newspaper read, CHARLES RAPPAPORT, 62, DAMARISCOTTA LAKE. The news brief, just two sentences, said he had "passed away suddenly," which was usually a journalistic euphemism for suicide, but not always.

An alarm went off in the back of Ryan's head. "Charles Rappaport" was one of the four names he had given just the other day to Lily Thornfoot. Indeed, according to the Gulf of Maine checking account records, he had been one of her bigger payers. Was his death a message from Lily? That is, he wondered, had it really been a suicide?

His mind began to race. To calm himself, Ryan went for a walk on his mile-long dirt driveway, out to the Bangor highway. As he walked, he thought: What if Lily had made it look like a suicide, and somehow forged a suicide note, or forced Rappaport to write one? What if that note pinned the death on Ryan? Lily was capable of such an act, he sensed, and would do it if she thought it would benefit her. He mulled how she would compose such a message. It might state: *I am killing myself because the pressure from Ryan Tapia has become too much for me. For nearly a year, he has been extracting payments from me of $5,000 a month in a blackmail scheme. The payments were sent to a cutout, a lawyer named Lily Thornfoot. I retained her services in order to prevent further contact between me and Tapia, who I came to fear. I didn't tell Thornfoot why I was sending the money, but only gave her instructions that she forward it to him every month. I am terminating this arrangement in the only way that I can see available, in order to prevent further damage to my family and friends.* That's the way she'd do it, Ryan figured.

Ryan dialed D'Agostino at the State Patrol. "It's not about that traffic accident," Ryan said quickly. "It's about a death near Damariscotta. Guy named Rappaport."

"Look, Tapia, you're kind of kryptonite around here these days," D'Agostino said. "I'm not going to the well for you again."

"On Rappaport, I'm assuming it was suicide. I just want to know if he left a note."

The officer said, "Do you have an interest in Rappaport's death?"

"Not directly, as far as I know. But I have a client who may have been in the same situation as him." He meant, of course, Roger Robichaux, another victim of Thornfoot's blackmail scheme.

D'Agostino sounded puzzled. "You mean, pancreatic cancer?"

Now it was Ryan's turn to be confused. After a moment he said, "No, that wasn't what I meant. Is that what really killed Rappaport?"

"Sort of," D'Agostino said. "He left a note saying that the pain was getting worse, so bad it made death seem like a relief. He'd been saving up morphine pills and took enough to knock himself out fast. His oncologist down in Portland confirmed that he had, let me see my notes"—Ryan heard some quick typing on a keyboard—"'pancreatic adenocarcinoma, T4, advanced and aggressive.' The doc said it probably was the best move for Rappaport, given the prognosis. In fact, they'd just told him to get his affairs in order."

When Ryan hung up, he felt almost disappointed. If Lily Thornfoot had tried to pin the death on him, he could have countered by sending investigators to look at the other eighteen people she had been blackmailing. Seventeen of them would have said they'd never heard of Ryan Tapia. The eighteenth, Roger Robichaux, would have said that he had hired Tapia to get Thornfoot off his back.

He realized that he had misjudged Lily Thornfoot. She would not endanger her entire scheme directly by going after him. That would mean losing a lot of revenue and no financial gain. No, he calculated, she would strike at him indirectly. But how?

31

RYAN VISITS THE DISTRICT ATTORNEY

Ryan went out for a drive. He couldn't shake a bad feeling, one he knew was separate from the grief he'd always carry. He randomly headed up north from Bangor toward the Future Minerals tipple. You never know what you might see, just by being there. He realized that he was driving behind a Future Minerals freight truck, probably going for another load. The truck hit a pothole, the bane of Maine roads in the winter, and a small rock fell from it. Ryan, idly interested, pulled over and picked up the rock. It was about the size of a golf ball, and slightly reddish. He assumed this was cobalt-bearing copper. The rock that was ruining so many lives. He stood on the roadside and studied its sharp angles.

I should focus on the cobalt thing, he thought to himself. Not this blackmailing thing. Lily Thornfoot really is not my problem, he said to himself. Why make her one? Let someone else deal with her. Turn over the entire mess to someone else. After all, he was a private citizen. He had no police powers.

But who? He couldn't go to the FBI, because his name was mud at the Bureau. What's more, the new FBI agent in Bangor, an alcoholic with a good record in his earlier career, was counting the days until retirement and had made it clear that he wanted nothing to do with Ryan. The Bureau's dislike also made federal prosecutors wary of Ryan. And Scales, the state attorney general, already had sided with Future Minerals, which made Ryan a de facto enemy of the AG.

He side-armed the rock into the spruce trees along the side of the road. As he did, he decided to try another angle: The local district attorney down where Lily Thornfoot operated. He got back in his pickup and called the office of the Adams County district attorney, Dick Auger. He was connected after a minute to someone who answered the phone as "chief of staff." Despite that title, the person speaking struck Ryan's ear as probably a teenager.

"Sir, I assure you that I can convey to him anything he needs to know," the squeaky-voiced chief of staff told Ryan, taking on a formal tone that just didn't work. He sounded like a high schooler playing an old man in a school play, wearing a cardigan and talcum powder in his hair.

Ryan decided to use an old real estate trick he'd read about: Make the seller the bidder. "I'm sorry, but the more I consider it, this is such a large-scale case, involving multiple criminal charges, most likely," he said. "Probably better to take it to the state."

The chief of staff's tone became more solicitous. "Well, the boss does like big, interesting cases," he said. "How's tomorrow morning?"

Ryan drove down for the meeting. The DA himself was just thirty-two years old, in his first term. He came out of his office to greet Ryan. "Coffee?" he said.

"Where's Mister Chief-of-Staff?" Ryan said, looking around.

"Timmy?" said Auger. "Well, he's really just my assistant. The only staff is him and the office manager, who has been here forever, knows where all the bodies are buried, and runs the place. But Timmy thinks that 'chief of staff' will look better on his résumé. And it was cheaper giving him a title than a raise. I don't have a real big budget."

Ryan followed the DA into the inner office. Auger sat and said, "I understand you have a potentially large and interesting criminal case?"

"Yes," Ryan said, "I do, involving extensive blackmail."

"I like that," Auger said, leaning forward and actually rubbing his hands together. "People read news articles about that. Nice high-profile case."

"But maybe too large for a county DA?" Ryan asked, provocatively.

"Meaning?"

"Realizing this morning how meager your staff is here, I'm wondering if the state attorney general might be a better fit for it. Case like this takes a lot of hours to nail down, what with multiple witnesses, bank records, and such." Ryan had never been very good at bluffing and wasn't sure it would work here.

"Why don't you tell me more about it?" the DA said. "Then we can make a decision."

"Okay," Ryan said agreeably. He felt he had taken the real estate ploy as far as he could. Without naming names or providing identifying details, he laid out the case: A long-running blackmailing operation against nineteen people, one of whom had paid him to look into it. "The upside of it," Ryan concluded, "is that the paper trail is readily available. I've already seen part of it."

"And the downside?"

"The hard part will be what it always is with blackmail and extortion: The targets don't want to give evidence or testify.

They'll want immunity. The IRS won't grant that, but a competent attorney should be able to get the IRS to agree not to impose large punitive fines."

"Let me run some traps and I'll get back to you," the DA said. He rose and extended his hand. He was already forming a plan in his mind. But it wasn't the one that Ryan expected. Ryan didn't know it yet but he had just made one of the biggest mistakes of his life.

32

BETTY GOES SHOPPING

It was a quiet Monday in Augusta, and it was Betty Groleau's first day on the new job at Peligroso Consulting. The legislature was not meeting, nor even any committees. She had expected that she would have the usual first day of settling in—getting issued a company phone and laptop, setting up passwords and voicemail, filling out health insurance forms. That sort of thing.

"How do you feel?" Peligroso asked.

"Honestly?" Groleau asked. "You want to know?"

Peligroso said, "Yes, I do."

"What I feel like is, I dunno, I guess like I'm selling out." Betty sighed.

Peligroso nodded. "That's natural. You're making a big change. But think of it this way: In my view, you're moving from the losers to the winners."

Groleau was puzzled. "Why do you say that? We're all, like, Mainers, aren't we?"

"Yes," Peligroso said. "But consider the facts of the matter. For better or worse, money drives American politics these days. Nothing you or I do is going to change that. Nothing. It is the way things are. Over the last few decades that new system has been nailed in place by billionaires and ratified by the Supreme Court. So, I think what you are doing isn't selling out."

"Then what is it?" Betty said, puzzled.

"It is buying into the system," Diane continued. "My take is, you are getting smart. You are taking advantage of a system that you can't change. There is nothing wrong with being realistic. I say, the beginning of wisdom is accepting things as they are. And the second step is taking advantage of it." Peligroso believed all this. It was the pep talk she gave to herself sometimes.

"I need to think on that," Groleau said.

"How are your parents?"

"In Fort Lauderdale," Groleau said with a sudden smile. "And yes, they're loving it. Dad says he just lies in the sun and lets his back soak up the rays. He sounds happier than I've heard him in years. And my mom does too. I want to make it an annual thing for them."

"Maybe you could even think about buying them a place to stay down there the whole winter."

"Can I really afford that?"

"Yep. Doesn't need to be on the beach. The sun is just as warm a few miles inland." Diane stepped back and looked Betty up and down. The former reporter was wearing a sky-blue frock. It was old but her favorite outfit. She'd worn it for good luck on her first day at the new job.

"What's the matter?" Betty asked.

"New priority," Diane said. "We need to get you some new outfits. Winners look like winners, not like yellow tag day at Goodwill."

Betty winced. But, she reasoned, she'd been honest with Diane about her feelings, and she was getting a frank appraisal in return.

"How about we take a trip to Boston?" Diane asked.

"We can just do that?" Betty said.

"It's a sleepy Monday in Augusta and the legislature is not in session. I've got to make some calls, but I can do that from the car. Let's go. We can get you the phones and laptops tomorrow. You wanna try out driving a Benz?"

It was indeed a new and different life. Diane handed her a key fob with a Mercedes Benz logo on it. "It's the black car on the right, out back," she said with a light smile. "I'll join you in a few minutes."

Betty walked out, pressed the unlock button, and slipped into the driver's seat. The sleek sedan smelled like luxury, like being inside a warm, cozy, comfortable winter boot or something, she thought to herself. Or a plush cocoon. This felt like a private refuge from the troubles of the world. The black leather was soft to the touch. She ran her right hand along the dashboard's polished wooden paneling. It was walnut, she guessed. She had never sat in any car like this, let alone driven one.

She waited a minute or two. This is what having enough money feels like, she thought. Not just soft and clean, but safe.

She pressed the ignition button. "*WELCOME, BETTY,*" the screen on the dashboard flashed at her. Below the greeting, smaller letters stated, "*Please turn up the volume.*" She did. "Welcome, Betty," a plush British-accented man's voice said from all four speakers. "I am your new Mercedes Benz V177 Class A Executive Sedan. We will go places together."

Betty sighed. "Wow," she said. Everything about the car stunned her. She had known, intellectually, that some people lived like this, with rich food, expensive clothes, and luxurious automobiles. But to think that she was living that life, that her own stubby, ink-stained fingers were touching this creamy leather, that three-pointed Mercedes silver star staring back at her from the center of the steering wheel, that she could drive this car wherever she wanted—well, that will take some time to really believe, she told herself.

Diane slipped into the passenger seat. "Next stop, Boston," she said.

As they sailed down the Turnpike, Diane made calls, always in her pleasant, coaxing voice. The longest call was in response to a plea from a cruise ship association that wanted her to represent them in Maine. They were having problems with proposed "no discharge" rules that would prevent them from dumping raw sewage within three miles of the Maine coast. The problem, in the view of the state government, was that three miles out was prime lobstering territory. Betty, listening to Diane's end of the call, was nervous. One of her cousins was the clam warden down in Sagadahoc, and had told her that sometimes the discharges were carried in by the tides. "It's not just a piece or two of poop," he had said at Thanksgiving. "An average big cruise ship produces thirty-thousand gallons of sewage water a day." At that point Betty's mother had suggested they change the topic while at the table.

To Betty's relief, Diane turned down the offer. "That's very generous of you," she told the man from the cruise ship association. "I appreciate your interest. But I am sorry, my roster is full. If that changes, I will let you know."

After the call was over, Betty said, "I am glad you didn't take that."

Diane shrugged. "The smellier the client, the more they'll pay," she said. "I would have liked it, but until you get up to speed, we really already have our hands full."

They spent the rest of the day getting Betty some proper outfits.

33

THE DA VISITS LILY THORNFOOT

The DA could hardly contain his glee. Dick Auger had found the job of district attorney disappointing, even stifling. Every day in court seemed like an endless parade of drunk drivers and domestic abusers. Pretty soon the faces of defendants became familiar. They'd come around every few months on the carousel, he thought to himself. One day he suspected he already knew the defendant, only to be told that no, this was the son, he just looked like the father who was arraigned the previous week. "That was 'Sleepy Senior,' this is 'Sleepy Junior,'" explained the defense lawyer, who repped both father and son.

So the DA was ready to move on—and preferably to move up. But he hadn't seen a way to grab one of the next-up posts, such as running for Congress or angling to be state attorney general, a position that in Maine, unusually, was selected by the legislature. The leaps seemed too far beyond his reach.

But now this case had landed in his lap. He hadn't told Ryan, but he had been hearing rumors about Lily Thornfoot for some time, about how her law practice seemed unusually prosperous for someone who mainly handled routine and minor real estate and trust transactions, with occasional petty commercial disputes. Some people thought that Lily looked affluent because her lobbyist sister had shared some of her wealth. Others, after a few drinks, offered darker thoughts.

And now Ryan had given him a few specifics to attach to the rumors: At least eighteen instances of continuing blackmail. In them, Auger saw a way that might help his political ambitions. He called Lily, then walked slowly along State Street to her office on Main. He rehearsed his approach as he moved down the sidewalk and watched ducks land on unfrozen spots on the Union River, off to his right.

Lily met him at the door in her usual outfit of blouse, jeans, and cowboy boots. She sat down behind her desk. "I have a problem I need to discuss with you," DA Auger began.

She listened to his broad outline impassively. It took him several minutes to make clear to her what he knew, and what he suspected.

"Are you finished?" she said, with an edge of impatience.

This was not going as he expected. He thought she'd be taken aback, perhaps take her head in her hands. That's what he would have done if someone in a position of legal authority had said they possessed evidence that he had committed dozens of counts of grand larceny—that is, nineteen targets, each paying monthly for at least a year. Each count carried a sentence of five or ten years.

Instead, Lily waved a hand in the air, as if brushing away a black fly. "Well," she drawled, "you're not here with handcuffs, cameras, and little Timmy, so I'm guessing you actually are sitting here because you want something from me." She leaned back in her chair. She looked remarkably relaxed, he thought.

"You're fast," he said.

"Oh, please," she said, rolling her eyes. "I'm just not as slow as most of the sixty-dollars-an-hour lawyers you face. Without their steady stream of OUIs and domestic abuse, they'd be on food stamps."

Auger began to wonder if perhaps this was not the first time someone had tried to confront her about her operation. At any rate, she seemed to be one step ahead of him. So, he gave her the respect of telling her exactly what he wanted. "What I'd like is for you to set up a meeting for me with your sister."

"She's in the phone book. Why do you need me?"

"Let me break it down for you Barney style," he said, clearing his throat. "I want you in the meeting. And I want you to tell her that you've decided to help my political career. And so you are asking her to pull in some favors, to get the ball rolling."

She leaned forward in her chair. "And if I do, my case goes away?"

"What case?" he said, smiling and extending his hands far out to his sides. The nice thing about blackmailers, he was learning, was that unlike most criminals, they knew how to do business. "All I've heard are some rumors, wild talk. You know how Mainers go on after a few drinks on these long winter nights. Probably just envy of your success." He waved a hand sideways in front of his face, dismissing all that stuff with one grand gesture.

PART II

34

THE OPEN HEARING ON THE COBALT MINING

It was the day of the open hearing on the cobalt situation. Much could be revealed, but only to those who knew how to read the signs and signals. "It's days like these," Diane Peligroso told Betty Groleau in preparing her, "that we really earn our pay."

From the chairs reserved for lobbyists, Betty surveyed the audience and recognized several faces. When she was a reporter, she had interviewed many of these people, looked them in the face and written down in blue ink what they had to say. Indeed, that was how the committee had learned about some of them. Others in the room who were prepared to testify had been sent to the committee staff by Ryan Tapia, an investigator she heard was sniffing around, and Doc Healey. Also, the staff had requested that the state medical association have its members talk to affected patients about contacting their representatives. Through that channel, about forty people had gotten in touch. She saw that Tapia was in the back row.

She gazed over at the witnesses, who had been seated as a bloc in the front right of the room. Like the majority of the population of Maine, they were older than the rest of the country. But they also stood out for their drooping eyelids and rash-covered arms. Someone had prepared them well. They dressed like poor, hardworking people, in clean but aging clothes. Some wore hoodie sweatshirts—predominantly showing allegiance to "Patriots" and "Black Bears"—but before the hearing began, took them off to reveal T-shirts. Others were in short-sleeved shirts. They had been told not to be shy about displaying the rashes on their arms and necks. At the witness table, one empty chair was bedecked in black cloth, to signify the deaths of three old, sick people. Pushaw locals believed their demises had been accelerated by the cobalt pollution.

Diane Peligroso, on the other side of the audience, wrote a note on a pad and crooked a finger at a Republican staffer on the committee. He came over, took it, and delivered it to the senior Republican on the committee, who glanced at it and then said, "Madam Chair, I think that this black-covered chair is a stage prop, and prejudicial to our proceedings. I ask that it be removed."

She looked up and down at the faces of the members. "With no objections," she said, "so ordered." The point had been made, and the photographs had been taken, so no one was going to fight about it.

The press table was long and large, but mainly empty. It had fourteen chairs, a reminder of the old days when newsworthy hearings would attract representatives of three wire services, seven newspapers, and some radio stations. But that was before the internet smashed the business model of most media outlets. Today there were just seven chairs being used, by representatives of the Associated Press, the Portland and Boston newspapers, National Public Radio, and the *North Country Times*, this last by an intern brought in just a few days earlier to plug the hole left by Betty's resignation. The intern would produce a shaky account of the hearing that essentially was a "he said, she said" version of the day, with little understanding or explanation of what it all meant.

Linc Addison would clean it up to make it presentable, but he knew the final product was still quite thin. The editing process would remind him of that old newsroom admonition that, "You can't make chicken salad out of chicken shit."

Betty walked over and touched the shoulder of the seventh reporter, Monique Bouchard. The Canadian reporter looked up at her coldly. "You turned into a lobbyist?" she said. Her eyes were at once distant and piercing.

"Let's talk later," Betty said in embarrassment.

"I think not," Monique said. She was about to say something more when the chair rapped the gavel to commence the hearing. The first witness was Bap Salim, the bearded young geologist from the University of Northern Maine. "My academic endeavors focus on the essence of life on this planet, which is the interplay of rock and water," he said by way of introduction. He didn't notice that this elegant summary of the field of sedimentary geology sailed right over the heads of the committee. That was his first mistake.

He gave a quick, nervous overview of what his field research had found. "Now, the mineshaft is at the very center of this issue. It is narrow. It is excavating a vein of cobalt-bearing copper ore that mostly follows a horizontal plane, with a slight upward angle as it proceeds north and east. That is the result of the continental plate lifting, I should add. This part of the plate is being squeezed upward a bit even more, creating the hills, which subsequently were desiccated somewhat by glacial scouring."

One member of the committee looked at the ceiling. Another began reading a newspaper. They were not as interested in the geological history as he was. He turned to a big map on an easel that stood next to him. "Now, please, members, here is what we have come to designate as 'the Fan,' the area where the groundwater appears to be contaminated. It is technically called 'the plume.'

"To map it, we started at the northern edge," he said. "We began picking up toxicity at this point"—he tapped a pointer on the map north of the Beecher-Asbury town line. "It intensified as we moved south and west.

"We paid special attention to wells and springs, which gives us not just geographical range, but intensity. The aquifer, that is the water-bearing layer of porous rock or gravel, runs below the mineshaft, so seepage downward, through the force of gravity, is a genuine and pressing problem."

A member interrupted. "Can't they just build sumps?"

Salim hadn't expected to be interrupted. He paused, then said, "One could, but those would just leak out as well. If one made them leakproof, they'd overflow pretty quickly."

He wanted to get back on track. "So, as I was saying, the tainted water percolates downward from the mineshaft until it reaches the aquifer, which then can carry the contaminants quite a distance. We call that 'migration of toxicity.' In this instance, such migration ends at the Salmon River, which dilutes the injection and carries it southward."

The committee chair asked, "Are there any fixes?"

Salim gulped. "Not really. In similar circumstances that I have examined, both in the United States and in other nations, the authorities commissioned the digging of remediation wells. You put those in the location with the dirtiest water, to intercept it and pump it out of the aquifer. This step reduces contamination but doesn't eliminate it. Second, you can also filter every drop of water taken out of the ground. But that is hardly a complete answer. So, in my opinion, in such an exceedingly difficult situation such as this, one probably must rely on alternative water sources for a good deal of time."

"From outside the Pushaw area?" asked a member from Ellsworth.

"Yes, ma'am," Salim said.

"Sounds expensive," she said. That was legislative signal language for: Not gonna happen.

"The issue of purchasing and transporting potable water in Maine is quite outside my area of expertise," Salim deferred.

"Speaking of expertise," said the member from Kittery. "Your testimony is quite alarming. But I must say, I've seen these places with my own eyes, and, if you'll forgive me, they just didn't look like to me the ecological disaster you're describing. We saw animals grazing, birds flying, a fisherman casting in the Salmon River. It was pretty damn nice, to be honest."

Salim's eyes darted back and forth across the faces of the legislators staring at him. He thought to himself that this particular questioner didn't know what he was talking about. Unaccustomed to the world of politics, he said pretty much that, taking off his glasses to collect himself and then unloading. "With respect, sir, in your tour, you saw only that which the company's representative, Miss Peligroso, wanted you to see. Quite frankly, with your untrained eye, you did not have the slightest clue of what to look for."

"Like what, son?"

"When one does do this full time, as I myself am fortunate to be able to do, one notices things. And with additional experience, one especially senses absences. One learns to ask questions. If we are in late spring, where are the tadpoles and salamanders? In summer, one might notice that the plants along a given stream aren't as prolific as they were last year. Or in September, why are migrating waterfowl bypassing this pond?"

"So you ask a lot of questions," the Kitterian said a bit dismissively.

"Sir, I have been taught that posing necessary questions is the beginning of disciplined academic research," Salim countered, building up a head of steam as he went. He had sensed the condescension in that last comment, and resented it. But emotional reactions are always risky in politics. "One might say that this posing of questions is the starting point of any kind of wise approach."

The next senator, a heavy right-wing lobsterman from Corea, came at him straight from out of the gate. "I want to remind the witness that it is our job to ask the questions, not his."

Bap Salim was getting jammed up. It took him some minutes to realize that most of the state senators were hostile to him. They were not there to understand him, but to undermine him, to shut him down.

"Ladies and gentlemen, I most sincerely implore you," the graduate student said, scrambling to defend his position. "This is a most grave situation. Indeed, we were faced with one dead body that had multiple signs of toxicity. This corpse rang all the alarms, I will tell you with the utmost sincerity. It was what we call a 'concentrated specimen,' quite unusual as I understand it."

The lobsterman interrupted him. "And, uh," he said slowly, "where is that body now?"

"I sincerely regret that I do not know where it is," Salim said.

"And why is that, Mr. Salim?" He slowly pronounced out the student's name as if it were a stretch limousine, into "Sa-ah-ah-leeeem."

"Someone took it, apparently."

The senator shook his head. "Well, isn't that convenient. You had the evidence but it somehow walked away. Cut me another slice of that blueberry pie, mama."

"There is a great and persuasive abundance of evidence, sir," Salim shot back, trying to contain his anger as he caught the implications of the senator's remarks.

"Well, try not to lose any more of it, son," the senator said. "I have no more questions." He rose slowly and left the room.

Salim was angry. "Sir, I say this with respect. I very much think you owe something to the people here," he said.

Diane smiled inwardly at this outburst of his. "Miss Peligroso," as she had been called, at first was perturbed to have her name mentioned by him in the hearing. But as Salim rattled on, she saw that from the frown on the face of the member from Kittery that Salim was making a series of mistakes. Yes, Salim's testimony was accurate. But the members of the committee found his manner insulting. No one likes to be called a fool, especially at an open hearing when one is sitting among one's peers and under the eyes of the press and the public.

"The witness is dismissed," the chairwoman said. She gaveled his testimony to a close.

Salim rose and almost staggered to the hallway. His introduction to American politics had not gone as he had expected. Ryan was just outside the big white door, waiting for him. He introduced himself. "I'm impressed by your research," he said.

"Thank you most sincerely," the geologist said. "The senators were not, I must say!"

"Do you need money to continue it?" Ryan asked.

"No, no," Salim said. "I have a most generous backer, the Society for a Better Planet. They have supplemented the university's stipend and that has enabled me to focus almost exclusively on the Pushaw toxicity issues. I want to talk to my advisor about making this situation the subject of my dissertation. But at the moment, I have no need of additional funds."

Inside the hearing room, the next to testify was Lorenzo Dow, a lanky backwoods Methodist minister from the town of Asbury with surprisingly long black hair and a prominent triangular nose that extended far beyond his pointy chin. He had a frontier air to him that seemed almost old and formal in a contemporary context. His was the northernmost of the three affected locales, the most remote, with several roads where the pavement stopped and the gravel began, leading out into the deep, rolling forested ridges. People got lost back there, and some were never found. Dow sat up ramrod straight in the witness chair. His posture reflected the fact that this was a man who knew how to preach the Gospel but also how to hunt bear.

"We are ordinary people," he began. "We ask no special favors. All we want is common decency. Is that so much to ask? Brothers and sisters, I think not.

"What do we do when a plague is visited upon us? I use that word advisedly. A company's mining operation has become like a plague upon us. They are invisible to us, operating in the bowels of the Earth, wounding it so that our water sometimes runs like blood.

"Why am I here today? For the simplest of reasons. I am here as a witness. I am here to report to you, the mighty and powerful, to hope that the groans of our people might reach your high and wise ears. They are suffering afflictions of the skin of their flesh, bright spots—like this," he said, and held out his right arm to show the angry red rash. "Thank you. And may God forgive this company for its transgressions against the people and the land."

The chair looked up and down the table at her colleagues. No one wanted to touch this guy with a ten-foot pole. "Thank you for your testimony, Reverend Dow," she said. There were no questions. She gaveled again. Dow stood and left the room.

The AP reporter said whispered to her two colleagues, "This is getting kind of Old Testament, don't you think?"

Third came Hugh Bugby, a stout road worker from Beecher. "I am not a real good talker, so I hope you will bear with me," he began. "I don't work with words, I work with my hands." He held them up as if they were supporting evidence. "In the summer I cut grass and lay gravel and asphalt in the potholes. It's hot work, but it's honest. In the fall I go out and pick up the roadkill deer and haul the carcasses to the town dump. When I get a little free time, I trim branches so they don't hit power lines and phone lines when the wind hits heavy.

"But now," he continued, "with the water problem and all, the effects, you know, the bad symptoms me and my wife have, I am finding it harder to do all that." He turned his hands palms up, as if asking them to speak. "Not looking for a handout. We're not the type to take welfare money. I am not asking for anything but one thing: I want to be able to work. I don't think that is too much to ask. What I want to ask you is, what kind of corporation poisons people? And gets away with it? Pardon my French, but just what the hell are you people in Augusta doing here?" Bugby realized he was losing his self-control. He pushed his chair backward and walked out of the room. In the hallway he cried. His appearance had taken every bit of energy he had, but he did it in the memory of his deceased wife, one of the people commemorated by the black-decked chair.

Somewhat unnecessarily, the chair gaveled his testimony to a close and, seeing tempers rising, called a fifteen-minute break to let the building head of steam dissipate. Groleau took out her phone to check her emails and texts. A man in his sixties recognized her and limped over to her chair. He stood over her. "Can I help you?" she said, looking up.

"You're that reporter who interviewed me," he said. It wasn't a question.

"Yes, I did," she said, vaguely recalling him. Because of his age, and his pre-existing condition of diabetes, the cobalt and copper had hit him particularly hard. She remembered now that he had told her then that he expected to have some toes amputated. She glanced down. It looked like the entire foot had been taken. She couldn't summon his name. She recalled that he said he lived in a mobile home, hard up against the Salmon River, right as you came into Finney Junction. Odd, she thought, that she could remember the place but not his name.

"You were real nice to me, gave me a hug when I got tearful," he recalled. "We talked about how I used to feel that I lived in paradise. And it was ruined."

"Your story was moving. I am glad I could help tell it." Something about him made her uneasy. He wasn't telling her he was grateful. In fact, he seemed quite irritated, even querulous.

"But I hear you went over to work for the mining company," he added. Again, it wasn't really a question.

"Sort of," she corrected. "I joined a public relations outfit that does some work for Future Minerals."

"How could you?" His voice was getting louder. "You heard our stories. You knew all about what they did to us. Yet you decided to join them. Just for money?" People were turning to look at them. "Look at you!" he shouted. He pointed a reddened finger in her face.

"It was for my family," she said quietly. Diane frowned at her. She had warned Betty against engaging with the victims. Nothing good could come of it. And it looked unprofessional. Diane wasn't focused on the witnesses. She was ignoring most of what they said and instead concentrating, word by word, on what the committee members were saying, and even on their body language. And she was learning a lot. She had taken notes about phone calls to make and problems to consider. Diane looked at Betty and shook her head, conveying an emphatic no.

Betty noticed Diane's shake and grimace of disapproval and got to her feet. "You'll have to excuse me," she said to the man. She walked briskly out of the room and took a right down to the women's room, just in case he was hobbling along behind her. His name suddenly came to mind. It was Gary Rath. She remembered thinking that only old men have the name "Gary" anymore. It evoked a half-forgotten actor for her—Gary Cooper, was that the name? And this Gary had given off a distinct odor of being unwashed. He felt humiliated and betrayed, and that, she realized, was a terrible combination. It had made him volatile.

In the bathroom she washed her hands and studied her own face in the mirror. She searched her eyes. She had not taken a vow of poverty, she told herself. She had the right to move on from the dying industry of newspapers and find another, more prosperous path in life. She had exercised that right. But why, she wondered to herself, did she not feel better about that decision?

She waited fifteen minutes and then went back to the hearing room, but took a seat in the back row, so that Mr. Rath and the other witnesses she had interviewed would not see her—or surprise her.

The hearing was winding up. The chair asked Senator Tweedy, sitting in with the committee down at the end of the podium, if he had any questions. He declined, saying, "I've learned a lot today, and I want to thank the distinguished chair for holding this important and thoughtful hearing, and for the courtesy of allowing me to join your panel today. I think we need to keep the big picture in mind, seeking a balance between interests, jobs, and the environment, and this hearing has enabled us to begin that process. I do wish we had heard some testimony today about the economic benefits of the mining in my district. Unlike some city types, we in rural Maine can't afford to be picky about where our jobs come from. But that can come another day."

In the audience, Peligroso allowed herself a small smile. She had only to hint to Tweedy what she wanted to hear, and he had delivered the full load.

Her phone buzzed in her hand, informing her that her twin sister had texted her. "WHAT U C IN AUGER?" Lily asked. "HE'S A SIMPLETON."

Diane wrote back, "BUT NOW HE'S *OUR* SIMPLETON!"

35

THE DA MAKES HIS MOVE

Ryan was wondering why he hadn't heard from Dick Auger, the DA down in Ellsworth. He usually browsed news sites over his dinner. First, he read the account of the open hearing the previous day. But his eye was struck by the story next to it on the home page of the Bangor newspaper's site. That adjacent article was topped by a color photograph of none other than DA Auger. In it, his face was above a cluster of microphones. He was flanked by two other Maine politicians whom Ryan vaguely recognized. They were legislators of some sort, he thought.

DA AUGER IN SURPRISE BID FOR STATE AG, the headline read. Ryan stopped chewing on his haddock sandwich. He read the news story, which in providing context stated that, "The move took many political observers by surprise because there already are two better-known candidates who have asked to be considered by the state legislature. Auger, 32, is a political novice who lacks any base outside his Down East county. However, his candidacy was endorsed immediately by two political heavyweights in Augusta, the chairs of two key committees—Criminal Justice and Judiciary—who appeared with him at the announcement.

"Further boosting Auger's prospects," the article continued, "Diane Peligroso, an influential political operative consultant and lobbyist, said she had volunteered to serve as chair of Auger's effort. Peligroso is known for her extensive contacts with major political donors not just in the state but also in Boston and New York, which gives her unusual sway with legislators as they contemplate financing their re-election bids."

Ryan felt nauseous. He had taken his best shot against Lily Thornfoot. She'd counterattacked with speed, precision, and impact. Staring at the article, he realized that she indeed was playing chess, and at a level well above him. She had warned him. He had gone ahead anyway. Now what to do?

During the course of his middling career in federal law enforcement, Ryan had learned that there are two kinds of mistakes: The lesser ones you recognize in the moment, as you are making them or in the moment after. The really big mistakes, he had come to see, the real life-shaping whoppers, were the ones you commit full of vigor and certainty, absolutely sure you are right, only to realize some time after that fact that they were badly wrong, that you had screwed up. Usually these errors carried a number of aftershocks, where you made additional smaller errors in the belief that you are handling everything just wonderfully.

These latter mistakes were the material of sleepless nights, as one realized, oh, I did this, and then because I thought I was right, I did that. I was so full of myself that I flipped off my boss, and everyone laughed at him, and that night I told my wife to shape up or ship out, and when she did, and my best friend took me aside and asked me to cool down, I told him to fuck off. That was numbers one through three, and so on up to ninety-nine.

As he sat and considered his moves and the Thornfoot sisters' countermoves, he began to think that his approach to the DA had been one of those whopping mistakes. He had sought to shut down part of Lily Thornfoot's blackmail business. Instead, he had empowered her and her twin sister. This happened because he had gone to the DA without at least a sense of how the man might use the information Ryan provided. He had done so because he hadn't seen another course open to him.

Still, he realized as he lay awake hours later, staring at the ceiling and the cold moon outside the window, he could simply have done nothing. In hindsight, that would have been the wiser course.

Sleep was out of the question. He got out of bed and researched "ambulance service in Pushaw County." He had assumed he would have to scroll through dozens of news stories, picking out comments members of the unit had made after accidents and fires. Instead, almost the first thing that popped up on his screen was a link to the Facebook page of "Pushaw County Volunteer Ambulance Service." Next, he found the service's roster on the county's site. There were three EMTs listed, plus two dispatchers and several drivers. Ryan thought over the anonymous phone caller: He had referred to "the EMTs," which probably meant that he wasn't one. So he decided to begin with the ambulance drivers. After that, if needed, he would seek out the EMTs.

36

FUTURE MINERALS STRIKES PRE-EMPTIVELY

Will Payne, the company's chief of security, also read the news accounts of the previous day's hearing. When he finished, he picked up his cell phone to call Diane Peligroso. He didn't like all the testimony about the medical problems people in Pushaw County were suffering, but he was more puzzled than angry. He knew Diane must have a plan. "Diane, I know you probably could have prevented that hearing, discouraged the chair from holding it," he began. "So why did it happen?"

"Yes, we could have done that," she replied. It was time for another round of Politics 101. She was careful not to condescend, because she needed Payne as an ally. She saw this as a good opportunity to help move Payne from the level of tactics, where he was comfortable, up to the level of strategy, with which he was less familiar. "But stopping the hearing would have been a short-term play."

"Okay," Payne said. "What's your angle?"

"When you have a long-term problem, you should look for long-term solutions. Yes, I could have tried to stop the hearing. It would have cost us. We would have had to use up a good deal of political capital, of favors called in, of promises made about funding in the next election. And that would be expensive for us. But yes, I could have done it. But why go to all that trouble? The information would just pop out somewhere else, like on the TV news. And the hearing was useful to us."

"How could that possibly be?" he said. Now he was truly mystified.

"If we are going to handle this situation, we need to know who our friends are, who are foes are, and who is going to just try to stay out of this mess. The hearing brought that to the surface. The chair, we could see from how she oversaw it, she basically wants this thing to go away. That tells me she likely would support a general settlement. And that is very good news for us.

"More importantly, I got a better feel for who our enemies are going to be. There are four, maybe five, in the legislature. We'll want to make sure to recruit primary opponents to run against them, either to knock them out or at least bleed them of time, money, and energy. If they survive the primaries, we'll fund their opponents in the general. The rest of the legislature will see what happens and learn the lesson: Don't cross Future Minerals."

"That sounds good, but expensive," the chief said.

"First lesson of politics is the same as first lesson of business: You want to make money, you got to spend money. Think of it as an investment. First, we discipline the legislature. That clears the way for us to draft and offer a settlement they won't oppose, one that the attorney general can get behind."

"Why would he want to do that?"

"Because he wants to run for governor."

"So we get the settlement, he gets what he wants. Then what?"

"Then, I think, your guys can follow that seam of cobalt all the way to the Canadian border, if you feel like it. Dig all you like."

"What a great country," he said. "Thank you."

"Just doing my job," she said. "I've got some other things up my sleeve as well."

"You continue to impress," Payne said, with genuine admiration. "I look forward to learning more about those."

"Well, there's something on my mind this morning I was going to call you about," she continued. "It has to do with handling the effects of the hearing."

"What's that?"

"That hearing released a lot of negative energy. People are angry, and they want a scapegoat. If we don't want the company to get tagged, we need to give them something to focus their anger on."

"Any suggestions?"

"Not yet. But I'd appreciate your thoughts. I'm not inside the company. Maybe ask your corporate general counsel—tell him about this conversation. See if there are people we can offer up as a sacrifice."

"Like who?"

"Have you come across any indication that someone connected with the company, either on the payroll or a contractor, may have committed an illegal act in connection with the mining?" She had heard some things, but didn't want to be more direct with Payne about them.

"You mean, inside our own company? Throw one of them overboard?"

"Possibly," said Diane. "Could be that. The company could make sure they were well compensated down the road. Or maybe public officials."

"We've generally tried to avoid them," Payne said.

"But you've had to work with a few."

"I get the drift," Payne said. "I'll check."

Payne worked quickly. The next day, Future Minerals, normally quite reticent, issued a statement that took people aback.

In subdued tones of regret and shock, it disclosed that it had learned that a senior official at its in-state subsidiary, Future Minerals Maine, had paid cash bribes to three town managers in Pushaw County. It said that upon learning of the situation it had collected relevant documents and taken them to the state attorney general, whose office last night had seized the records of the three towns in question. Basically, that meant the AG's investigators had taken the towns' laptops and filing cabinets. The state also had frozen the bank accounts of the three town managers. All three had been suspended from their jobs by the selectmen in their towns.

Future Minerals also announced that, "out of an abundance of caution," it was suspending mining operations indefinitely, to see if any indication emerged from the new investigation that it had been operating improperly.

Ryan read the news on the site of the Bangor newspaper. He was in awe. It was a three-cushion shot. First of all, Future Minerals had seized control of the narrative, making itself appear a conscientious corporate citizen that had tripped across some corrupt local officials. Second, in that process, it had neutralized, even crippled, three possible potential opponents. The town managers knew the most of any local officials about the mining operation, but now they had lost all credibility. Third, and most subtly of all, Future Minerals had found a good excuse for stopping mining for a spell, which likely would give the water table a chance to rinse itself a bit before any official governmental inquiry got around to water sampling.

Ryan called Healey. "It's breathtakingly cynical," the doctor said.

"Yes, and it's brilliant," Ryan responded. "They have acted preemptively. To the casual observer, it looks like they have occupied the high moral ground."

"One thing I don't understand," Healey said. "To get the town managers, they had to throw one of their own executives under the bus."

"Oh yeah," Ryan said.

"Doesn't that make other employees nervous? You know, that they'll be next?"

"Nah, they'll think he's lucky," Ryan said. "The company will put out the word on the q.t. that he is getting a sweet deal—go along with the story, turn state's evidence, get a plea bargain. And when you get out of jail, come back on the payroll, and at the end of that year, you will get a multimillion dollar 'Christmas bonus.'"

"Wow," Healey said.

The town managers squirmed at the company's revelation. By noon, it was the only thing locals were talking about in Asbury, Beecher, and Finney Junction. People stared at the men angrily at the Hannaford grocery store, at the diner on the Bangor Road, and at the two Dysart gas stations.

When big money wants the wheels of justice to turn, they spin. By sundown, the lawyers for two of the three town managers had called the state attorney general to agree to plea deals: Disgorgement of all cash accepted, which was $15,000 each, plus fines of $15,000 each. Those two also signed statements admitting guilt and immediately resigning from their positions.

The third of the town managers, Finney Junction's Pete Skillings, turned down the state attorney general's offered deal. Skillings was a man of notable pride. He did not believe he was guilty of anything. All the cash he had accepted had gone to help townspeople in need, every penny. He had made sure that old people had heat and prescription drugs, that kids had breakfast and a coat to wear to school on winter mornings. He was pretty sure that the same was true of the other two town managers.

But he felt awful about what the toxic water had done to Finney Junction, and knew he was in some way partly responsible. He believed he had let down people he had known all his life who had trusted him. When he left the attorney general's office that afternoon, he went home and sat down against the maple tree in the backyard. Then he took off his right boot and sock, put the muzzle of his hunting rifle in his mouth, and pulled the trigger with his big toe.

His wife, Verdella Skillings, came home, called his name, looked around, felt the house was cold, and saw the back door had been left open. She looked out and saw his still-warm corpse slumped at the base of the big maple tree. The top of his face and the front of his skull were gone. She shrieked like a fox, a high, lonely, piercing cry of infinite pain. Then she fell to the ground and shook.

37

THE FAN

Even with mining operations temporarily ceased, the Fan lived on. The land and its towns looked pretty much the same as always, except for the rash of dermatitis cases of the residents. But for those living on it, under its influence, the Fan was like the tormentor in a Stephen King story, some kind of vast supernatural beast that inflicted a thousand pains on their flesh. Every new shock of pain carried implicitly the question: Is that another effect of the Fan? It wore people out.

Even worse, the Fan had creeping social effects, its acids corroding the ties of local society. Unspoken understandings unraveled. People who had agreed for decades to disagree now felt it urgent to make their differences explicit. Felicity Grubb, pumping gas into her Honda Civic outside a grocery store, saw her old friend Jane Wilson pull up at the pump opposite her. They had known each other for decades, ever since they were in elementary school. Felicity blurted out, "At the July 4 parade last summer, your husband grabbed my ass."

Jane snapped back, "Well, if you stopped twitching it at him, maybe that wouldn't happen." She jabbed the fuel nozzle back into its holder, got in her Toyota, and drove away.

Four men who had met every Tuesday night at the Carcass Pile for a few beers now found two of their group engage in similarly bitter exchange.

"Oh, fuck you and your liberal talk. I'm sick of it."

The other one replied, "Why don't you ever talk about the fact that your son moved to Portland because he's gay?" They stopped meeting for their weekly beers and bullshit session. They all missed it, and didn't know what had happened. People withdrew into their houses.

But even while at home, they still managed to erode relationships. Lee Metcalf had always wanted a better view from his house of the mountains in the northwestern distance. But there were three tall pine trees blocking that magnificent perspective, standing on his neighbor's property. He dumped several gallons of the herbicide called Tebuthiuron 80 WWG around the trunks of the pines. Their needles soon turned brown and began to fall. The three dead trees then had to be cut down before they toppled onto his neighbor's house.

Winston Jones thought that Johnny Aftergood talked too much, too loudly, and too stupidly in the annual town meeting. So to punish Aftergood, he began trapping racoons and squirrels in his Havahart and releasing them next to the man's garden. Some moved into Aftergood's warm basement for the winter.

When Marty Flurry developed kidney trouble, with fever, chills, and severe back pain, he had to stop working at the post office, which deprived the town of a key communications asset. Everyone missed him, even the children. At Christmastime, he was unable to play his usual role of Santa Claus at the annual party thrown by the Pushaw Volunteer Fire Department. A substitute was found, but to many children, it just wasn't the same. "We want the real Santa!" shouted one four-year-old boy. A toddler picked up the phrase, shouted "WANT REAL SANTA!" and then began to weep unconsolably.

Dwight Haskell, who ran the local U-Haul franchise, had a rash on his back, but was happy because his business was having its best year in more than a decade. People were moving away, and they were renting his trucks and trailers to do so.

Others were moving in—people with an instinct for where cash was flowing in new ways, especially if you kept quiet about it.

And some locals picked up the scent as well. Senator Tweedy sensed that that there might be some money to be had in being a member of the legislature in the next term. He decided to end his bargain and run again, even though it was Bill Dunn's turn. Dunn was shocked. Their campaigns against each other would prove to be memorably bitter, raising eyebrows across the state.

The Fan kept on trickling, day and night.

38

BETTY GROLEAU'S BAD HEADACHE; VERDELLA SKILLINGS'S BAD DAY

The rising sun illuminated Betty Groleau's face. She had been awake since five in the morning with a piercing headache. She was in her new apartment near Augusta. She was lying in bed, gazing vacantly out the window at the ice floes in the Kennebec River below her new apartment in the small, somewhat chic town of Hallowell. But her mind was on the ache that resided just above her right eye, and when it worsened, it reached down the side of her eye socket. On this particular morning, it was almost touching her cheekbone.

She lay her head back on her pillow and considered it. That's just the tension of a new job, she told herself. I've got a lot to learn and it is hard. Also, she told herself, there was stress in moving in social classes, in her case from lower middle class to upper middle class. It was a bigger leap than she had realized. She was pretty sure that no one she knew from high school or college drove a brand-new Mercedes Benz sedan.

Half of her believed that. But deeper inside her there was another half, probably more solid, more connected to her past.

And that other half wasn't buying it. That part of her was saying that it hadn't taken Miss Groleau very long to sell out. You'll regret it, that part was muttering this morning. She wanted to strangle that second voice.

She got out of bed and made some espresso with the machine Diane had given her, a smaller version of the powerful commercial one that was in the office. She took the cup of rich coffee out onto the snow-covered balcony and looked over the town and river while she sipped it. The landscape before her was cold and lonely. She wondered again if taking this new job had been the right move. She wrote an email to Monique Bouchard that said, "I am not sure I am doing the right thing. Will you call me?" She gave a number. Then she posted on her blog, "Cub Reporter is wandering in the woods."

Meanwhile, thirty-five miles to the north, Verdella Skillings was having another bad day. Ever since her husband had shot himself, she had retreated from the world. She was going through a bottle of coffee brandy a day. For breakfast she mixed it with hot milk. For the rest of her day she just sipped at it. Many days, she just sat out back and stared at the maple tree where her husband had breathed his last before shooting off the top of his head.

But on this gray day, she told herself that she needed to get away from the house. She drove the dirt back road up into the hill overlooking the town. Where the power lines crossed the road, she pulled over. She sat there, looking through the windshield to where the electricity towers marched down the hill and crossed the Bangor Road. She remained there for more than an hour. She sipped on the brandy. She saw a pickup truck go by on the highway below her. She thought she saw the round Future Minerals logo on its door. "Fuckers," she muttered aloud.

39

A SETTLEMENT DEAL

Ryan was en route to a meeting with the three leaders of the Afflicted Citizens' Group. He stopped at the IGA to pick up some bananas, kale, and cheese. It would make a dinner to keep up his potassium levels. At the checkout counter, he saw the new issue of the *North Country Times*.

The cashier picked up the paper and, instead of bagging it, looked at the front page. "Shit!" she said. She looked at Ryan. "Well, damn," she added. She pointed at the headline across the top: TOWN MANAGER DIES SUDDENLY.

Ryan sat outside in his truck and read the article. It was still on his mind when he walked into the meeting of the Afflicted Citizens. He had just sat down when several of their phones began to ring. People in the state house had just been briefed by the state attorney general on a proposed settlement offer from Future Minerals. "It's pretty generous," said one of the legislators who was calling.

"Praise God from who all blessings flow," said one of the ACG leaders, quoting the beginning of the Common Doxology.

The company had gone over everyone's head to offer to the state's attorney general a universal settlement to handle the problem of the toxic water in Pushaw County. Under the proposed terms, it first would "remediate" the situation with the groundwater by endeavoring to pump 90 to 95 percent of the water from the shaft into a steel-lined settlement pond. Second, it would set aside a fund of $30 million to cover current and future medical treatments for those who lived in the Fan in the three towns and had health problems that appeared related to the groundwater. On top of that, each adult citizen of the three towns who applied would get a cash payment of $10,000 if the towns ratified the settlement. That amounted to roughly an additional $10 million. And until the water quality improved, the company would truck in potable water for free distribution in the three affected towns.

What the attorney general did not ask, and what Future Minerals did not disclose, was how much the company had profited from its cobalt operations. That remained a closely held secret, even from the US government, because much of the money went to a limited liability company with large overseas accounts.

Ryan asked Ted French, the local lawyer Doc Healey had mentioned, to step outside the meeting. "What's your take?" he asked.

To his surprise, the lawyer shook his head. "There's something off here," he said. "I don't know what. I think it smells. I wonder what they're up to. I'll look into it."

French called Ryan back a day later. "The settlement is not with the parent company, it is with the subsidiary," he said.

"Does that matter?"

"Yeah, it could," French said. "It's an oddly structured deal, and there's probably a reason for it."

A day later, French and Ryan met at Doc Healey's house. French said, "In sum, Future Minerals Maine filed a document with the court stating that before the settlement was reached, it had sold almost all its assets to the parent for the sum of $50 million.

In return, the subsidiary had assumed all current and future liabilities from the mining operation in Maine."

"Why would they do that?"

"I think it's a bankruptcy play," French said.

"How so? They're not going to get out of paying, are they?"

"No, it's more artful than that. They'll pay what they agreed to pay up front, that lump sum and the cash to each citizen. That's what fifty million is for. But after that, the subsidiary will declare bankruptcy. Not chapter 11, but chapter 7—and go out of business. So all the potential problems down the road, the unknown hazards, they're not the parent company's problem—and the subsidiary will no longer exist. It's nasty but elegant."

"And we can't do anything?"

The lawyer shook his head slowly. "That's the Machiavellian beauty of it. The deal was constructed to look like they were taking care of everything, but really what it did was move Future Minerals out of target range."

"What do you mean?"

"The parent is sealed off from liability. The whole deal is with the subsidiary, Future Minerals Maine—which I bet you won't exist a year from now. So people get their cash, and the medical bills paid, and they move on. But if the remediation effort goes to shit, and it probably will, there's no way to force it to improve. The water table can remain a ruin and we can't do anything about it."

"How is that possible?" said Healey. "Why would the attorney general of Maine agree to that?"

The question hung in the air. French shook his head slowly.

In Augusta, some people already knew the answer. Betty Groleau asked her new boss about the settlement. "Oh, it's perfect," Diane Peligroso replied.

"How?"

"Well, the medical bills in the towns are taken care of, right? And the politics works out. Scales, the state attorney general, is going to move up to governor. Governor Harrison is going to run for the US Senate—it hasn't been announced yet, but the current occupant is going to retire. Solid already has lined up heavyweight endorsements that will be rolled out when she announces her bid. She also has some good financial backing from Wall Street."

40

VERDELLA MISSES RYAN

It was a February day in Maine, and that usually means gray and cold. Ryan was driving to Asbury to follow up on that tip about the paramedics who responded to the death of Ned Meddybemps. The sun was just a fuzzy pale disc that appeared occasionally on the southern horizon when the clouds lightened.

Verdella Skillings was driving back to what she had come to think of as "her spot"—the place on the back road where the power lines crossed. Down below was the pull-off spot on the highway where during his heyday Donut Michaud had peddled the fish he dynamited. As before, she had packed the day's bottle of coffee brandy. But this morning, she also had brought a plastic-and-nylon folding chair, a blanket, and her husband's hunting rifle.

Verdella sat and sipped. She noticed that if she concentrated, she could see a spot about a quarter mile away where vehicles were coming up from Bangor on the two-lane road. Then, about twenty seconds later—she counted "one thousand, two thousand," and so on—each vehicle would appear at Donut Michaud's old spot where the power lines crossed the highway. She played a little game. See a vehicle. Take a sip of brandy. Count the seconds. And then, when the vehicle appeared, she would make a pistol with her finger and thumb and say, "Pow!" It amused her as little had since the death of Pete. A tear ran down her cheek.

Then she saw a white pickup in the distant gap. She thought she saw the logo too, but couldn't tell in the slight glare. No matter. She picked up the rifle and aimed down under the power lines.

Ryan was driving when a hole popped in the right side of his windshield. His immediate thought was that it was made by a rock kicked up by a vehicle in front of him. But in the same moment he realized there were no vehicles close enough to do that, nor any that had gone by in the southbound lane. He pulled over to the side and touched the hole. It looked like it had been made by a bullet. Only then did he examine his side window and see that the same round had exited there. That meant it passed just inches in front of his chest, and that it had come from the right, the hill where the power lines descended to cross the highway. That didn't seem like something Lily or Diane would arrange, he thought to himself. Too sloppy, too chancy, and leaves too much undone.

But if not them, what? And who?

He unholstered his ankle pistol and walked up into the evergreen woods. He climbed the hill quietly, step by step, staying among the trees but parallel to the opening cut through them for the power lines. The snow on the ground helped muffle the sound of his footsteps. He would take a few steps and then stop, sometimes five, sometimes ten, varying the number to make himself less predictable. After ten minutes he came to the back road, which was dirt but was plowed and still passable. He walked along it for a moment and, standing behind a large spruce tree, he saw just down the road about twenty-five feet an old Honda Accord parked on the side. Next to the car, sitting in a folding chair, and holding what looked like a liquor bottle, was an old woman in a worn sky-blue ski parka. The low winter sun, dipping toward the southwestern horizon, cast a twenty-foot shadow northeastward from her and her chair. She was facing away from him. She took a sip from the bottle and placed it in the snow. He studied her for a moment and realized he had met her at the basketball game that was forfeited. He remembered her unusual name: Verdella Skillings.

Then he saw a hunting rifle propped up between her knees.

"Mrs. Skillings?" he shouted. "Verdella Skillings?" He was ready to slide sideways, getting more behind the protection of the big spruce, if she shot at him. But she didn't. When she turned to look at him, her rifle fell forward. She used both hands to stand up, unsteadily, from the chair.

"Who's there?" she said in a shaky voice, looking around nervously.

"Ryan Tapia," he said, coming near enough to her to speak at a normal volume. "We met at the basketball game."

"Oh," she said vaguely. "That was before Pete shot himself." She sobbed a little, the way people stricken by grief do when they are reminded of the departed. Her life now had only two parts: Before and After. And she hated this second part. She examined Ryan up and down. "Why did you sneak up on me quieter than a game warden?"

He walked closer. Speaking of shooting, Ryan thought to himself. He leaned over to pick up the rifle. "May I put this in your car for you?"

"Sure," she said, hazily. "I'd offer you a seat but I only have this one chair."

He came back from her car, carrying a plastic milk crate that he'd found in the trunk, and said, "I'll take a sip of that brandy." She handed over the bottle. He sat on the crate and sipped some of the stuff. It tasted wretched, but also somehow appropriate to the moment. He winced and sipped again. It spoke to him of bitterness and despair.

He thought it was time to let her know. "Mrs. Skillings," he began.

"Oh, please," she said, waving a hand above her head. "I'm country. Call me Verdella."

"Okay," Ryan said. He handed the bottle back to her. "Verdella, I think you just shot into my truck."

"Was that you?" she said, only mildly interested in the news. "I am so sorry." Again she looked him up and down, her blocky chin lifted. "But you look okay. So I guess I didn't hit you." She sounded almost disappointed. "I used to be a better shot. Only girl on the shooting team in high school. Always got my deer, and usually Pete's too, truth be told. The one time he went out and hunted his own deer, he brought it home with his brother. They'd been drinking and wanted to drink some more, you know, so they carried the deer's body down into the cellar and then sat in the kitchen and opened up some more whiskey. They heard a ruckus down the stairs. Turned out his shot had hit the deer in the skull, only stunned it, and now it was awake again and tearing up the whole cellar. They were laughing and drinking too hard to stand, so I went down and finished it off."

She snorted through her nose as she remembered the incident. "Neighbors came over, knocked on the front door. I answered it covered in blood. They'd heard a shot. Looked me up and down and asked if I shot my husband. I laughed, and then they heard him laugh." Now she was laughing and crying at the same time. "Oh my," she said, wiping both cheeks with the back of her gloved left hand.

"Verdella, why?"

"Why what?"

"Why did you shoot at me?"

"Don't be a silly goose," she said, grimacing and waving a hand dismissively. "I wasn't shooting at *you*. I thought you was the Future Minerals guy, that supervisor who has a white pickup."

"He has a big brown beard. I don't."

"Well, it's goddam hard to see with the sun so low this time of year," she said, defensively. She tipped back the bottle of the coffee brandy and took a big gulp, as if to compensate for the missed shot.

"What are you doing up here?"

"I can't be in my house anymore. It—it—it—just creeps me out."

"Verdella, you are stuck inside a tragedy. I've been there, a few years ago, when I lost my family. It was hard, real hard."

"But?"

"But you can't do this," he said. "Have you thought through what you are doing up here, shooting at passing traffic?"

That got a rise out of her. She turned and looked at him, irate. "Oh, so now I have to obey the law, when no one else seems to be?" she said, almost shouting in her indignation. Then, in a softer tone, with tears on her cheeks, "Those fuckers poisoned our town and pinned the blame on Pete. I feel so bitterly." She picked at a scab on the itchy red rash on her neck.

"This is not the way to go," Ryan said.

"Well, then, smart guy, what is?" she said.

That took Ryan aback. "That's a good question. I don't know. I wish I did." He took another sip from the brandy bottle. They were both silent for some time. The sun, which had struggled all day to climb above the southern horizon, gave up and rolled down into the bare limbs of the maple, birch, and oak trees at the top of the ridge on the far side of the Bangor Road. A dozen crows perched on the bare limbs of a nearby maple began squawking at each other. "My mother said that when crows beef like that, they're 'politicking,'" Verdella observed.

"Good word," Ryan said.

With the sun gone, the air began to cool rapidly. He walked her back to her car. She drove him around to the cross road, then turned out to the highway and left him by his truck.

"You be more careful, okay?" she advised him. She did a wobbly U-turn on the road and headed back toward Finney Junction. Ryan stood for a moment and considered her admonition.

41

AN INFINITE CORPORATE ARSENAL

Ryan sat in his truck and checked his messages. The first was from Nina. "Ryan, I just can't see you anymore," she said in an unusually low, slow voice. "Thank you for what you've done for me. But all this mining stuff, I think that's what you're concentrating on nowadays. Maybe call me when that's all done. But I can't do it. It is too much for me. I am feeling overwhelmed."

He sat a moment and tried to digest Nina's message. But more voicemails swept it to the side. A guy from the town of Malta, located to the northwest of Finney Junction, said they were worried about their water. So Ryan took down the contact info and called Bap Salim, the geologist at the university. "Hey," he began, with some urgency. "I've got a new indication, outside the north side of the Fan. Can you come down tomorrow to check it out?"

Usually Salim was eager to dive into new problems. He loved getting the data and seeing the pattern change. But today he responded with an unusual silence. "Mr. Tapia, I have had the intention for the longest time to place a telephone call to you," he finally said. He hemmed a bit more.

A bell rang in the back of Ryan's head. "Mr. Salim, what are you saying?"

"I fear that I must withdraw from this project, no matter how much I have reveled in it. I must tell you that I regret this action most deeply but feel that I have no alternative."

Ryan thought that over. "The company reached you too?"

"Yes," Salim said glumly. "Half my funding comes from the SBP."

"Which is?"

"The Society for a Better Planet. It is an important organization for funding innovative research in environmental change."

"And?"

"I never inquired with SBP about their sources of financial support. I now have learned, quite belatedly I must say, that almost all of it comes from people working in high finance, mainly on Wall Street. They do indeed want a better planet—but I have learned they want it on their terms. They made it painfully clear to me that it is quite unwelcome to criticize one of their donors."

"Future Minerals?"

"Yep, some of their partners of that company. Because this company is supplying material for batteries for electric cars, they are perceived by many as being on the side of the virtue. I strongly believe now that if I persist in research in the Fan, my funding will end. And I also was made to worry about my immigration status. Mr. Tapia, I am getting too old to start over a third time. So I did as they asked. I am ashamed of following this course, and I apologize to you with all my heart."

"I'm sorry," Ryan said. "Thank you for your work so far. And be careful." He hung up and stared through his windshield. His eye fell on the bullet hole. He knew Verdella wasn't working for the company, but the hole kind of summarized for him the situation. He was amazed at how many different ways the company had for reaching out, for touching people, for breaking resistance. It seemed to possess an infinite arsenal.

They hadn't reached Nina, at least. She had dumped him on her own. But she had done so because Future Minerals seemed to have reached into his life and grabbed it. She was right. The company was occupying a big part of his brain and soul.

42

A TALKATIVE AMBULANCE DRIVER

Ryan drove up to the town of Beecher, where the headquarters for the area's paramedics was located. It was striking to him in these towns that even in the winter, there were lights on inside, albeit behind curtains drawn to keep out the cold. And there were still cars parked on Main Street while people ran into a convenience store or the town library. Down on the coast, by contrast, with all the summer people gone, it seemed like at least half the windows were dark and the main streets empty, giving the state's coastal towns a ghost-town feel on winter nights.

He first knocked on the door of a female EMT, who wasn't home. Next, he tried the other EMT's house. The man's wife slammed the door in his face. Third, he went to the house of the next-door neighbor of Zach Pelletier, one of the ambulance drivers. A man answered the door and said, "Yeah, what's up?" He held up a fist to his mouth and coughed.

Ryan instantly recognized the voice—and the cough. Both belonged to the anonymous caller. "I'm Ryan Tapia. I'm looking into a recent road accident."

The man's eyes got big. He took a step back. "I don't know how you found me," he said. "Leave now." He closed the door.

Bingo, Ryan thought to himself. He walked to the next house, where one Zach Pelletier lived. He knocked on the door. It was answered by a large man in a Red Sox baseball cap and an expression of mild astonishment—eyes open wide, lips slightly parted—that made Ryan think of John Candy, the Canadian comic actor who was prominent in the 1980s.

Ryan said, "Hi, I'm Ryan Tapia. I'm looking into a recent road accident, one dead, down in Finney Junction."

The big man looked left, not at Ryan but over at his neighbor's house. "That asshole! I told him not to tell anybody." But as he said it, he gave a slight chuckle and a wave of his hand. "Way of the world," he said.

"May I come in?" Ryan said. "I think you can help me out some here."

"What the hell." Pelletier shrugged with surprising equanimity. "Cat's outta the bag. Come on in."

They sat at the kitchen table. "You seem to know I was the driver on that call," the man said. "I had a few beers with that dumbass the other night"—he nodded his head in the direction of the house next door—"and I guess he's been blabbing. That's my fault. I mean, I was the one who talked in the first place."

"What struck you as strange about that night?"

"You know that too?" he said. His eyes got big.

"I suspect it, but I want to hear what you saw and did that night."

"Okay," Pelletier said, spreading his hands out in front of himself. His short, fat fingers, Ryan noticed, looked like ten sausages stuffed into an unbaked loaf of bread dough. "We didn't do nothing wrong, so I don't mind talking. And I'll tell you, I don't like what I've been seeing that mining company do." He leaned forward and waved a finger in the air. "Let me think," he said.

He wrapped four stubby fingers around the can of Bud Light on the table, took a long swallow, then said, "So this is how it went down. So, we get a call, maybe eleven at night. I'm the duty driver that night. I meet the duty EMT at the town hall. We leave our privately owned vehicles there and get in the ambo. We drive down to Future Minerals, their place. We're on site in, say, fifteen minutes. State trooper is standing there holding a flashlight. Says he hasn't touched the body, except to determine the lack of a pulse and breath."

"And?"

"I follow my EMT over to the body. It looks funny."

"How?"

"I dunno. Different. Not the usual corpse."

"Different how?"

"Well, we see a lot of these. Typical one, an adult hit by a vehicle has major injuries, lacerations, to the legs or lower torso, from the impact itself. Then, usually, higher up, secondary blunt force from hitting the ground with some energy—maybe contusions on the head, more often on shoulders or arms."

"How was this different?"

"Didn't see none of those things. Seemed to me like the body must have been lying down when it was hit. The EMT, she looked at it, said, 'Supine?' Like she was asking a question. She's got good training and is pretty precise in her language. You know, 'supine' means lying flat on his back. He was that way when we looked at him, but we were guessing also when the vehicle had driven over him. And the tire tread. It was heavier than most cars, so probably a heavy pickup truck, it had run straight over the chest." Pelletier ran a finger across the "NYFD" emblem on his shirt to illustrate the movement. "And there were some holes from the studs in the tire." He dotted a finger across his chest.

Ryan said, "Have you ever seen that before, that flat on the back sort of accident?"

"Coupla times. When someone was drunk or stoned, just passed out on a road or driveway."

"Was there any indication of that in the blood sample she took from Meddybemps?"

"Nope," he said, shaking his head. "Traces of THC, but not nearly enough to knock him out."

"Was there anything else that bothered you?"

Pelletier thought for a minute. He held a round index finger in the air. "Now that you ask, yeah. There was one other funny thing. I didn't notice it, I'm not that smart, but my EMT did. She's real observant. She said, 'Look, his arms weren't touched by the tire.' She was right. Neither one. Not a mark. That means they were not by his side. They were up over his head." He held both his arms up straight above his head to show what he meant. He was a man clearly disposed, even compelled, to physically illustrate his statements.

"What does that tell you?"

"Nothing," Pelletier said, shaking his big, square head. "But it is damned unusual. Don't think I've ever seen that."

"Tell you what," Ryan said. "It makes me wonder if he was dragged to that spot by the arms. Someone pulling on them, just let them flop down, didn't bother to move them after they got him to where they wanted him."

"Could be. Those mining company people, they're bastards. You poking around like you are, you'd better watch yourself."

"Think it was homicide?"

"What do I know?" Pelletier said. "I'm just a driver for a little local volunteer ambulance service." He put out two hands in front of himself and moved them up and down slightly, as if he were at the wheel of a vehicle.

Ryan thanked him and headed south to see Doc Healey. It had been a long day, from Verdella Skillings's random rifle fire to being dumped by Nina to Bap Salim's withdrawal to Zach Pelletier's account of the way the Meddybemps corpse was laid out. He felt like the world was closing in on him.

While Ryan was talking to Pelletier, the head of the company's surveillance unit thought it wise to notify Mr. Payne of Ryan's location. "What is the tracker telling you?" Payne asked his subordinate, who not only tracked vehicles but could intercept some cell phone communications.

"He seems to be going around talking to people who are on the local volunteer ambulance unit," the chief of surveillance team, a retired Maine state trooper, reported to Payne. He was relying on the tracker they'd put on Ryan's truck. At least once a week, Ryan checked over his truck for such devices, but he did not know that there was a new generation of trackers on the market, much smaller and more difficult to detect than the ones he had used during his time at the FBI. These new devices were quite expensive. They did not need to be placed on the outside of the vehicle, and they could be configured so that they only emitted a signal after being pinged by their owner. The one on Ryan's truck was, in fact, attached magnetically to the inside of the gas tank.

"Is that going to be a problem for us, this guy talking to the ambulance crew?"

"Could be."

"Is there any surveillance video of that, of moving the body?"

"Yeah, there was some, of when they caught him near the tipple. It's gone now."

Payne considered. Tapia was slow but persistent. Letting him run around turning over rocks and poking into problems like the termination of Meddybemps was just asking for trouble. "It's time to put your plan for Tapia into motion," Payne said.

"Will do," said the junior man. His team members not only had studied it, they had even rehearsed it once.

43

HEALEY'S EXOTIC BLISTERS

As Ryan drove south toward Doc Healey's place, he considered the state of play. The company was picking off its opposition. They had bought the reporter. They had scared off the geologist. They had crushed some of the townspeople, from Pete Skillings to Gary Rath to, literally, Ned Meddybemps. They seemed to have the state attorney general in their pocket.

And now Doc Healey appeared to be fading away. He had told Ryan over the phone that he no longer went outside. Ryan drove down the doctor's long driveway, parked, and knocked on the door. "Come in, Mr. Tapia," he heard a thin voice say. Ryan found Healey sitting in a rocking chair by the woodstove, trying to stay warm. He was alone. He looked to have lost perhaps sixty pounds. Once a hearty slab of a man, he now had the wheeze and shakes of someone on his last legs. Dark creases ran vertically down his gray face from the corners of his eyes to the edges of his mouth, as if he were collapsing in on himself.

They talked a bit. Healey showed Ryan how his fingers had curled in and couldn't be unfolded without great effort and some pain. "The body conserves itself," Healey said, looking at his hands.

"If it is low on supplies, it retreats from the periphery. The fingers and toes go first, in order to keep the big three going—the heart, the lungs, the brain."

Healey continued gazing at the fingers of his left hand, flexing them a little bit. Unusually, just above the furthest knuckle on each of the four fingers grew a half-inch high blister, the size of a large blueberry, but conically shaped, like Mount Fuji. At their bases, they were an angry red. Above that each had a thin ring colored a sinister blue-black. The tops of the blisters were glistening white, with a clear center, a little like that snow-capped Japanese mountain. To Healey, they burned like little volcanoes.

The fingers were oddly shiny, as if they were exuding decay. The five nails at the end of each digit were going soft and crumbly. Red streaks and rashes speckled the inside of his left arm. After spending a life helping others be healthy, it was a hell of a way to wind up, he thought.

Ryan looked over at the doctor's right hand, holding the arm of the rocking chair, but there was no similar affliction there. Healey noticed Ryan's look. "It's the damnedest thing," he said. "These popped up about ten days ago. I went in and had the nephrologist, the oncologist, and an orthopedic surgeon look at it. None of them had ever seen it before. Then, in the hallway, when I was leaving, I ran into an old friend, a senior cardiologist, Dumas Malone. Wonderful guy, and smart as a whip. He said he was glad to see me back in the hospital. I told him I wasn't working, that I was having my left hand looked at. He took it, examined it for a moment right there, and asked me to come back to his office with him.

"We did," Healey continued. "Malone probed, took some photographs, then took a sample of the fluid from one of the odd blisters. Sent the sample down to Walter LeDroit, that technician down in the basement, with a note on it: 'Rush for Doctor Healey.'

"While we waited for Walter's results, we chatted a bit about this and that, the hospital management, squirrelly as ever, that weird lawsuit against me. Finally I asked, 'What are you thinking about these weird blisters?'

"Malone asked me, 'Why do you call them weird?'

"I said, 'Because most blisters I've seen are kind of round. Like from burns, friction, or pemphigus. But these little guys are pointed, as you can see.'

"'You're right,' he said. 'And thereby hangs a tale. The shape of these guys is the result of internal pressure, intense pressure. And that takes me back to one of the things I love most in life, the human heart.'

"'How's that?' I asked. Malone says, 'The organs of the body are not all equal, as you know. Most look out for themselves, as they are designed to do—the kidneys, liver, larynx, lungs, and so on. The lungs are the most obvious—they figure they have enough work to do without worrying about anything else. But the heart and brain, they look out for the others. And in your case, when the heart noticed that heavy metals were coming along its way in the blood when they should have been filtered out and expelled through urine or feces or perspiration or respiration, well, Mr. Heart stood up and issued some orders. He forced the toxic materials, as much as he could, into the closest extremity he could find, the fingers of your left hand. With luck, he figures, the metals will get pushed out somehow, or pulled out. And worse comes to worse, you can live without some fingers.'

"I was skeptical. I asked, 'You think the heart is that smart?' And Malone said, 'I know it is that smart. We don't know how intelligent it really is. Especially when it and the brain cooperate, as I think they are doing in your case.'

"Then we discussed treatment. He basically said it depended on what Walter down in the basement found. 'If it's benign, just serum, that's one thing,' he said. But I think we both knew it wasn't going to be.

"Just about then, Walter LeDroit knocks on the door. 'Doc Doom, Doc Healey,' he says. 'May I come in?'

"Doom—that's the hospital's nickname for Dumas—waves him to a chair. Walter sits down, staring at the fingers of my left hand the whole time. But kind of afraid to touch them. Doesn't say anything. Finally, Malone says, 'Care to share, Walter?'

"Walter looks up and says, 'Doc Healey, I am sorry. Those blisters of yours, they're bad news. They're loaded with traces of cobalt, copper, hexavalent chromium—'

"'That's the worst type of chromium, isn't it?' I interrupted him.

"LeDroit nodded in agreement. 'Deadly. Also, tiny bits of arsenic and gold.'

"I said, 'So basically, each of my blisters is a miniature toxic waste dump, my own private Superfund site?' Walter nodded. Malone nodded. And that's about the size of it."

Ryan meditated on that for a moment, and then asked, "Why didn't the blood cleaning get this junk out of your body?"

"Because the stuff already was embedded in the tissue, and only comes out slowly," Healey said. "The liver, kidneys, spleen, they're feeling overworked already. That's why I've been so poorly."

"And what are they doing about the blisters?"

Healey held out his affected hand before the desk lamp next to his chair. He contemplated the odd blisters on his spread fingers. They glistened, lethally. He winced. "Three times a week, someone comes and drains them. Takes the material away in a little hazardous waste can. The blisters grow back up in a day or two. Doom Malone says that's a good thing, because it means the heart's plan is working."

Observing Healey, Ryan found him a Job-like figure. A man who used to rise at dawn to pull on his fishing gear now was in his pajamas and wearing slippers, clearly not having been dressed all day. He was carrying afflictions that he simply did not deserve, Ryan thought. Healey had worked all his adult life to help people, either curing them or easing their pain. Now he had all but lost his wife—she was still down at her sister's in New Hampshire, with no sign of ever wanting to return—his occupation, the value of his home, and his health.

Healey rocked forward and placed both feet flat in front of him. "I keep thinking over that day when I found that toxic brookie out in the river, going over the whole morning in slow motion," he said.

"Why?"

"Beats me. It isn't like I could have done anything different. I guess it's because that's the day my life turned upside down. I've treated victims of car accidents, especially the drivers—they tell me they replay the whole thing, second by second, over and over."

Ryan hardly spoke at all. He sat with Healey and watched his great grief. He didn't want to waste the man's energy on small talk. They sipped the doctor's mediocre Scotch. Ryan gave him his time and space.

Finally, Ryan got the sense that Healey had collected his thoughts. "Why do you think they haven't come after me?" Ryan asked.

Healey considered the question. "I've been mulling that," he said. "They will, I expect. But they've been careful with you. They know you have money from that big settlement from the crash that took your family, so they can't try to bribe you. And they're probably a little wary of you, given your background in the FBI. They don't know what you might have up your sleeve."

"But?"

"I'd guess they will come for you in good time. When they do, they will have it well planned. It will happen so fast you will be surprised. You might want to retain a good lawyer."

"A gloomy thought," Ryan said.

"That's all I have these days. I don't mind dying, really. I've seen a lot of that. You can't have life without death. I think my earthly race is run. And I am going relatively quickly, which is a blessing—believe me. So many times I have seen people desperately trying to live longer, when all they really are doing is dying longer, extending the agony."

"So what is it that's making you miserable?" Ryan asked.

Healey chuckled. "I am sorry it is so obvious. But since you ask, what I hate is the feeling that I have lost my country. You know, we've always had rich people in this country. But I've never seen it like this, where the super-rich are running everything, including politics. I don't believe we live in a democracy anymore. I think it has the trappings of democracy, like elections and a Congress and so on. But the American oligarchs are calling the shots. I was never a big fan of Bernie Sanders, but I think he was right when he said Congress doesn't regulate Wall Street, but instead that Wall Street regulates Congress. So really, I am not sorry to be going."

They sipped their drinks in silence as that mournful thought sank in. After more than an hour of this, and at least three more tumblers of the doctor's Scotch, Ryan said he should be going. "I'll see myself out," he said.

Healey nodded. He was wondering when he would lose his hearing and eyesight. He wanted to go before then.

44

RYAN BEHIND BARS

At the end of Healey's long dirt driveway, Ryan turned right onto the highway south to Bangor. As he gained speed, reaching perhaps thirty miles an hour, a car with its headlights turned off lurched out of a side road and directly into his path. Ryan's Ford F-150 crunched straight into its side. It was a classic T-bone collision, albeit at a fairly low speed.

Ryan pushed aside the airbag in his truck, opened the door, and walked over to the car, a Camry. "Are you okay?" he asked, leaning down and peering into the car, where the driver sat looking straight ahead. It was a man in his thirties. He looked up at Ryan, neutrally.

"I've called the police," the man said.

Ryan heard a car or pickup pull over to the side of the road, behind his truck. He paid it no mind, assuming it was just a passerby stopping to offer help. He was looking over the Camry, trying to figure out what else he should do to assure that no one was hurt. Someone ran up behind him and splashed some liquid over the back of his head. Ryan smelled it—it was whiskey. He spun around and said, "What the fuck?" The splashing man ran back to a waiting pickup truck and drove away. At this point, Ryan knew he had been set up. He thought he saw the Camry driver crack a brief smile. Ryan retreated to the side of his truck and awaited the police. He could almost feel the long, thin fingers of the company tightening around him.

Ryan heard a siren in the distance, and then saw flashing red and blue lights reflecting on the low clouds over the highway. A sheriff's deputy parked and approached Ryan, holding a flashlight in his right hand. He shone it on the driver of the other car, and ordered, "Please remain in your vehicle." He turned to Ryan and sniffed. "How many drinks?" he asked.

"Several," Ryan said.

The deputy looked him up and down. "I need you to turn around," he said. "Place your arms behind you."

Ryan did, and felt the handcuffs slip around his wrists, and then click. "Deputy," Ryan said over his shoulder, "you should know I have three weapons. There's a Glock in my left ankle holster. There's another in the glove compartment, which is locked. And there's a large hunting knife in a metal box that's screwed to the inside of the back bumper."

Unconsciously, the deputy's right hand went to his holstered pistol. "Why all the firepower?" he asked. "You some kind of Rambo?"

"Just former law enforcement. FBI."

"What do you do now?"

"Confidential investigative work."

"A PI, huh?" Cops tended not to like them. "Let's give you a breathalyzer."

A state trooper who apparently had been patrolling in the area arrived to provide backup. He eyed Ryan for a moment, then said to the deputy, "Hey, I know this guy."

"How?"

"He was fired from the FBI a couple years ago, after that bombing in Wiscasset."

The deputy assessed Ryan again. He didn't much care. He put a clean nozzle on a little handheld breathalyzer device. "Blow, steadily, until I tell you to stop," he said. Ryan did so. The deputy said, "That's an oh-nine." He placed Ryan under arrest and informed him of his rights.

"Sit here," the deputy ordered, opening the back door of the patrol car. From there, Ryan watched the officer begin to search his truck. A moment later the officer stood back and held up the bag of marijuana that Ned Meddybemps had given Ryan, who had tucked it under the seat of his truck and promptly forgotten about it. Then he pointed to the hole in the windshield. "Made by a bullet, looks like," he said to the state trooper.

The trooper nodded and walked a few feet over to his car radio. "Guess who the county just OUI'd?" the trooper said to someone on his two-way, using the Maine law enforcement abbreviation for "operating under the influence," a term that covers the operation of both motor vehicles and boats, and the use of alcohol and narcotics. "That FBI guy who went rogue during those Indian protests a couple of years back. Used to be a special friend of the governor, if you get my drift." There was a pause while the person at the other end spoke. "Yeah, before she was elected." There was a staticky response Ryan couldn't make out. The trooper said, "Yeah, he hit some guy on the Bangor Road. Blew an oh-nine. Also looks like they found several ounces of marijuana in the truck, which might figure in the OUI inquiry as well. Several weapons, too. Some indication of gunplay. This guy looks like bad news."

Just a few miles away, Will Payne, Future Minerals' security chief, monitoring the police radio channel, allowed himself a smile. Occasionally, everything went according to plan. This was one of those times. Ryan Tapia had been nettlesome and persistent. But he had just been taken off the chessboard. Payne picked up his cell phone and pressed a button. "Diane?" he said. "Yes, it's me. Feel free to let interested media know, without your name or the company being involved, that Ryan Tapia, a key figure in the opposition to Future Minerals' local operations, was arrested tonight. OUI and a collision. Weapons and drugs in vehicle."

Diane Peligroso asked, "Will the company be issuing a statement?"

"We'll have no comment on the arrest of Mr. Tapia. But you might suggest to a friendly commentator that perhaps Mr. Tapia, who talks a lot about corporate responsibility, needs to reflect more on his own personal responsibilities."

"Will do," she said. Then she smiled to herself.

Two hours later, Ted French, the lawyer and friend of Dr. Healey, appeared outside Ryan's jail cell. "They got you," he said. He handed a Styrofoam cup of coffee through the bars to Ryan.

"I think it was a setup," Ryan said.

"As sure as the sun rises in the east," French said.

"What do I do?" Ryan asked.

"Speaking as your lawyer?"

Ryan nodded.

"They will play this to the hilt. They have you right where they want."

"What do you mean?"

"Your biggest problem isn't the OUI charge. I am thinking more about the driver of the car you hit. This is just guesswork, but I would bet he almost certainly is a Future Minerals contractor of some sort, probably in security work. They'll say he was legitimately tracking your movements, doing nothing illegal, not on private property, not infringing on your rights."

"And?"

"That driver almost certainly is going to turn out to have neck problems, back problems. Real ones. Certifiable. That's why they picked him to be the driver of the vehicle tonight. He will be examined by a credible, board-certified specialist who will state, in an affidavit, that some of the driver's pre-existing back and neck conditions appear to have been aggravated by the energy of the collision. And this makes you liable for medical costs—and, they will assert, also for punitive damages for operating in a criminally reckless manner."

"Meaning?"

"They will sue you for every penny you have. The longer it takes, the better for them. Bleed you with legal bills."

"What should I do?"

"Speaking as your lawyer?"

Ryan took the hint. "No, you've persuaded me that's a losing cause. What would you tell me if I were family—say, your brother?"

The lawyer looked around, lowered his head, and whispered, "I'd say, let's talk when you are out of here and you have more privacy."

45

VERDELLA HITS SOMEONE

Verdella Skillings tried. She made herself stay away from that spot under the power line for several days. But every new morning was as bleak as the last. After staying away for three days, she woke up on the fourth morning in a particularly black mood. It was like she was wearing those blinders that are sometimes placed on horses to make them look straight ahead. All she could see was that she hated her life. She saw no real future. Just red anger and dimming light.

Without quite admitting to herself what she was doing, she opened the trunk of her old Honda Accord and put in her chair, her blanket, her binoculars, and Pete's rifle. She didn't put the big, heavy bottle of coffee brandy in the trunk. She kept that by her side, putting it on the passenger seat. It was like family to her. She even put the seat belt on it, partly to stop the car from beeping at her, but also to keep the bottle safe.

She set up her chair in her little cleared patch in the snow under the power lines. She wrapped herself in the old sky-blue ski parka. She sipped the brandy and watched the road through the binoculars. She didn't want to make another embarrassing mistake.

It was one of those days where the snow remained frozen when it was in shadow but melted where the sun hit it. Hence, the highway surface was intermittently muddy and then icy. Through the binos, she spotted a white pickup truck passing through the distant gap in the woods. She thought she saw the Future Minerals logo, splashed with mud. At least she was pretty sure. She put down the binos and lifted the hunting rifle to her shoulder. She counted, and as the truck appeared in the power line opening, she put her finger on the trigger. This time her angle was better. Through the scope she glimpsed a brown beard, so she gently squeezed the trigger. The bullet went through the windshield and plowed into the chest of John Skratsbud, the assistant principal of the county high school, and tumbled through his heart. His dying hand jerked the driver's wheel hard to the left. The truck flipped and skidded sideways and upside down along the asphalt, pushing up slush and gravel. By the time it stopped moving, the assistant principal was quite dead. He did not know that he had been shot. At one moment he was driving, thinking about the girls' basketball team's morale problem. The next moment, he wasn't thinking anything.

Verdella picked up her binoculars and looked through them at the truck, upside down under the power lines. "Damn," she said. She had been wrong again. She was still sitting there in her chair, weeping and drunk, about fifteen minutes later when a state police car crept up the hill, its roof lights flashing. "What is the world coming to?" she said aloud. Then she slipped off her boot, placed the muzzle of the rifle in her mouth and put her big toe on the trigger. She mused for a moment that she had known this ending had been her fate ever since she had first come up to this spot with her lawn chair, coffee brandy, and rifle. Then, steadying the rifle barrel, she followed Pete into oblivion.

46

A LAWYER'S FAMILY ADVICE

Ryan's bail hearing was held up for forty-eight hours, he suspected at the behest of Future Minerals. After he was released, he drove home, showered, and called Ted French, who asked him to come back and meet him in Finney Junction.

French was standing out in front of the building that held his small office. "Not in the office," he said. "Might be bugged. And let's leave our cell phones there too."

"You think they can monitor them even if we turn them off?"

"Who knows?" said French. "Let's drive out of town."

Oddly enough, French took them to the same spot where Verdella Skillings liked to sit, drink, and shoot. He parked under the power lines. They got out and began walking under them. "The electricity might help interfere with any long-range eavesdropping," French explained, pointing upward. "This is a spot we all used to come to and drink on Friday nights, back when we were in high school. Maybe they still do."

"Yeah, I've seen Verdella Skillings out here," Ryan said.

"You know she shot herself out here yesterday?" French asked.

"I heard some talk about that in the jail," Ryan said. "The guard said she also killed Assistant Principal Skratsbud."

French nodded slowly. "Two more victims of Future Minerals, I think," he said. "I mean, Verdella was never herself after she lost Pete."

They stood in silence, mulling that comment. Finally Ryan said, "So, what's the family advice?"

French sighed. "If you were my brother, this is what I would say, in private. I'd say, first, move your assets out of the country." He handed Ryan a card. "This is a good lawyer in Boston who does that kind of thing every day. Probably will send the money through the Caymans into two or three Swiss bank accounts, and maybe one in Macau, just to spread the risk. He'll charge you a percentage, but it'll be worth it."

"And after that?"

French stopped walking and looked at him. "Are there any places overseas where you've wanted to live?"

Ryan was taken aback. "You're serious, leave the country?"

"I am," French said. "These people are playing for keeps, and they are not playing by rules. I'd even consider getting a new identity once you are out of the country."

"Well," Ryan said, "I've always been intrigued by Bali. And I liked Nice, France. But if I have to live somewhere, actually put down roots, I think Ireland."

"That's a good one," French said. "With your looks, you almost certainly have Irish forebears.

"So here's what you do. This afternoon, drive up to Montreal. Go through Vermont—your OUI charges won't be in the Canadian computers there yet. In Montreal, apply at the consulate for an Irish passport. They'll tell you they need documentary evidence of your ancestry. I will arrange that and express it to you. And don't come back into this country without calling me first."

"You're getting in pretty deep here, for a country lawyer," Ryan observed.

The lawyer sighed. "You are correct, I am. But at some point, we have to take a side. This country is slipping out of our hands. Future Minerals is basically a criminal organization—but one with its hands deep in the pockets of the authorities."

"That sounds a lot like the conversation I was having with Doc Healey just before I was set up on the highway."

"He and I have talked about this," French said. "A lot." He frowned. "I am sorry to be such a bearer of bad news."

47

A RICH DINNER AND A LONG DRIVE

Betty Groleau was invited for the first time to a Future Minerals celebration dinner in Boston. It was to be held at The Laughing Pig, one of those high-end restaurants that reveled in ostentation. No bare wood and exposed bricks here. This was all shiny brass, low lights, and heavy red velvet curtains. The entrees began at $39 and climbed to multiples of that. Sides were extra. It was a definite departure from the old New England culture of always making sure to appear poorer than one really is. "You should feel honored," Diane had said when handing her the engraved invitation. "The top guns at the company want to meet you."

On the day of the dinner, Diane drove her to the Saks Fifth Avenue store in Back Bay, just off Boylston Street, and in just a few minutes picked out an outfit for her—a black silk mini faux wrap sheath dress. "You want to project a look of remote but sexy, elegant but fuckable," she had instructed. "This fits the bill." She lent Betty a single string of pearls to set off the dress.

That evening, a waiter led Betty to a private dining room in the back of the five-star restaurant. It was set apart from the main dining area by a thick black curtain hanging from bronze rings.

She recognized two people from Maine, but the seven others around the long table were all from Future Minerals' headquarters in Cos Cob, Connecticut. She wasn't accustomed to the heavy French food. There was filet mignon in a sauce of brandied cream and green peppercorns, mashed potatoes with truffle oil, garlicky spinach. Even the butter she spread on a crust of bread tasted richer than what she had eaten in the past. A thought crossed her mind: Was there one kind of butter for the wealthy and another for everyone else? Apparently, yes.

The wine theme of the night, the maître d' announced, was "monster reds from California." Betty hoped a couple of glasses would wash away the headache above her right eye. The table began with a few bottles of a Sonoma cabernet and moved on to a booming reserve petite sirah from Paso Robles. The moment her glass was empty, an arm would reach from behind her and refill it. The food and drink weighed on her brain—and on her lower intestine. She guessed that the evening's meal for the eight people at the table would cost about what she used to make in a month. Then she picked up the wine list and realized that the bill for the twelve bottles of wine alone, plus a tip, would actually be more than her old salary of two thousand dollars a month.

The headache was gone but she felt a little loopy. She realized she had consumed too much food, too much wine, too much money—and too little oxygen. She looked around the table at the blotched white faces, reddening with the night's repast, and tried to remember the name of the guy sitting on her left. Languid? Lambent? Langouste? Something like that. She needed air.

She was dining with a bunch of sweaty White men with red faces, self-satisfied in the extreme, raising their intoxicated voices in a curtained room. She idly wondered, was this what she had worked toward in college? She knew it was not.

She excused herself to go to the ladies' room. There she vomited a rich mix of beef and red wine. She flushed, sat, and passed a long rush of gas. She washed her face and reapplied her makeup, then sat and rested for a few minutes. On her way back, she paused outside the curtain to primp for a moment and also to make sure all the gas was out. She heard through the curtain the rising mix of their intoxicated chatter:

One voice: "Sure, sure, I know, there's a lot of crying about the water. But look, if we didn't take that cobalt, someone else would. Dude, it's called progress. Get used to it or get out of the way. Let the market work its magic."

A second: "The way I see it, the question wasn't whether the cobalt would be taken, it was who would take it. Luckily for us, we did!" This was greeted with guffaws, as if he had unveiled a witticism.

"What about the people up there?" asked a third voice.

From across the table, a fourth shot back, "You mean Mainers? What a bunch of dumb fucks. Sometimes I feel like they deserve everything that's happened. For people who are pretty poor, you know, they seem to me pretty stuck up. I mean, if you're just as good as me, then, why are you so poor? That's what I think."

Another voice, the guy who had been sitting on her left. "Groleau's not bad. But she's still a little clueless." She remembered his surname—Lambert.

"About what?" asked someone.

"How the world works," Lambert said.

"I'd do her," volunteered a voice from across the table, a little wobbly.

"Of course you would. You have a weakness for little lost lambs," someone parried.

"Oh, give it up, would you?" someone said with apparent boredom.

Groleau took a deep breath, nodded, and parted the curtain. She saw the man who had been talking snap a finger and point at his empty wine glass. A waiter scurried over with the tardy refill and a soft, swift apology.

"What'd I miss?" she tried to ask brightly as she sat back down. She took in the scene—herself and nine plump men, most of them intoxicated, raising their voices in a curtained room.

"Nothing, just us chickens squawking," the boss, sitting at the end of the table, said quickly. He looked around the table, which quieted for a moment.

After a few minutes she excused herself. "It's been a long day," she said, standing. "Thank you for inviting me." She walked outside and down the street to where the little black Benz sedan was parked. She sat in it and put both hands on the wheel with the window down, hoping the cold air would sober her up. She drove away with the breeze blowing on her face. Without thinking much about it, she drove for hours, hitting I-95 before midnight and following it through New Hampshire and up into Maine. As she drove she rocked back and forth in her seat, glancing up occasionally at the array of stars, so numerous in the skies of rural Maine, especially on a cold night.

At the little town of Sherman she took the familiar exit to Route 11. At the stop sign, she turned left and gassed up at the twenty-four-hour Irving station, the only place open for miles in any direction. Then she plunged into the darkness of Route 11 as it sliced through the fir and spruce of the lonely north woods. Without quite thinking it through, she was driving to her parents' house in Ashland, in the far north of the state. As she passed through the empty night, she thought about that shocking moment at the hearing when Gary Rath had confronted her. His words had stirred her. And then about the comments the company executives had made when they thought she couldn't hear them. She bit her lip. She did not feel like a winner, as Diane Peligroso had assured her she would.

The roads were clear and the car fast and sure-footed, so she made it from the restaurant in Boston to Ashland in just over five hours. She arrived at 3:30 A.M. and parked down the street from her parents' dark house. She stared at the moonless sky, at the Milky Way. *What have I done?* she asked herself. She examined the leather interior of the automobile as if seeing it for the first time. *Was this really worth my soul, some chromed metal and soft leather?* She needed to do something to make it right. To change course.

She sat and stared at the sky. A dog barked, shaking her from her reverie. There's no time like the present, her parents had always taught her. She would do it. She pressed the ignition button on the Benz. It hummed to life. She turned southward and drove two hours nonstop to Finney Junction, generally seen as the worst part of the poison fan. Just having the intention to chart a new course in her life was elating. She felt liberated, like she was shooting upward into the sky after losing a great weight. Her hands were on the wheel but her mind was in the stars.

She sang as she drove, trying to recall old gospel tunes she'd heard on the radio as a child. She soon ran out of them, so she turned on the car radio. The sole local station popped up, a feisty little outfit broadcasting out of Presque Isle. She had grown up listening to its unusual mix of country and pop oldies and potato crop reports. Sure enough, Hank Williams's plaintive version of "Lost Highway" came on. She sang along, "Neither good nor bad, just a ki-iiii-id like you."

When the potato crop prediction reports began, she hit "seek" on the radio and a CBC station came on. It was the top of the hour. She heard a warm, familiar voice, one that made her comfortable, and realized that Monique Bouchard must be anchoring the late-night local news, exactly the kind of task that might be assigned the station's newest reporter. She pulled over and texted Monique.

"MB, I think I am going to quit," she wrote. "This lobbying isn't for me. Call me, okay? BG." As she drove she found herself idly daydreaming about Monique's breasts. She wondered if her nipples were as deep brown as her eyes.

It was still dark at about seven in the morning when she arrived outside the mobile home of Gary Rath. She knew it was early, but it was the beginning of an entire new phase of life for her. She was eager to apologize to the people she had let down, like him. And she would quit this job working for Diane. She was seized by the wild joy of the newly converted. She wanted Mr. Rath to know that she had heeded his words, was grateful for them, and was changing her ways. She pulled up next to the mobile home, hopped out, and walked up the four wooden steps. She knocked on the thin metal of the front door. She wanted to shake his hand.

Rath came to the door, rubbing his eyes of sleep, and suspicious of being visited so early. He held an old police revolver in his right hand. He opened the door and said one cryptic word: "You?" And then, on sheer angry impulse, he pointed it at her face. She stepped backward. The round tumbled through her left shoulder, shattering the scapula, or shoulder bone. It spun her entire body around. She tried to lift a foot but instead toppled to the bottom of the four steps and passed out. Rath walked down the steps and looked at her. He cocked his head when he heard a plummy British-accented voice say from the idling Mercedes Benz, "Betty, we've been driving for several hours. Are you ready for a rest break?" He looked but didn't see anyone in the vehicle. Rath dropped the pistol next to her still body and went back to bed. He was awakened minutes later by a police siren in his yard responding to a neighbor's call of a shot fired. Betty lay at the bottom of the steps, her blood running over the string of Diane's pearls that hung from her neck.

48

A VISIT WITH A NATIVE AMERICAN LEADER

Montreal, cold and icy, felt weird to Ryan—not quite American, but insufficiently foreign. It was like a familiar song being performed in an off-key voice. He did the initial paperwork at the Irish consulate. He walked the slushy streets until he got bored. Then he walked some more.

He waited for several days. He did not want to stay in the city for the months the nice woman at the consulate had said it might take to complete the process. He called the office of Ted French, the lawyer in Finney Junction. There was no answer. He called the lawyer's cell and left a message. Then he called the man's home. Again, no answer. Finally, he called Ed Healey and asked why French seemed so out of touch.

"You haven't heard, have you?" Healey said weakly.

"No, I'm not in the country," Ryan said.

"He went off the road yesterday at Brewer's Falls, just before the bridge. Crashed through the ice. They're still pulling him and his car out of the river."

"Foul play?"

"Does it matter?" Healey said softly. "He's gone."

"I'm sorry," Ryan said. "I know he was a good friend of yours."

"And a good man," Healey said. "We need more of them, not less."

Ryan hung up and went to a coffee shop to think about what Plan B might be. Goddamn, he thought. He called and left a message for James Reveur, who was co-head of the IZORIP, as people referred to the new International Zone of Refuge for Indigenous People that had been established by the governments of the state of Maine and the province of Quebec, and Indigenous groups in both places. The purpose of the new zone was to give Native Americans and Canadian First Peoples a place to experiment freely with alternative means of living with global overheating. Ryan told Reveur that he needed to speak about a sensitive matter and could only do so in person.

"I don't know why you think I can help," Reveur said when he called back. "We've had enough of White peoples' trouble."

"I wouldn't call unless it was serious. A matter of life and death—for me, personally."

"I don't know," Reveur said hesitantly.

"It involves something that will interest you, which is outsiders poisoning the land in Maine."

At this Reveur snapped to attention. Any land in Maine was land that might one day be reclaimed by Indigenous people. "Come on down tomorrow," he said. "I'll be a the gate at eleven."

In the morning Ryan drove through the dreary towns of southern Quebec. His phone noted that one town formerly had been called "Asbestos." Another area mauled by corporations, he thought to himself. He saw the IZORIP sign and parked at the visitors' center, just outside the zone. He called Reveur, who came outside the fence to see him. Ryan was struck that the man actually looked younger than he had three years earlier. Back then, he realized, Reveur had been carrying the enormous weight of a sustained protest, one that ended with the bombing that killed several, among them Reveur's best friend, Paul Soco, the co-leader of the protest march. After that, Reveur had led a band of about forty tribal members deep into the Maine woods and then across the border into Canada, which welcomed them. After months of negotiations, they had arrived at the agreement to establish a new international zone of refuge, where Indigenous people from both the United States and Canada would seek to revive ancient customs that might help them prepare for climate-driven changes in temperatures and water distribution.

The two men sat on either side of a wooden picnic table, facing each other, Reveur's moon-like face was intent and somber as he listened. "Your work here at the zone seems to agree with you," Ryan said. "You look younger than you did back during the March."

James Reveur nodded. "Fewer worries," he explained. "Only one world, ours, to handle."

"Is it, like, primitive living?" Ryan asked.

"More like, sensible," James said. "Electricity and internet only one hour a day, and none on weekends. It keeps things a lot quieter, the mind less jangled. You can focus on what's important instead of what industrialized civilization chooses to put in front of you. And the more independent we are, the better off we will be when western society collapses."

Ryan nodded. "Sounds good. I need a place like that."

"So what troubles drive you here to our quiet, remote, and peaceful lives?" James asked.

For two hours, Ryan told the story of what happened when Future Minerals began mining cobalt in north-central Maine. James listened intently. He asked only an occasional question. Ryan talked about the discovery of the poisonous Fan, about the toxic effects on people and fish and other animals, and about the company's fierce and comprehensive campaign of lies, manipulation, and violence against its critics.

"And that's it, what brings me here today," Ryan concluded. He waited.

James remained silent, turning over his thoughts before sharing them. Finally he said, "What do you want me to say?"

"You're a wise man. How do you assess the situation?"

James nodded. "First, and I say this with respect for the people suffering from this: These towns are being treated like the United States has always treated Indians."

That hadn't occurred to Ryan. "How?"

"Look at the patterns of behavior. You got in the way of Big Money. In America, and maybe in most places, the rich take what they want. Big Money trampled on your rights. You were lied to. It acted without mercy and broke the rules whenever it needed to. If it has to, it will kill, and then it will prosecute the surviving victims."

"So what do I do?"

James paused, made as if to speak, and then stopped again. He said, "I can't—" and then broke off, shaking his head.

"Why the hesitation?" Ryan asked.

"You see, if you were an Indian, I would tell you to find strength in the old ways."

"I have your example right here," Ryan countered. "Why can't I follow that? Make a new way of life out here with your people."

"We were fortunate, in retrospect. We had old ways to reclaim. Many of them had been lost, but we still had many others. We are learning new ways to uncover the old ways. These were modes of living that had been tested and improved on this soil for ten thousand years. I mean, my people were actually brought to this part of the world by climate change, by the glaciers receding. We still have myths, stories, about encountering the People of the Ice, which presumably were like today's Eskimos."

"But?"

"More an 'and,'" James corrected. "I say that because, it seems to be that you, Ryan Tapia, have none of that, no old ways to fall back on."

"Can't I learn them here?"

"No," James said, vehemently shaking his head and crossing his arms. Ryan was surprised by how emphatic he was. "Having White people around, that's something we strive to avoid. Right now we are more or less left alone, once we made it clear that almost no one is allowed past the visitors' center. But if we became a sanctuary for those fighting the power structure, we would be crushed. We need to stay out of the Anglo world's squabbles. That was our big mistake, back when the Europeans came to this continent, making alliances with various European factions. We thought we could manipulate them.

"And another reason. We are working hard to strengthen our culture, and any Anglo presence would dilute that work. We have enough problems without taking on yours. I believe with all my heart that this mining company or its allies would track you down here. It would be White trouble. But the headline would be, 'Violence at Indian refuge.'"

He paused again, and held up his hands, palms facing up. "If America had a more stable, deeper religious tradition, I would suggest you find refuge in a monastery. But I haven't heard of one that can withstand the pressures that would follow you into their cloister. There is no rock of refuge." He shook his head and repeated, "There is no rock." He stared down at the picnic table, running an index finger along its grain as he thought.

Reveur didn't mention it to Ryan, but he had studied the early history of Western monasteries intently, out of the belief that the IZORIP was in some ways a modern version of the medieval monasteries. Those Christian refuges had formed in Europe during the

Middle Ages partly as a way of preserving knowledge during a time of extreme social turmoil. Many monasteries had by design been located far from the cities whose wealth attracted Vikings and other raiders. And, Reveur had learned, the upheavals wrenching society back then were caused in large part by what historians called "the Little Ice Age," a period of several decades when the European climate cooled sufficiently to depress normal harvests and so caused groups to migrate in search of food and productive land. Old social structures could no longer feed or protect people, so they collapsed. The climate refugees gathered around the castles of local lords who could help them. They offered their fealty, trading their freedom and labor for bread and security.

Ryan felt stuck. James, who had led the beleaguered Indian protests so adroitly, seemed to despair of helping him. James finally looked up. "I do have one idea, or really the beginnings of one," he said. "Indians in your kind of fix, sometimes they followed a mode of quiet struggle."

"What was that?"

"Adopt the identity of the oppressor—but all the time, inside your head, remain yourself."

"Pretend to be one of them?" Ryan asked.

"Exactly," James said. "But at every sunrise and sunset, remind yourself that you are not."

"A life of secret resistance to the company and to the oligarchical power structure?"

"Yes."

"Sounds hard."

"It was, for me," James said. "We call it 'walking in the two worlds.' There's a real strain in doing that. Which is why I smoked weed and drank every night. It was only when I stopped playing along with the Anglo world that I got sober and sane."

"What kept you going?"

"For me, it was the growing belief that the American Machine—the term I came to use for the whole damned power structure—is doomed. That gave me energy and urgency. Still does."

James stood. "Which reminds me, I have a lot of work to do right here, right now. It isn't easy preparing for the collapse of American society."

Ryan walked with him slowly to the gate of the Zone. "What if you're wrong?" he said. "What if western civilization doesn't collapse?"

"Possible," James said. "But I think unlikely. But no matter. We will still be living better lives, here in the deep woods. And every year that the oceans heat up, the storms grow more intense, tornadoes take down power lines not designed for that, the species move northward, the bugs and ticks get thicker—we'll stand back and watch. And as each season passes, I will be more certain that we are right. Here, in the Zone, we are moving from thinking annually to thinking in terms of centuries."

"What does that mean?"

"Well, consider that my people have been here in this area for at least one hundred centuries. The last four centuries have been bad for us. But when my people got here, the glaciers were retreating about a mile a year. That means it took around two centuries for the land to reappear from the coast to where we are now. It took a few more centuries for it to flourish, as flora and fauna moved northward. The caribou, moose, and beaver came, and my people moved with them.

"So yes, we have to be patient. But every day I see more signs that we are on the right track in the Zone. Yesterday I saw a sand-hill crane land in the swamp below here."

"What's that?" Ryan asked.

"Southern bird, supposedly good meaty eating. But we'll keep our hands off for now, let them establish themselves as a population. They've never migrated this far north before. It could take years, but we will wait until there is a sustainable flock." James paused. "Patience, that's a word I try to teach every day to our people here. We all were taught in the capitalist world that time is money. But we may be moving into an era when money is just irrelevant, just doesn't matter. It may be that as the globe heats up, and large parts of the Earth become uninhabitable, that patience is a great power, perhaps the essential one."

"And what does that lead you to think?" Ryan asked, genuinely curious.

James smiled. "Me, I think that our Indian civilization may gain the upper hand in the coming times. If there is a hidden flaw in western civilization, a bug in the American Machine, it is that it rewards impatience. If there is one thing Indians know, it is how to wait, and even to appreciate the waiting. For us, patience is an art form, or really a part of our religion. I'm coming to see it as a form of silent prayer."

He held out his hand. "Thank you for coming." As they shook, he said, "One last thing: I want to thank you even more for taking care of Moolsem. How's he doing?"

"Good," Ryan said. "Hobbles a lot, but I think enjoys life." He thought for a moment. "If something happens to me, can you take him?"

"Of course!" James said. "He's a veteran of the march. And now I must go." He waved to the guard at the IZORIP gate and went back into the refuge. Ryan drove through the deep spruce and fir forests back to Maine.

49

BETTY AWAKENS

Betty Groleau, peering through the fog of her half sleep, saw Diane Peligroso standing like an apparition at the foot of the hospital bed. She was solicitous, carrying flowers and candy, and bristling with nervous energy. After some small talk about how Betty was feeling, she got to the point. "Don't make any rash decisions until you feel better," she advised as she paced about the room.

"Like what?" Betty asked. She had considered quitting but hadn't told Diane. Yet the moment Diane began to instruct her on what to do, she decided against doing that. Instead of resigning, she would work the inside and comment about it, anonymously, from the outside.

"Just don't do anything foolish," Diane said. "You don't need any more trouble," she added, patting Betty's good shoulder. She left. Betty knew Diane well enough to understand that implied threat. But if Diane was already acting defensively, she calculated, it was because she was scared. She had sensed that Betty, in her short time working for her, had learned a lot about the lobbyist's business. But Diane couldn't know exactly what Betty had picked up. That made her nervous.

After Diane left, Betty lay in bed, looking out the window at the ice floes in the Penobscot River. She thought she saw a doe standing on a big chunk of ice that was floating down the middle of the river, probably trapped on it when her weight broke it off. That's me, Betty thought to herself. Drifting along toward the rapids. She decided that she shouldn't be a scared deer, that she needed to take action. But what?

50

ADDISON SELLS

Lincoln Addison, the editor of the *North Country Times*, braced himself for an argument with his wife, Mary. They were sitting at the kitchen table, where they ate their dinners unless they had company.

They'd been shaken by Gary Rath's shooting of Betty Groleau. They had known both people, of course, and saw them both as additional casualties of the Fan. To try to recover a bit from that shock, they had retreated into their small, cozy home for a long weekend. They watched some basketball on television, walked their dog, Steno, in the woods, did some cooking, and read their current books. She was deep into Elizabeth Strout's latest novel while he was reading a collection of essays by Anne Lamott. It was now early Monday evening, the Presidents' Day holiday celebrating the birthdays of George Washington and Linc's namesake. He waited until Mary dug into his garlicky meatloaf, her favorite dish. Steno lay under the table, snoring lightly.

"I've been meaning to tell you," he began.

"Oh?" she said, her fork pausing. She cocked her head. From experience she knew that's how he conveyed big news.

"I've had an offer for the paper. I think a solid one." He studied her face for her reaction.

"Linc, that's wonderful." She smiled. She had long assumed that the *North Country Times*, given its dwindling revenue, was almost worthless. Thus any offer at all was both surprising and welcome news. She had expected that when they retired, they would have to live off her meager pension from her thirty years of teaching English at the high school, plus their savings, which were, frankly, not much. They'd scrape by in their declining years, but they'd be watching pennies the whole time and hoping their two old cars kept going.

"Yes and no," he said, pursing his lips. "It's not a bad offer, but I don't like it."

"Linc, why not?" she said, putting her fork back on the plate without eating the steaming chunk of meatloaf on it.

"It's a generous offer, considering."

"But?"

He looked at her. "But it's from an investment banker in New York."

She stared at him, holding back her incredulity. "Are you going to let regional enmity get in the way?"

He had been worried she was going to say that.

She continued: "How much is it for?"

"Six hundred and twenty-five thousand," he said.

"Not bad," she said. "In fact, quite generous, given the current state of the business. Is it cash, or just promises of payments down the road?"

"Cash," he said, but not happily.

"Don't make a mistake, take it!" she said.

"But—"

"But nothing!" she cut him off so loudly that Steno slowly raised his old head to see what the matter could be. He wasn't accustomed to raised voices in this house. "Lincoln Addison," she said formally, "your pride and prejudice is showing."

"It's more than that," he said. "I googled the guy. He's a kid in his early thirties. Was president of the Federalist Society at Harvard. Libertarian. Born on third base and thinks he hit a triple. Made millions overnight by buying up nursing homes that are funded by Medicare. Gets rich off government spending and then wants to stop it. Big Trump supporter back when that was a thing. Kind of a right-wing nut. Selling to him, that makes me feel like I'm giving up."

"Got it, he's not our cup of tea," she agreed, softly.

"Think of what he'd do to the paper." Lincoln Addison had dedicated his life to the *North Country Times*. He hated to think of it peddling anti-government nonsense to the unsuspecting readers of Asbury, Beecher, and Finney Junction.

"And when you do that, maybe also think of us having food on the table and oil in the furnace in our old age, and even able to afford our prescription drugs," she responded.

"So you are for it, really?" he said in a quiet voice.

"Linc, I know it may be hard for you." She reached across the table and took his hand. "But yes, I am."

He sighed in relief. Her bright certainty burned off his fog of vague doubts.

With that settled, she added, "You need to visit Betty Groleau in the hospital, you know."

"She quit the paper. Why?"

The sale closed quickly. A week later, a friend sent them a clipping from the *Wall Street Journal* that mentioned the investment banker who had bought the paper had been the college roommate of the current CEO of Future Minerals.

51
FAREWELLS

It was the depth of the Maine winter, four months into it, the thermometer sometimes hovering all day at zero. Even the lobstermen had headed to Florida for a month to wait for more reasonable weather to return to Maine.

The politicians kept busy. Scales, the state attorney general, looked to have a lock on winning the governorship in the upcoming election. He formally announced his candidacy, resigning the attorney generalship as he did. Dick Auger was picked by the legislature to succeed him.

Ryan stopped at Dysart's convenience store on the Bangor Road to gas up. Inside, getting a coffee, he saw the headlines in the *North Country Times* about the political moves. He bought a copy and sat in his truck, reading the stories. It seemed like the forces of corruption and oppression were winning across the board.

He turned the page and saw two editorials. One welcomed the new leaders of the state as "a breath of fresh air after years of oppression by micromanaging bureaucrats and socialist-influenced Democrats who never met a government spending bill they didn't like."

Below it was a second editorial titled CLOSER TO HOME. "We don't mind from-aways advising us what to do," it began. "Sometimes they have good ideas. But we think it is high time to make some distinctions." It continued:

> The people of the North Country have labored long and hard for what they have. Should they risk it on the say-so of a disgraced former FBI agent from—of all places—California? We think not.
>
> The "Afflicted Citizens' Group" is no doubt well-meaning. Many of its members are longtime friends and neighbors. But they have come under the influence of that former FBI agent, one Ryan Tapia. Earlier this month, he was at the wheel of his pickup truck when it crashed into a car on the Bangor Road. According to the State Patrol report, he had a bellyful of whiskey in him, as well as a bag of marijuana in the cab of his truck.
>
> So we ask the ACG: Is this the type of person you should rely on?
>
> We notice, with appreciation, that another group, the Concerned Citizens of the North Country, has emerged. They are, we think, following a more reasonable course, one that seeks to balance the needs of commerce and the demands of nature. Nor do they seem to have come under the sway of Mr. Tapia.

Later that day, Lincoln Addison opened up the new edition of the newspaper he had just sold. He turned to the same editorial Ryan had read. Within a moment or two, Addison was clenching the newspaper in balled fists. He threw the newspaper down on the kitchen table, then picked up his cell phone. It rang twice, and then he heard a "Hello."

"Robin, I want to cancel—" Addison began. He had called the number of the woman who had answered the phone and taken classified ads for over fifteen years at the paper. She was married to Sandy Bay, who laid out and printed the paper every week. He stopped when he realized he was talking to an automated answering system that was offering him a number of options. He hung up on that call and made another, to the sports reporter at the paper, Johnny Boyle, who had toiled at the *North Country Times* almost as long as Addison himself had.

"Yesterday they laid off pretty much everyone except me and the new kid," Boyle said wearily. "And they've told her she has to cover both education and business. And obits. They also put the meetings of the selectmen on my plate."

"For all three towns?"

"Yep," Boyle said quietly. Even his voice sounded worn out.

"Do they know that the selectmen's meetings and the high school games often take place at the same time?"

"I don't think they care," Boyle said. "They don't know how important the sports are to our readers."

"What about Robin?" Addison asked, inquiring about the woman who answered the phone and took the dwindling numbers of classified ads.

"Laid off, along with Sandy," Boyle said. "They're thinking of moving back to Greenville, trying to live off the land up there."

"That's crazy," Linc said. "There's no growing season up there."

"What else are they gonna do?" Boyle said. "By the way, word is the new publisher is paying himself two hundred thousand dollars a year."

"That's nuts," Addison said. "The paper can't carry that kind of salary."

"It's a brave new world," Boyle said. "Not sure I want to be in it. Bye."

Linc put down the telephone, covered his eyes with his hands, and let the tears flow. Only now was he beginning to comprehend what he had done by selling the newspaper.

He decided to check the online version. He'd never paid much attention to it, leaving it to younger staffers born to the digital world. Now, as he scrolled through it, he was impressed by how much better the layout was, how much faster the stories came up. But it was the advertisements that struck him most of all: There was page after page of pop-ups pushing books and articles by right-wing thinkers. Weird products like "super pillows." Odd patent medicines. Very high-end "all-natural hand-caught" tuna that cost $6 a can, a price that Linc doubted one in one hundred of his readers could afford. He realized that he was seeing the new business model: Focus on the online newspaper and support it with generous ad placements from right-wing billionaires from across the country. They weren't looking for sales, just looking to support a right-wing voice in the north woods of Maine.

52

RYAN'S JOINT CONVERSATION WITH DIANE AND LILY

Ryan, mulling the death of Ted French, had come to realize that his money made him vulnerable, that money without power is just an invitation for predators. When he got back to his leased house on Lost Pond, he wrote four checks for $1 million each. One was for Doctors Without Borders, the second for Earth First, and the third for a foundation that paid for the education of children of police officers killed in the line of duty. The last one he was sending overseas, to a monastery in Ireland called Inishturk that he had read about. The small, obscure friary had the reputation of declining to disclose the identities of its residents to anyone outside its doors. He wrote his landlord a letter stating that he would be giving up the house, enclosing a check for two months' rent. He drove to Bangor and sent the four checks by express delivery. With that, his bank account was just about cleaned out.

Ryan remained curious about these two women, the sisters who were cutting a considerable swath through Maine. He called Diane Peligroso, who said she actually was down in Ellsworth, visiting Lily. "Why don't you drive down and meet us at Flynn's at half past five," she said. She added, "I believe you know the place," signaling that she was aware of Ryan's previous meeting at that bar with Lily.

He parked, made sure his phone was set to record, and found the sisters in the rear room, at a corner table. Diane was wearing tight jeans and a soft, plush sweater of light gray cashmere. Lily was in cowboy boots and a brown suede jacket, wearing a Red Sox baseball cap. Ryan stood at their table. Diane's shiny long black hair, smelling of aromatic argan oil, contrasted with the gray of her posh sweater. As he was about to speak, Diane's smartphone rang. She looked at Ryan and held up a finger, meaning, *Give me a moment.*

"Yes, that offer still stands," she said into her phone. "Lunch tomorrow in Bangor? I'm glad you're still interested. As it happens, we have just had a slot come open that would be a perfect fit for someone like you, a smart, energetic young political reporter. Noon at Tomlinson's."

Listening to the appointment being made, Ryan thought to himself, another one bites the dust. He realized that Diane truly enjoyed her work.

He stood at the table, his hands in the back pockets of his jeans. He was conscious of being on Lily's turf. "May I join you?" he asked.

"Of course," said Diane. Lily said nothing.

He sat. "I'm sorry about Betty Groleau," he said.

Diane waved a hand in the air. "I saw her today. She'll be okay," she said airily. "But that's not what you're here about. What can we do for you?"

Ryan leaned forward. "I need to know: Why are you two like this?"

Diane reached out, took a sip of her Scotch on the rocks, looked over the rim of the glass, and almost drawled, "Like what, Mr. Tapia?"

"Manipulative, cynical, predatory," Ryan said casually, as if talking about the weather. "That sort of thing. Siding with a company that destroys people and nature."

Lily Thornfoot's cap emphasized her short, chopped haircut. She rolled her eyes. "Oh, grow up," she said. She took a sip of her dark pint of draft Guinness. She hadn't been pleased when Diane told her that Ryan Tapia was coming to see them. "You know what I say?"

"What?" he asked.

"Checkmate," she said. She reached out to the saltshaker between them and tipped it on its side, symbolically referring to how chess games end.

"You're right," Ryan murmured.

Diane held up a hand to her twin. "My sister means, you sound perhaps, well, a little naïve. A better way to put it is, we understand power, and she suspects you don't."

"Maybe so," Ryan conceded. "What is it that I don't understand?"

"Power is all around us," Diane said, looking upward and waving her right hand in the air. "It just floats out there, waiting to be taken by those who can. My sister and I, we're the kind of people to find it, grasp it, use it. We were born to it." She clenched her right hand into a fist and brought it down on the table.

"And then what?"

"We win, we move on. We look for more power. It's a game that never ends. Your old friend the governor? She's the same. She's term limited, so she'll run for senator, and win. The state AG is running for governor and likely will make it. And Auger, the old DA from here, has the state AG job. So everyone's happy."

"Is it really possible to arrange things like that, so neatly?"

"In most states, no. But Maine is pretty small. People think of it as big, because it has so much land. But it has the least population density east of the Mississippi. Just about one-point-four million people, total."

"Why does that matter?"

"Because there are so few levers to pull—you have mayors of a few cities, a handful of newspapers and TV stations, and a few big corporations. The congressional delegation is just four people, compared to, what, forty for Texas, and even more for California."

Ryan mulled that, then said, "Do you ever think about the people you chew up and spit out?"

At this point, Lily had heard enough from him. She leaned forward and pointed an index finger at Ryan. "Here's what I think," she said, spitting the words at him. "I think you are being sexist. I think you're unhappy, chagrined, shocked, to see women exercising power. I think you want us back in the kitchen and the bedroom, being meek little creatures. That is not going to happen, mister. We are acting as men have acted for eons—and you don't like that, do you?"

Ryan again took a moment to think that through. He had not expected a feminist defense of Lily's criminality. He had been more successful in interfering with her operation than he had with Diane and her allies at the company. But he saw now that his intervention almost certainly had just been a temporary setback for her.

"There's probably something to that," Ryan conceded. "But here's where I think you went wrong, Miss Thornfoot. The richer guys, the retired executives who moved here from away, they saw your blackmail as a cost of doing business. Easy come, easy go. They'd cheated the IRS, you caught them, and they paid up, and a lot less than they would have had to send to Uncle Sam. And honestly, I think they were kind of intrigued by you—this smart, attractive woman confronting them."

"But?" Lily asked.

"But you made a mistake with my client. To him, it was a matter of principle. To him, you were robbing him of the sweat of his brow."

"I'm guessing you don't know that your client profited on insider knowledge of where the interstate junction would be when the highway was extended. He bought the land cheap from people who didn't know the construction plans, then sold it for millions more."

That gave Ryan pause. "Okay," he conceded. "Didn't know about that. But still, the land was bought with hard-earned money, in his view."

"Thanks for the free advice." Lily snorted. "But it's not really free, because you cost me a lot of money."

"Yours was a tactical error, nothing more," Ryan said. "I am sure your scheme is still rolling along." A waitress came by. Ryan asked for a club soda with lime. He was being careful since his arrest.

"But," he resumed, "there's something else that perplexes me. You, Lily, have engaged in criminality. By contrast, I think that you, Diane, have acted generally within the law, even if the company hasn't. Despite that, I think you have committed the greater sin. There's a bit of Robin Hood in Lily's operation. But yours, the work you do for Future Minerals," he said, looking into Diane's black eyes, "that's really robbing the poor to give to the rich."

Lily retorted, "Now you're sounding more like a minister than a cop. Different tack—but still the type that can't stand strong, independent women. I guess when you've lost the fight, you retreat into moralism. You're basically telling us that we are going to Hell."

Ryan said, "But what if you are?" He believed in Hell because he felt that he had been there, on a temporary visit, during the year after his wife and children were killed.

"Me, Future Minerals, we did what we needed to do." Diane shrugged. "We took care of the right officials. We knew what we were doing. Your interfering just made it harder for us, maybe a little more violent. Bumps in the road."

It occurred to him that it was time to leave. He had asked the questions he wanted to pose to Diane Peligroso and Lily Thornfoot, and they had given their answers. He understood what they had told him, but still he felt better than he had before they spoke. "That said, I think you two are more at home in this country than I am these days. More comfortable with who has real power, and how it is being used."

"I still don't think you really grasp what power is," Diane said, glad to be back on her own specialty. "I study it every day. Financial power, political power, personal power."

"What do you mean?" Ryan asked. "I don't understand."

"Well," said Diane, "how would you define it?"

He thought for a moment, then said, "I guess I'd say, power is the ability to get things done, to make people do things they otherwise might not do."

"As a definition, I'd say that's naïve but passable," Diane said.

"What a Boy Scout," Lily snorted.

Ryan was stung. He turned to her. "Okay, you're so clever, Miss Thornfoot, how would you explain power?"

"Simple," Lily said, with a slight sneer. "Your definition also describes money. But power is more than that. My motto is this: *Money insulates, but power protects*. I'll tell you what real power is, most of all: *The ability to break the law with the confidence that you'll get away with it*. That's how I define it."

He stopped and considered what she'd said. Her definition applied equally well to both her blackmailing business and the business model of Future Minerals. He feared she was correct. He felt like he'd been hit. She was taunting him. "I am not sure I would ever want to live in that world," he said. He felt a surge of bitterness.

"Wake up! You already do!" Lily said, leaning forward, the heels of both hands on the edge of the table. "This is life! How do we know? What we are telling you is the wisdom that comes from being abused. If you want to understand power, be one of its victims. They know how power works and they remember those lessons, because they have the scars to show it. In America, people with enough money live by another set of rules, which is basically that there are no rules. None! Small deals, they ignore. But if you move up into the tens of millions of dollars and higher—well, then, the gloves come off, and the laws go away."

Diane held up a hand to Lily and said softly, "That's enough." It was one thing to pretend to be candid, quite another to actually discuss what they did. In her triumphalist candor, Lily was getting much too close to the reality of the situation. And something about Ryan's ease with his apparent defeat nagged her. Diane turned back to him. "What I sense you are saying, in a fumbling, roundabout way, is that you have realized that we are winning. That we've won."

"So you just see me as roadkill?" Ryan asked.

"Not really," Diane said, soothingly. She wanted to let him down easy. Provoked, he might still be dangerous, be able to cause a bit more trouble. "I see you as someone who attaches to lost causes. A romantic, if you will. In your case, I'd say a religious dreamer."

"Maybe so," Ryan conceded. He stood.

"Bless me father, for I have sinned," mocked Lily.

Diane shushed her. "Be graceful in victory," she admonished her twin. "You've had a setback. But he's giving up."

"And he never understood that we come from a long line of witches," Lily said, referring to the family's centuries on their isolated little island.

"Thank you for your time," Ryan said, and turned away. He had realized during this conversation that he had just been a bump in their roads, perhaps even a warning sign to them to be more careful. He walked out of the pub and turned right, heading down two blocks to where Main Street crossed the dark, tannin-laden waters of the Union River. He stood there for nearly an hour, leaning on the rail, watching the shallow water slide under the bridge. He thought about the people who had been destroyed in various ways by Future Minerals—literally in the cases of some, such as Jacob the Growler, Ned Meddybemps, Ted French, Pete Skillings, and Verdella Skillings; in soul-warping ways for Betty Groleau, Ed Healey, Lincoln Addison, and Bap Salim. And for Gary Rath, who almost certainly was going to spend a few years in prison for shooting Groleau.

Ryan wasn't contemplating suicide—at any rate, it would be hard to drown in that cold, shallow river—but he was frozen by a sense of futility. Had he really lost, as Diane had said? Was he giving up?

He walked back to his truck, got in slowly, and followed Route 1A northwest back toward Bangor. "I'm out," he said aloud to himself as he drove. His view of life, of what was important, was changing. The frame was shifting. It was like trying to climb a mountain during an earthquake.

As he turned onto his long driveway to Lost Pond, he pressed the button for the audio in the truck. A song from the list Nina had emailed to him began playing. It was Cat Power, singing, in a fragile tone of defeat, "Once, I wanted to be the greatest . . ." He thought to himself: I didn't even want that. I just wanted to do my duty well. And I feel that in this situation, I have failed as an American citizen. But, he added to himself: What if your country no longer wants people like you, dutiful followers of the law, to succeed? When it belongs to the rich and powerful, people like you, Ryan, are just an impediment.

Again, he said to himself out loud, more certain this time: "I am out."

That night he dreamed of his dead family, Marta and the two children. They were at the beach, reveling in summer weather, running in and out of the shallows, the dog happily bounding behind them. His wife turned and saw him, and waved her hand, inviting him to come in and join them. Oddly enough, Nina Daigle was also at the beach, standing in deeper water, waving at Ryan as well.

But in the dream he did not wade into the water. He opened his eyes and thought to himself that it was time to get out, yet it was not time to cross over. He sat up in bed and stared out the back window at the morning mist on Lost Pond. He wondered why in his dream Nina Daigle was in the water near his dead family. A mourning dove was cooing on the pond's eastern shore. A rooster cock-a-doodled somewhere on a farm near the western side. It was time to get up and move.

He had coffee at the family altar. He said to it, "I'm out—but I am not completely done." He reached for his smartphone and listened to the recording he had made of his conversation with the two women last night. Assured that it came through loud and clear, he loaded it on to a thumb drive and put that in his jacket pocket.

53

A LAST APPOINTMENT

Even then, the final toll had not been called.

Ryan drove down to Hallowell to see Dot Williams, his grief therapist. She had been a big help, pulling him up out of his hole. They sat, as usual, in armchairs facing each other, a table between them holding a box of tissues.

Few people in life are harder to deceive than a grief counselor. Dot Williams had seen and heard it all. She knew the human mind was immensely resourceful in trying to avoid pain. She had sorted through thousands of emotional cover-ups, elaborate denials, and last-ditch lies. Her superpower was that she not only heard every word that was said, but she could also even hear the words all those evasions left unsaid.

Understanding that, Ryan, when he sat down in the old gray armchair, let it all hang out. When she asked how he was doing, he first said, "Okay, I guess," but then quickly amended that to, "But really, not good. Unfocused. Distracted. And you probably know that Nina broke up with me."

"I do," Dot said. Her gaze was penetrating. She waited.

"So life kind of sucks," he said. "But that's why I'm here, right?"

Dot looked out the window and then at him. She realized he didn't know. She drew a deep breath and then, with the calm but concerned eyes of a human being about to present terrible information, said, "I have bad news."

"Yes?"

"She's dead."

"Who?"

She saw that his mind was racing away from the reality she was about to present. "Nina," she said simply.

His heart sank. Tears filled his eyes. He doubled forward in his chair.

Dot stood and put a hand on his back. "Breathe," she said. "Slowly. In. Pause. Pause. Out."

He did. Then he said, "No, I didn't know." Some time passed. "When? How?"

"Yesterday," Dot said softly. "She drove up to the cabin where the hunter shot her husband. It's on Ambajejus Lake, near Millinocket and Grindstone. She sat on the steps of the cabin and called me. She thanked me for my help, and, she said, for introducing you to her. She said she had enjoyed her time with you, that it was the one thing that kept her on this side for so long."

"But?"

"But she said she was ready to cross over and rejoin her husband. Which of course was why she was standing on the spot where he was killed. She said she'd decided that's where her life really had ended. Used a phrase that she said had haunted her."

"Was it 'vale of tears'?" Ryan asked.

Now there were drops welling up in Dot's intelligent eyes. "Yes, that's it. Said she was 'ready to move on from this vale of tears.'"

"Gun?" he asked.

Dot shook her head slowly. "She told me she planned to walk out on the ice of the lake in front of the cabin, to a spot she knew where there was a spring under the lake. 'Its flow keeps the ice thinner there,' she said. She planned to fall through and just keep going. She told me she had walked along the waterline and filled her coat pockets with stones. She said it was the least violent way she could think of to go, except for sleeping pills, and she didn't have those, didn't know how to get enough either."

"How do you know she went through with it?"

"When she hung up, I called the police chief up there. He knew the case of Nina's husband getting shot, of course. He sped there and found her car in front of the cabin. Engine was still warm. He couldn't safely go out on the ice but called and patched through to the game warden pilot, who was aloft. The game warden flew in low and saw the tracks on the snow and ice—they were one way—and the hole where the tracks ended. He dropped a weighted buoy on a line to mark the spot. After ice-out they'll get divers in there, but right now it's risky, getting out on soft ice, or trying to swim under it."

Ryan leaned back and looked up at the ceiling. Dot waited. Five minutes passed. "This is too much, just too fucking much," he finally said. "I want to look up to God and yell, 'Knock this shit off, man.' I mean, he took my family. Okay. Can happen to anyone. But I have kept faith, I built a new life. And then Nina dumps me and kills herself. I mean, what the fuck?"

"It doesn't make sense," Dot said.

"It sure doesn't," he said. He was weeping now.

She waited and watched. When, after about ten minutes, he finally made eye contact, she unloaded. "There's a line in a song by Tom Waits you reminded me of—'there's no Devil, that's just God when he's drunk.'"

He looked at her in surprise. Where was she going with this? He tilted his head in puzzlement.

"That's what you're feeling now, I think," Dot said in explanation.

"Yeah," he said, "that's pretty much where I am. If I saw God today, I'd punch him in his big fat nose."

They both sat in more silence. There was a lot of emotional energy whirling around the room. During this breather, it occurred to Ryan that Dot Williams must feel that she failed with counseling Nina.

It was as if Dot saw that thought. "On days like this, I have to remind myself several times that my job is to try to help the living," she said. "To that end, I need to know whether you are considering hurting yourself."

He looked up. "You think I am?" He felt a great fatigue. Getting out of this life would be fine with him, but at this moment finding the way out was just too much damn work to contemplate.

"No, I really don't," Dot said. Her big, round face was intense, her eyes glistening. "Yet I do have the sense that you are considering doing something, taking some kind of action."

"I am," he agreed. "You're right. But it doesn't involve harm to myself or others."

Dot mulled that, then said, "So the vibe I am getting from you, right now, is fight or flight. And you say you are not going to fight. I believe that. So?"

Ryan stood up. "You would have been a great detective," he said, with genuine admiration. It was as if she had peered into his future. She had sensed his pulsating impulse to fly. It was uncontainable. He thanked her for all her help, shook her hand, and walked out the door to his truck.

He sent an email to James Reveur asking for someone to come collect Moolsem. Reveur wrote back that he had a friend at the Penobscot reservation in Old Town who would come by in the morning.

54

A RECORDING AND A KISS

The third morning in the hospital, Betty awoke feeling remarkably better. This time, standing at the end of her bed was a redheaded man she thought she'd seen before, but in her addled state couldn't place.

"You feeling okay?" he said.

"Just stiff," she said. "I really can't feel anything in the wounded shoulder."

"That's better than the alternative," the man said. "Let those bones knit."

Betty was puzzled. The previous days were a fog. "Are you my doctor?" she said. He didn't look like one, she thought, in his jeans, white shirt, and leather jacket.

"No, I'm Ryan Tapia. I'm an investigator. I've been looking into Future Minerals. So of course I read all your articles. I mean, before you . . ."

"Before I sold out, you mean."

"Yeah," he conceded. "But reading your stuff, watching you at that hearing, I had the sense that your foray into that world wouldn't stick. What are you going to do now?"

"I don't know. Why do you care?"

"Because I have something that might help you decide." He took out his phone. "This is a conversation I had the other night with your boss and her twin sister." He pressed the "play" symbol.

Betty heard Diane's unmistakable smooth voice say about her at the beginning, "She'll be okay."

"That's pretty cold," Betty observed to Ryan. "She sounds like she doesn't care I got shot."

"That's hardly the worst of it."

The conversation at Flynn's went on. Lily Thornfoot seemed to acknowledge that she was blackmailing tax dodgers. Ryan smiled. "There's more of that."

"That would be of interest to the bar association, at least," Betty said.

They heard Diane Peligroso's acknowledgment that the company knew what it was doing when it "took care" of local officials. "I wonder what federal law enforcement might say about that," Ryan said. "Also the hint that the company resorted to violence when necessary."

On top of that, there was all the talk of political deals that Betty couldn't quite follow, but it sounded pretty awful to her anyway.

By the end of it, Betty had tears in her eyes. "Those two are rotten motherfuckers," she said.

"They are indeed," Ryan agreed.

"What are you going to do with it?" Betty asked, wondering about his next move.

Ryan dropped the bomb. "Nothing."

Betty stared at him. "What?" she shouted. She tried to sit up but her left shoulder stopped her with a stabbing pain.

"You heard me on the recording. I'm out."

"But?"

"I'm giving it to you."

"Me?" Betty asked. "What do you think I can do with this? And why would you trust me with this?"

"You decide. I think you were seduced to the wrong side, and I bet you are now reconsidering. Maybe that conversation will help you. I think you're a fighter. I think you can carry on. You're young, resilient, and adept in this new digital world." He reached into his jacket pocket and handed her a red plastic thumb drive.

"Do Diane and Lily know they were recorded?" she said, staring at the drive and turning it over in her right hand.

"Not yet. I am leaving it up to you."

She laughed. "Then they are in for a surprise." A moment later, her mind adjusting to this new circumstance, she asked, "Where are you going to go?"

"Better you don't know," Ryan said. "Good luck." He turned toward the door.

When the door closed, she plugged the drive into her phone and listened to the conversation again. Then she tucked it into the nightstand drawer and fell asleep. Hours later, she awoke with a plan. She called Monique Bouchard.

"Radio One," Monique said, answering her phone.

"It's Betty Groleau. I'm in the hospital," Betty said. "I got shot."

"*Tabernak*!" Monique said, using a particularly colorful Quebecois curse. "You have better stories down there," she said enviously.

"Not as much fun as you might think," Betty said. "I need help."

"From me? A big lobbyist like you?"

"Yes, I was wrong about that. But I have a plan."

"What can I do?"

"Get here as soon as possible, if you can get away. Can you?"

"Well, let's see. I work in New Brunswick," Monique said with insouciance. "When King Charles the Third was in the British military, he served here, and called it 'the middle of nowhere.' So what would be happening here? The fire department wants more money. The health commissioner says youth make poor choices. Dairy Queen is expanding. There's a new exhibit at the forestry museum I need to check out. These are my top four stories. Want me to go on?"

Three hours later, Monique strode into the hospital room, her brunette hair waving behind her, as if trying to keep up.

"That was fast," Betty said.

"Well, you don't have speed limits here, yes?"

"We do, but no one obeys them."

"Land of the free," Monique said sarcastically. She eyed Betty's shoulder bandages, and said, "My little cub reporter got shot. Who did it?"

"Some poor guy," Betty said. "Nothing major."

"Then *pourquoi* the big emergency?"

Betty handed her the thumb drive. "It's on this. This is hot stuff. I can't have it traced to me. That's why I didn't email it to you. There are no electronic footprints connecting it to me. Tell no one where you got it. Ever. I need you to go back to Canada, post this anonymously online there. Add a simple headline like, 'Dirty Politics in Maine.'"

"I think you have moved over to *le côté des anges*, the good guys, again, yes?" Monique said inquiringly.

"I was stupid, okay?" Betty said. "I'm not going to leave the job. But I am going to use it for good ends."

Monique considered that. "That's very hard to do," she warned. "I have a friend, he is First Peoples, he calls that '*les deux mondes*,' like 'walking in the two worlds.'"

"I think I can do that," Betty said. "When you post it, use a secure VPN based in Canada, okay? One with dynamic tunneling if you can."

"Oh, you with your big tech talk," Monique chided lightly. "If I recall correctly, you worked at a print weekly in the woods. Look, I'll use a semi-whitelisted PPVN, okay?"

"Point taken," Betty said. "Anyways, send me a link as soon as it's up. And don't get in trouble—this is potent stuff."

Monique turned up her hands. "What are they going to do, transfer me to Fredericton? I liked you the first time I saw you." She leaned over Betty and gave her a long, gentle kiss on the lips, finishing with a tongue flick. Betty's right hand reached up to cup one of Monique's breasts, the size of an orange. Monique smiled.

"Oh, my," Betty said out loud, feeling a flicker of passion through the dull pain.

"Until next time," Monique said with a wink. "We need to spend some serious time together." She turned to leave the room.

Monique worked fast. That evening, the link arrived.

55

FLIGHT

In the morning, Ryan was surprised at how little time it took to pack up his entire life. He filled a daypack with a change of clothes, a sweater, and the contents of his kitchen altar. Looking over his bookshelf, he decided to take with him a book of essays by Edward Abbey. The rest of the books he boxed up, along with some unneeded clothes.

He took his two pistols and the knife out of his truck, wrapped them in an oiled T-shirt, and bagged them twice in trash bags. He counted off ten steps east from the maple tree nearest the house, then dug a three-foot-deep hole and buried them. If he ever came back to Maine, he thought to himself, he'd probably need them.

An old black pickup truck pulled up. "James Reveur asked me to come by and get a dog?" the driver, wearing a t-shirt that said 'Penobscot and Proud,' said.

Ryan gave the dog a last hug and then lifted him into the cab of the pickup. "This is Moolsem," he said. "He's a sweet dog. His front legs are bad, so you need to lift him in and out, okay?"

The driver nodded. "Good name," he said. He headed back down the long driveway.

And then Ryan was ready to go. He poured a second cup of coffee. He took it out to the back deck, sipped it, and bade farewell to his life on Lost Pond. An anomalous warm front had blown in, bringing with it a swirling winter fog that obscured the trees at the far end of the pond. Crows wheeled in and out of the mist, cawing their unhappiness with this irregular weather. Ryan heard a rumble of thunder in the distance, totally out of season. The overheating of the planet seemed to be accelerating.

He dropped off the clothes and books at the Goodwill store on Stillwater, not far from the Orono Bog, where he had walked with Nina. Then he cut down I-95 to the Bangor NPR station, which was nestled in a building that during the Cold War had been part of a big Air Force base. He went inside carrying a letter stating he was donating his Ford F-150 to the station. He gave the letter and the truck keys to the security guard at the front desk. "It's parked outside. The title is in the glove box," he said. Then he swung his daypack over his shoulder and walked the mile west to the little airport's quiet terminal.

When he came to a retaining pond, he stopped to check his phone. "Dirty Politics in Maine" had been posted in Canada and reposted on dozens of American sites. Politico, a site specializing in American political news, just a minute before had posted an "exclusive" on "Maine Politics Roiled by Secret Tape of Lobbyist."

Ryan read it over, pleased that he still had that one big punch left in him. Then he threw the phone into the pond, irritating two ducks that had been napping. They quacked at him. He boarded the noon jump to Boston.

Later that afternoon he was on the Aer Lingus overnight flight to Shannon, Ireland. When the wide, aging Airbus was forty-five minutes out from landing, the attendants turned on the cabin lights and served good coffee and buttered Irish bread. As the huge aircraft descended, Ryan gazed out the oval window at the gray Atlantic below and considered his journey of recent years. In retrospect, he had moved steadily eastward—from San Diego on the Pacific, to Maine on the western side of the Atlantic, and now he was about to be in Ireland, on that second ocean's eastern shore. He was running against the movement of the sun, it seemed. He felt like he was trying to push against the currents of history. Yet at the same time he felt he was moving in the right direction, at least for himself. He was not just being carried along mindlessly, he hoped.

He deplaned, passed through a cursory passport inspection—just another planeload of Yanks from Boston come to harass their cousins in the Old Country, said the tired eyes of the Irish officials on the receiving end—and walked out of the airport to a leaden, wet, windy Irish morning. He hiked and hitched his way fifty miles to the Inishturk monastery he had read about, hoping they had received the check he had sent by express a few days earlier.

He saw the roadside spring he was looking for, a rough cross of whitewashed stone above it, a weeping ash tree behind it. He knew from the internet that this spring served as the sole sign for the monastery that was a quarter mile off the road. He knelt and washed his face, then cupped his hands below the spout and drank. The water was cool and clean. He remained on his knees and felt waves of tension, so deep he had hardly been aware of them, release from his back, his calves, his thighs, his arms. He tapped his right hand against his heart and said, "I am grateful for this." It was like a single ray of sunlight breaking through ominous storm clouds.

Then he rose and walked slowly up the long driveway behind the spring. He was surprised to see that it was unpaved, not even graveled, more a mossy pathway than a road for vehicles. It clearly did not get a lot of visitors. There was an old gray stone building in the distance, a big farmhouse. Behind it stood a barn and other outbuildings. This was the small, secluded monastery he had read about online, the most reclusive in all of Ireland.

The horses in the front pasture glanced up at him, but the three cows didn't. Two dozen more cows grazed on the low hill rising behind the farmhouse. He walked up to the building and knocked on the front door. He waited more than two minutes. Eventually, he heard footsteps inside.

The rough wooden door, grayed with age, opened. A man in a brown frock said, "Brother Ryan? I'm the abbot. We've been expecting you." He gestured for Ryan to step inside. And with that, Ryan Tapia disappeared from the modern world.

56

DIANE'S NEW LIFE ON THE DEFENSIVE

Diane Peligroso was curious that she hadn't heard from anyone at the company for several days. She had left voicemails on Payne's cell. She had emailed. She decided to drive up to the Future Minerals tipple. When she saw a chain across the entrance road, she was only half surprised. She parked her blue BMW sedan on the side of the entrance road, by the small sign that simply stated, FUTURE MINERALS, and stepped over the chain.

She stood in the parking lot and surveyed the complex. The mining operation was dead quiet, absolutely still. The mobile home that had contained the operations center was gone. There was a thick chain and solid-looking heavy-duty alloy padlock on the tipple doors. She walked over to look through the garage door window of the maintenance shop and saw no one. She called Payne's office and heard, for the first time, a terse recording stating that Future Minerals had ceased operations in Maine and informing the listener that any questions concerning the Maine operation should be directed to a law firm in Portland. She realized the rumors she had heard were true: The company had extracted most of the easy- to-reach cobalt from the Maine vein. The subsidiary had been cut loose to deal with the terms of the settlement.

Diane walked back out the entrance road to her BMW. She liked to use her driving time to mull business opportunities. On the road back south to Augusta, she began thinking about encouraging Dick Auger, the new state attorney general, to look into the finances of a Nevada company that owned a nuclear power plant in Rhode Island and wanted to sell expensive electricity to the Maine grid. They had some shady dealings and other vulnerabilities, she knew, and those problems meant they'd need someone who could represent them in dealings with the attorney general. That could be a good long-term contract for her.

A day later she learned from a reporter who covered mining for an industry publication that Future Minerals was rumored to have abandoned Maine after it quietly located a major new source of cobalt-bearing ore, in the desert just north of a national park above Moab, Utah. Nothing had been said in public yet, the reporter said, but it already had contracts signed with the county officials there who controlled non-energy mineral rights. The operations center was in place, and in a few days the company would begin drilling the primary shaft.

She could see it in her mind's eye, and she kind of admired its stubborn profit-making persistence: The company was even now, at that very moment, a chewing, relentless, blind subterranean reptile, rarely resting, always burrowing on, delivering its minerals to a world that craves them and had shown that it is willing to live with its poisons and violent actions. It was the way of the world, she thought to herself. The price we all pay for what we want.

In the following days after the posting of "The Conversation," as it came to be called in Maine, Diane Peligroso's life spun out of control. Lily Thornfoot took off for an extended trip to Morocco, which made Diane remember that nation had no extradition agreement with the United States. There Lily established an internet-based business called "Expats with Assets" that offered financial advice to people who fit that description. Some would become clients, and others, targets. With Lily, the distinction was never quite clear.

In Maine, reporters began digging into the details of the recorded remarks. Their queries led politicians to distance themselves from Diane and her business clients. Governor Solidarity Harrison was first, issuing a statement that she deplored the tone of the conversation and promising that Peligroso would play no role in her future campaigns. "This is not us," her statement concluded, even though she suspected that it was exactly what America had become.

Perhaps because she was accustomed to being on the offensive, Diane was slow to fathom how much damage the posting had inflicted. Seeking to shore up her business, she called the man at the cruise ship association and left a message saying she was happy to tell him that she was now able to take on their business. When she didn't hear back, she called again the next day. This time there was a long pause at the other end of the line. Finally, the man said, "Uh, this is uncomfortable for me, but I have to say that we're looking for someone with, uh, a lower profile. You're kind of controversial right now."

"A hot potato?" Diane asked.

"Well, your words, not mine," he said. "Goodbye." She noticed he didn't say "good luck," which would be customary. Man, she thought, when even the cruise ship people look down on you, you're pretty low.

A few minutes later, her phone rang again. It was a partner at the law firm in Portland that she used. He was a fatherly figure, a retired judge, the firm's wise, old troubleshooter. Did that mean she was now considered to be trouble? What was he shooting today?

"May I speak frankly?" he began.

"That's what I pay you guys for," she shot back.

"Well, put it this way, I want to speak to you in confidence."

"Aren't all our conversations privileged?" she asked.

He coughed. "All right, I will be as clear as possible. I want to make damn sure that our conversation isn't being recorded."

"Why would I do that?"

"I don't know," he said. "But then I don't know why your conversation with that investigator was taped." He was saying she was no longer to be trusted. Might there be other recordings out there, or embarrassing documents?

"It sure as shit wasn't me," she said. "What do you want?"

"I'm calling to advise you that we are a civil firm."

"Which means?"

"In our opinion, you probably should seek counsel more experienced in the criminal realm."

"You think I'm going to get charged?"

"Not necessarily," he said smoothly. "But I would expect that sooner or later, you'll get a grand jury subpoena. Maybe not from Dick Auger—I know he's in your pocket. But even you can't control the feds."

"So?"

"Here are two names for you. They're pricey, but that's because they're the best criminal lawyers in the state."

It was the same pep talk Diane often used to tell her potential clients as she informed them of her fee structure. She hung up and considered that in just one hour, both the cruise ship guy and a lawyer had cast her adrift.

She was beginning to realize that she had underestimated Ryan Tapia.

57

JACOB'S EVERLASTING WAVE

One hundred miles to the south, down on Penobscot Bay, in Witches Hole, just west of Witch Island, the ancestral home of the family of Diane Peligroso and Lily Thornfoot, down below the waves, the corpse of Jacob the Growler waved slowly at passing fish. When he had been dumped in the cold sea water and plunged into the depths of the underwater valley called Witches Hole, Jacob's arms had been held in rigor mortis at his sides. But constant tidal action had eased the stiffness, so now his arms and hands pointed up above him, moving back and forth slowly in the dark, cold water. Below them, his feet were bound by chains that were tied to the engine block of an old pickup truck. Here in his resting place, forty fathoms deep, Jacob's flesh was left all but undisturbed. Occasionally a herring or seal would take a tiny nibble, but after tasting the metallic tinge of his flesh, like biting on aluminum foil, they soon would spit it out. Preserved by almost-freezing bottom water, the salt in that water, and the avoidance of the marine life, he hung there, waving his hands in a never-ending warning that no one would ever see.

ACKNOWLEDGMENTS

Once again I want to thank Jessica Case for her fine editing of this book. Her suggestions improved it a lot. Also, Susan McGrath turned in another round of smart copyediting. The two of them make revising a manuscript a pleasure.

This view of the world in this story was inspired by the works of David Simon (*The Wire* and much more) and also by *Cobalt Red*, an important book by Siddharth Kara about the impact of cobalt mining in the Congo. The two accounts of basketball matches were influenced by Dawn Potter's lovely poem "First Game," from her collection titled *How the Crimes Happened*. Bap Salim's statement that life on our planet is about the interplay of rock and water is borrowed from page 194 of *Reading the Rocks: The Autobiography of the Earth*, by Marcia Bjornerud. The thought about people today not living longer but dying longer is from my friend Samuel Harrington, whose book *At Peace* explores that idea. As I wrote this book, I was also thinking about the writings of Paul Kingsnorth, which is why this story ends the way it does.

Morning is my writing time. Much of the writing of this book was fueled by the marmalade produced by Nervous Nellie's of Deer Isle, Maine. I believe it is the world's finest orange preserve.

For those who are interested, Peace Ridge Sanctuary, mentioned by Ryan to Roger Robichaux, is a real place. Located in Brooks, Maine, it is open occasionally to visitors. I loved meeting its horses, donkeys, cows, dogs, pigs, goats, and sheep. If you can't visit, you can still donate.

And yes, some Mainers do suffer from the cold in the winter for lack of money. You can help some of them by sending a check to the Island Heating Assistance Program, P.O. Box 383, Stonington, Maine 04681, with "IHAP" in the memo line.

Again, I am pleased to acknowledge the inspiration I get daily from dozens of photographers of Maine's mountains, rivers, lakes, coast, and animals. The photo on the cover, which shows Moxie Pond as seen from Mosquito Mountain, was taken by Tanya Buzzard.

Other Maine photographers include these, who have what might be called two first names: Mark Albert, Gary Allen, Mark Allen, Janine Andrew, Steve Bart, Bob Benjamin, Scott Carl, Myrna Clifford, Kevin Christopher, Andre Curtis, Johnny Dallas, Jan Davis, Kelly Delano, John Edgar, Justin Elliott, Lee Evans, Erik Francis, Donald Frederick, Laura George, David Harris, Julie Harvey, Cindy Joyce, Christopher Lawrence, Samantha Lee, Tim Lewis, Sarah Lizabeth, Joseph Lowell, Megan Lowell, Kay Mallory, Donna Marie, Pamela Martin, Trish Martin, Justin Matthew, George Melvin, John Michael, Andy Nelson, Susan Oliver, Nathan Pablo, Rick Perry, Liz Quinn, Steve Ramsey, Bruce Randall, Bob Rich, Scott Richards, Travis Richards, Josh Robert, Nanette Roberts, Adam Rodgers, Sara Rogers, Lewis Rudolph, Jeff Ryan, John Stephen, Erika Thomas, Megan Thomas, and Mary Valerie. And not to forget Jordan Samuel Adams.

Others who have posted wonderful images online, in various Maine photography sites, include Kathryn King, Corey Cain, Claire Collinson, Cindy Case Chandler, Dave Darrow,

Devta Doolan, Jon Jewett, Joni Jacobson, Teig Tyrson, Tatania Tadenev, Towle Tompkins, Lisa Lebo, Megan Morong, Penny Polakoff, Peter Prinz, Gwendolyn O'Guin, Eillen Euton, and Ethan Eisenhaur.

Let us not forget Earl Marsh, Bob Sabo, Ret Talbot, Lovena West, John West, Mark Estes, Richard North, Loretta Coty, Cody DeLong, Rachel Price, Joel Ferguson, Peter Slovinsky, Gary Jansen, Gary Vanidestine, Charles Vandersluys, John Vander Meer, Tracy Van Buskirk, Vonda Lavway (and her chipmunk), Sue Mahaka, Floyd Tanaka, Florine Wyche, Julia Chase Bailey, Jill Turner Odice, Tricia Young-Chappie, Patti Trottier Basiliere, Kimberly Bertkau Mosca, Kyle Anne Manzie, Sharon Smith-Gavenda, Bitsy Holt Copp, Mike Scott, Scott Loring Davis, Scott Meyer, Debbie Gallant, Debbie Chatfield, Don Powers, Kenny Ames, Mark Rowe, Troy Frye, Jeff Frye, Paul Gase, Sandy Holt Heal, Vickie Ketch, Brenda Ketch, Susan Lynch, Deb Boxer, Jeff Glaser, Stephen Paynter, Justin Thatcher, Paisley Turner, Kirk Horner, Michele Booker, Blair Weaver, Bob Warner, Dan Wagner, Jared Smelter, Brandon Barter, Brandon Wyatt, Peter Duckett, Steve Cutting, Jeff Cutler, Keith Carver, Anna Seekins (and her underwater loon), Emily Cannon, Bob Spear, Eric Spear, Eric Storm, Karl Ramsdell, Jan Walker, Reena Walkling, Peter Just, Eric Orkin, Frank Owen, William Pead, Mike Poirier, Diana Presson, Donna Dodge Baker, Dick Brubaker, and Deb Boulanger.

Wait, there's more. Here come Jacqueline Robidoux, Kathy Bishop-Heroux, Mary Jo Marquis, Warren LaBaire, Martin Thibaudeau, Jodi Cyr, Janet Marie Cyr, Paul Cyr, Susan Pierter, Laura Pelletier, Richard Plourde, Robert Saucier, Chris Michaud, Clifford Dupray, Todd Dechaine, Tim Grillot, Traci Labash, Phil Lapierre, Jason Morneau, Bonita Poitras, Tom Ventura, Anthony Gedaro, Susanata Baguni, Mike Vadas, Macayla Fortin, Jiaxin

Wang, Rachel Heiss, Crystal Stockbridge, Doriann Cetina, John Saleda, Svieta Beliveaugale, Karl Chopelas, Armin Kososki, Mariusz Potocki, Bruce Coryell, Bruce Grover, Jason Smith, Matthew Lankford, Carol Behan, and Michael Overton.

In addition, Ted Russell, Russell Hall, Ricky Hall, Junior Stahl, John Day, Cathy Knight, Jack White, Bob Black, Shirley Whitenack, Tyler Pascocello, Dan Marino, Tina Philbrick Richard, Lisa Philbrick, Lisa Jordan-James, Lisa Morgan Cass, Cassady Kay Austin, Julie Watson King, Karen House Prock, Patty Ann Larrabee, Peter Maffly-Kipp, Nancy Logan Tobin, Helen Webster Drake, Laura Sego Dexter, Beverly Brennan-Overberg, Shanna Downing Goodine, Marcy Pluznick-Marrin, Amy Parker Zupancic, April Hundley-Gilmore, Pamela Gagnon da Silva, Patsy McGould, Maryanne Marie Chipman, Ann Marie MacLean, Jane McIntosh, Alison McKellar, P. J. McKraken, Bryan McDonnell, Cal Mackenzie, Josh McPhail, Ameryss Stewart, Achille Bellinger, Will Crowe, Bill Byrd, Randy Swan, Richard Schwanhausser, Dennis Haarsager, and of course, Cindy Willigar and Bumpa Hennigar.